THE GIRL IN THE YELLOW SCARF

A NOVEL

Book 1 – Opus Series

C. R. FRIGARD

ti

Treebones Inc

Copyeditor: Pamela Illies
Cover and Interior Design: Peter Wocken

Published in the United States by Treebones Inc.
ISBN-13: 978-1983575419
ISBN-10: 1983575410

First edition
Printed by CreateSpace,
a DBA of On-Demand Publishing, LLC

ALSO BY C.R. FRIGARD

NONFICTION

Funthink: 12 Tools for Creative Problem Solving

Arthink: Creativity Skills for 21st Century Careers

FICTION

The Piano Man – Book 2 – Opus Series – Fall 2018

The Opus Café – Book 3 – Opus Series – Spring 2019

"But hope that is seen is not hope at all."
- Rom 8:24

For Janet…forever

She reached in for the small wooden box.
Just touching the rough-hewn surface,
knowing the story of its contents, gave her hope.

Manhattan, February 1982

Mike Monroe rocked back from the shouts of a huge crowd, as he was about to leave the Plymouth Theater on 45th Street. A bit stunned by the clamor he stepped out under the blazing lights of the marquee, followed by his family who gaped at the fans and photographers straining to get a glimpse of the young composer. Heading out from under the portico into a confetti-like snowfall, Mike suddenly stopped, leaned back and let the cool white flakes caress his face.

After a moment gazing skyward, he patted his chest with a smile; then continued, shaking hands and posing for photos while shepherding members of his family to a double-parked Cadillac stretch limousine.

Everyone laughed and talked at once as they dropped into their seats and toasted Mike's first Broadway musical with waiting glasses of champagne.

"Where to, Mr. Monroe?" asked the driver.

"Crown Plaza Hotel," Mike said, grinning. He glanced over at his friend Jesse and his sisters, Trina and Persis. "Can you believe these crowds?"

"Why not?" gushed Persis, "it was wonderful." The others nodded enthusiastically.

As the black limo carved its way through the congested after-theater traffic, he replayed the audience's roar when he bowed to his adoring fans. He had made it. His long sought after dream was finally a reality.

"You did great, Michael," his mother said, beaming with adoration.

"I don't know. I was so nervous. I should have said . . . something." Mike frowned, recalling the moment the spotlight found him in the theater.

"No one could tell," she said, waving her hand in dismissal. "You came across calm and confident."

He smiled, his heart warmed by his family, who had stuck with him through painful years of loss and frustration.

When the limo reached the hotel entrance, they were met with more excited fans rushing up with shrieks of delight and instamatics flashing. The hotel manager whisked them through the chandeliered lobby to the elevators and up to an elegant suite for the cast party. Cheers roared through the group as he entered the marble foyer and thickly carpeted room arm in arm with his radiant sisters, followed by his mother and Jesse. Leon Kohn, producer of the play, immediately grabbed Mike for a hearty handshake and a slap on the back, and then called out to get everyone's attention.

"As most of you know, I've backed a few projects in my day. But I have to say, none can match the joy I felt watching this phenomenal cast of musicians and actors perform this incredible story to Mike's music tonight." Beaming, Leon raised Mike's hand high over his head as the room erupted in agreement.

Mike humbly bowed, overwhelmed by the accolades. He then circulated about the spirited gathering, thanking each cast member while searching for Elizabeth Shepherd, the leading lady who had seized his soul with her tender performance. But before he could find her, the buzzing crowd hushed to a murmur with the first reviews coming in over Radio WBLS.

"Inventive," "Outstanding," "Inspired," "Sure to be a lasting hit"— Mike's knees went rubbery.

"Oh, Lord, I can hardly stand it . . . it's too sweet," Mike said, hugging everyone within reach. All the people he cared about were there to share this glorious moment—except one.

As suddenly as he was struck with joy, Mike knew he had to leave. With his pulse beginning to pound, he got the crowd's attention, thanking them again with heartfelt words of gratitude and apologies for his unexpected departure. He then quickly ushered his family to the elevators and down to the crowded lobby and out to the waiting limo.

Sitting silent for a moment in the luxurious leather seats, he scanned the faces of his loved ones.

"Sorry," he said, dropping his head. "She made it all possible. I need time with her—"

"Michael, don't say another word; we understand," his mother said, reaching for his hand as the limousine eased out into late-night traffic, heading home to Harlem.

After giving everyone a warm embrace on the steps of their Strivers Row townhouse, Mike climbed back into the car.

"Where to now, Mr. Monroe?" the driver asked.

"Breezy Point in Queens," he said, then fell back in his seat and stared out into the night.

1

Mike - Manhattan, September 1979

Rudy grunted "Hey" as Mike entered Johnny's Piano Bar in the Flatiron District of Manhattan.

The familiar reek of stale cigarettes and spilled beer, tinged with a dash of mold, met him as he paused to adjust to the cave-like surroundings. *One more night playing in a hole— how much longer can I stand it?*

"Ready for a rip-roaring Tuesday, Rudy? Hmm . . . maybe I should be a poet," Mike said as he wove his way through a scatter of tables and chairs to the vintage grand piano. He glanced back at Rudy, who busied himself wiping down the bar, silhouetted by the sparkling glow of backlit bottles and glasses, a frustrated scowl permanently etched on his face. A recently retired NYPD detective, he'd owned the bar now for two years, a dream Mike knew wasn't meeting his expectations. With his rough-and-tumble looks and demeanor, Rudy was also the bouncer.

"Honey working tonight?" Mike called out as he propped up the ebony lid of the grand.

"Yeah," Rudy said.

"At least something to look forward to," Mike muttered to himself, switching on the spotlights and adjusting the single microphone over the piano.

He usually began his five-day workweek at eight p.m. Lately though, he'd had to prod himself to the aging club, which once featured notable musicians of the '40s, '50s and '60s— Erroll Garner, Art Tatum, May Lou Williams, Ray Charles— who played till early morning to crowds that gathered after the curtains fell in the theater district. But those glory days were long gone.

When entering Johnny's from Gramercy Park West, under the faded blue awning with peeling white lettering, patrons saw the baby grand piano against the left wall with tables and chairs radiating out. The bar, an endless slab of mahogany with stools and an attached brass foot rail, extended the full length of the room on the right, backed by a mirror with glass shelving for liquor and glasses. He had been thrilled at first, getting a paying gig while attending NYU for his MBA, but after a year at Johnny's, the once cozy and welcoming club became claustrophobic—dark, stuffy, and leading nowhere.

Sitting down at the worn but resonant piano, he moaned as he gently stroked the very keys the masters had touched. If it weren't for the heartwarming timbre of this seasoned instrument, he would have quit long ago.

After a brief warm-up, Mike sat back staring at the keys. He had come so close to making it big. Major clubs uptown had been on the schedule, with a possible tour in the works— then Miranda, his beautiful collaborator and love of his life, decided to jump ship and join a rock band now on a world tour. He was still recovering, his heart severely trounced along with his career. After searching for months for a decent replacement, his dream of headlining fame was sinking out of sight. On top of it all, he had lost touch with many of his friends from college, who were now launching successful careers and getting married.

As he slumped in thought, Honey burst through the door with her dark eyes flashing; offering an unoriginal excuse for being late. Rudy once again threatened to fire her, but they all knew he wouldn't – being the only waitress that hadn't quit within weeks of dealing with the ex-cop. Mike couldn't help but chuckle at the sight as he got up and strolled to the bar. Nodding at a couple perpetual patrons, he gave Honey a one-armed squeeze as he reached for his second bourbon and water from Rudy, who peered at them both through his bushy black eyebrows.

"What are you doing after work, beautiful?" Mike asked with an exaggerated seductive grin.

"I'd drop everything to spend time with you, sweetie, but I know you're not serious," Honey said. "When you going to get over that Miranda person and give a real woman a chance?"

"The *M* word has been struck from my vocabulary. I'm no longer imprisoned," he said, grimacing with a thought of Miranda's extraordinary beauty. Maybe if he said it enough, he could convince himself.

"We both know that's not true." Honey cradled his face with her hands. "Mike, you deserve the best. She wasn't it."

"Please . . . enough already." He looked over at Rudy, who was busying himself polishing glasses with his usual scowl. "It's show time, Honey. Time to get to work."

More regulars began dropping in for a little courage after a long day in the nearby publishing houses, law firms, and garment shops. No matter their occupation, he knew he had the power to transport people, giving them a break from whatever they were facing. His music was a gift, and he loved both singing and playing. He'd just thought Johnny's would have been one of many gigs on his resume, not the only one.

Mike launched into the first set, singing "Piano Man," "Georgia on My Mind," and many other requested standards. Later, winding down for a break, he sat staring at the dimly lit keyboard for a long minute thinking of having to do the same old thing for the rest of the week. *Crap, maybe the rest of my life.*

Shaking his head to reconnect with reality, he got up, went for another drink, and swizzle it around as he walked to the end of the bar. *I gotta find something else.*

He dragged a stool to the wall phone, set his drink on the phone book, dug in his wallet for his agent's number, and called.

"Jimmy here."

"Hey, Jimmy, Mike. I'm serious, man," he said, dropping down on the stool and fidgeting with the cord, "you've got to help me. I can't keep playing the same old songs to the same old crowd."

"Look, my friend. I thought I explained it," Jimmy said. "I had you lined up with some great venues before Miranda bailed, but now . . . it's tough selling a one-man act, and you've said many times you won't play backup for anyone."

Mike squirmed. "Okay, Jimmy, listen. I'm working on some new material, and I'm checking out the Village clubs for talent to replace what's-her-name."

"Mike, you've *got* to move on." Jimmy chuckled. "She sure was a looker, though."

While Mike searched for something to say, Jimmy added, "Something will turn up. I promise. Hang in there, kid—you got talent."

"Sure, Jimmy, sure." Mike hung up with a clunk. He reached for his drink, pushed the ice around a couple of times, and downed the last of it. He really wasn't sure of anything anymore, except where he stood on Jimmy's priority list—somewhere near the bottom.

Play backup—that was what Jimmy was always riding him to do. He had tried playing with small combos that were in demand in the uptown clubs, but it just didn't suit him—he needed to do his own thing.

Noticing a dark look from Rudy, Mike rose from the stool, trying mightily to mask his frustration. He got another drink and returned to the piano. Picking out the loose change and two one-dollar bills from the tip jar, he sat down, straightened his shoulders, and sang to the bottle blonde at the table next to him as if she were the only person in the club. Her sad eyes brightened slightly and gazed back as if recalling some happier time. Her melancholy struck him in the chest. He wondered if she had lost hope. He was beginning to understand how that felt.

Halfway through the second set, with all the regulars in their places and a few new faces, he threw in a "request from the table in the back." It was an improvisation—blending classical, jazz, pop, and blues into a composition that lasted over fifteen minutes, drawing inspiration from happy family memories at the Jersey Shore, the chaotic throb of city streets, and the melancholy of a dank late-evening fog sweeping down Long Island Sound.

He closed his eyes as he played, but opened his imagination to his favorite dream. The dark cloud of anxiety drifted away, replaced by warm golden spotlights upon his face. He was seated at the monstrous concert grand on stage at Carnegie Hall, where a packed house took in every nuance of his début performance, which was also being recorded and soon to be released on Capitol Records. His dream had come true. He had finally reached the world with an opus of his own.

As the last chord diminished, his whole being stirred, enlivened. He was about to rise to a standing ovation, when, looking up from the keyboard at the dozen tables scattered about the piano, he realized only the sad blonde had listened and taken the journey with him. The rest of the drinkers continued talking without a hint of interest. Mike's face fell as he drew in a deep breath. He stood, shoved back the bench with a scrape, and pointed an accusing finger toward the noisy table of four.

"Hey, you guys! Could you keep it down? Someone might want to listen!"

Rudy spun around behind the bar with eyes blazing. He slapped his hand down with a smack and gestured for Mike to come over. A little surprised at first but somewhat numbed by four bourbons, Mike stood, tossed back the last of his drink, and sauntered over to Rudy.

"What's with you?" Rudy said, trying to keep his voice down. "People don't come in here to listen to you. They just want some background music while they're drinking. Keep this up and you'll be out of here." Rudy paused and stuck out his chin. "And another thing—try shaving once in a while. You look like crap!"

Mike pulled his head back for a moment as he thought about walking out the door—but he had nothing else going, so dug down deep.

"Sorry, man, I . . . it won't happen again."

Rudy remained brooding behind the bar as Mike turned back to the piano. *Man, I've got to get serious about finding something else.*

Home late after his row with Rudy, Mike entered his fourth-floor flat in Greenwich Village and poured another tall bourbon and water. He started pacing. Music teachers throughout his school years had encouraged him to pursue his obvious gift in music, claiming he was a prodigy. His father, however, had other plans. Mike was sent to college to get an MBA as soon as possible to help grow the family grocery store business into a chain that would serve the poor communities of Harlem.

Mike loved and respected his dad. He drove himself to meet his expectations by graduating from Cornell in Ithaca. But after moving to Greenwich Village and a year at NYU to get an MBA, while working evenings at Johnny's, he'd hit the wall. As depressing as Johnny's had become he couldn't imagine taking over the family business. If Johnny's were purgatory, going into business would be hell.

Emptying his glass, he flopped down on his bed resolved to make a change. He would head home tomorrow, talk to his father about quitting NYU, and focus full-time on music so he could break free from Johnny's. *It's my life, after all.*

2

Sarah

For a brief moment, she had to work to recall where she was. Then it came to her as a whiff of musty canvas and sputter of snoring hit her. Turning to her side, Sarah wished she could sleep more but knew she wouldn't. After a week in and out of shelters, she longed for her own soft bed and some privacy.

Sitting up she swung her legs over the edge of the canvas cot and scanned the sea of rumpled blankets and tousled hair in the basement shelter. She had trouble sleeping with all the moaning and hacking, but it was still better than the slatted wooden bench in the park. Twisting her body from side to side to stretch her aching back, she groaned. *I'm only nineteen. How am I going to feel when I'm thirty?* Then thought how bad the older folks must feel.

Sarah reached under her cot for her shoulder bag and pulled out a peanut butter sandwich wrapped in waxed paper she had made last night at the soup kitchen. She learned the hard way to eat something first thing in the morning to keep her blood sugar up to avoid a diabetic reaction. She did her best to eat regularly, but it wasn't always possible.

Munching on her sandwich, she looked out over the dark forms on the creaking cots. Her heart ached for them. Then it struck her: she was now one of them.

Standing, she grabbed her bag and stepped carefully, weaving through the scattered cots. The dim bulb at the end of the room was barely enough to find her way through the maze to the bathroom—diabetes had diminished her eyesight over the past year. Once inside, she gently closed the door so to not wake anyone and switched on the flickering overhead florescent light.

At the sink, she studied herself in the mirror and wondered what the day would bring. Her once silky red hair, now rust-colored, was beginning to mat under her yellow scarf. She longed for a hot shower, but all she could do was splash icy water on her face and dry it with a coarse paper towel. Standing a moment at the mirror, as she fingered the silver cross around her neck, she gasped, suddenly picturing her mother's face.

Stumbling back against the cold tile wall, she slid down to the damp floor. Breathless for a moment, she bowed her head, let her arms fall limp at her side, and began sobbing as her shoulders heaved.

With no tears left, she lifted her head, wondering how long she had been sitting on the floor. It could have been minutes or an hour—she didn't know. Why at least hadn't Aunt Clara come to the funeral? She had called and written to explain her mother had died of a stroke, but she never heard back. There was always some upheaval in the family Sarah never understood.

A few friends came to the funeral, which meant a lot with no relatives showing up. But when they offered to help, so she could keep her apartment, Sarah declined. She needed to prove she could make it on her own. She told them she expected to be moving in with family. The truth was, when all the medical bills and funeral expenses had been paid, she had less than a hundred dollars to her name and was completely alone.

Sarah shuddered at the vision of her mother in the casket—the face so much like her own. The voice of Grandma Mae then came to mind, bringing some comfort. *"Put your faith not in what is seen but what is unseen."* Her grandma had died when Sarah was young, but memories of her were vivid. Grandma Mae always had a Bible verse at hand to fit the circumstance. Sarah could still envision her sweet wrinkled face and hear her saying, "Sarie, we have to be tough to make it in this world. But with God's help we can handle anything. Right?" Her grandma would smile broadly, then pull Sarah in and give her a hug that took her breath away.

Revived by the thought of her grandma, she got up from the floor, wiped her face, and nodded to herself in the mirror. "You have to be tough, Sarie. You can make it."

She was careful again not to make noise as she left the bathroom. She crept to the back stairs and out the side door to the shadowy alleyway. Stepping over trash, around oily puddles, and past a dumpster that smelled bad enough to gag a maggot— something her Grandma Mae would have said—she made her way to the alley entrance and into the cool, misty morning air. When she reached the street she stopped, took a deep breath, said a prayer, and started walking west up 31st Street.

She was determined to make it to Madison Square Park by the time the sun broke over the East River. Sounds of early morning began to waken Manhattan, born anew each day with murmuring motors, backup beepers of garbage trucks, and the clanking of sliding store shutters. Soon cab horns, delivery truck motors, and police sirens would add their voices to the symphony.

As she walked in the lifting veil of dawn, her thoughts turned from the noisy city to memories. To peaceful, sweet hours spent with her brother fishing in a leaky wooden rowboat among the lily pads and cattails of a small Kentucky lake.

She would use this happy memory as inspiration once she got to the park. She tried each day to draw in her sketchbook, from visions of her past or sights in the city. She'd been doing this since tenth grade art class. Her teacher, Mrs. Morgan, had inspired her to become an art teacher herself, but that had to be put on hold, at least until she could find a job and got off the streets. But so far stops at the unemployment office had turned up nothing.

Her eyesight was getting worse, with things not as crisp as before. But she loved to draw, so more and more drew from memory than from what she saw. The sketchbooks and a small wooden box she carried in her shoulder bag, along with the handcrafted silver cross around her neck, were her most prized possessions.

Doctors had warned about her weakened heart, so she learned to pace herself. By the time she crossed Broadway and 5th Avenue to the park entrance, a shaft of golden light streamed through the stately elms and onto her favorite bench in front of the fountain. The fountain hadn't worked in years, but the azure sky, rustling green leaves, and chitter of birds was salve for her soul. Sarah stooped to pick up the trash strewn around her bench, then sat down and pulled out a napkin full of breadcrumbs. Being shy around strangers, some days the birds were the only living things she would talk to.

When the sun slipped behind a band of dark clouds, despair began to seep in. She squeezed her eyes shut and began humming to herself. Soon she was singing softly with thoughts of harmonizing with her mother while folding clothes at the kitchen table in their Chelsea apartment. Humming and singing were like a prayer she used to ward off sadness.

Another memory arose, out of nowhere, it seemed. She recalled her mother saying she had "eyes as beautiful as a Monet painting." When they went to see the luminous picture at the Metropolitan Museum, Sarah had cried with delight, standing close as possible to the exquisite masterpiece.

A slap of wind and rain suddenly jerked her into the moment. An angry squall had rolled in from the northeast, with clouds casting a dark shroud over her. Her mother's old raincoat wouldn't be much protection against an all-out downpour, but pulling it over her head, she got up and shuffled as fast as she could across 5th Avenue, trying to miss puddles and dodging cabs to the entrance of the Toy Center Building, where she waited twenty minutes for the squall to pass.

Chilled and soaked to the bone, she started to shake. Her teeth chattered uncontrollably. At the shelter, she'd overheard you could get a shower at the 23rd Street YMCA for two fifty, and that was only a few blocks away. *A hot shower would be heavenly, and I could wash my hair*.

On her way down 23rd, she was getting faint. Knowing she must look a fright in her sodden raincoat and stringy hair, she walked into Samson's Market to get something to eat before she passed out. It always amazed her how much could be packed into such a small store. Walking down the narrow aisles, turning sideways to pass other customers, she picked up what she thought she could afford— a bologna-and-cheese sandwich, a half-pint of milk, and for a treat sugar-free strawberry Twizzlers. Digging in her pocket for the last bit of cash, she realized she was down to thirty-one dollars and some change. She put back the Twizzlers.

She finished her meal as she walked, so by the time she got to the Y she was rejuvenated. Entering the wide-open first floor, she was unexpectedly caught up a current of energy and joy as people laughed and talked in the busy café to the left. Straight ahead was a checkout desk for a small library and reading room, with people standing around a bulletin board, and to the right and up the stairs were the locker rooms, showers, and gym. After paying her two fifty at the desk, a surge of hope came over her as she made her way up the stairs to the gym and a glorious hot shower.

Sarah soon learned you had to be creative, living on the streets. So figured as long as she was taking a shower, she would wash her clothes at the same time. Everything she owned, she wore or carried in her shoulder bag: underwear and socks for six days, sweatpants and a shirt that she wore during the day, and slacks and a blouse she was saving for a possible job interview. The rest of her clothes she had washed and boxed up, leaving them for Goodwill at the apartment she could no longer afford.

Sarah got out of her street clothes and tossed them into the shower stall along with her other dirty laundry, then jumped in and closed the curtain before someone could see her. Getting the water as hot as she could stand, she began to giggle as she stomped around on her soapy clothes, as if mimicking some ancient grape-crushing ritual. After ten minutes of steaming, sudsy water, Sarah and her clothes were squeaky clean.

Just about the time she was done rinsing and wringing out her clothes, a loud voice echoed just outside her stall.

"Hey . . . you okay in there?"

Sarah screeched. Then gathering her wits, said, "Yes, uh . . . yes, I'm fine."

"Doin' your laundry, are ya?" came the reverberating voice.

"Oh, uh . . ." Sarah sputtered. It was no use. What could she say?

"Honey, it's okay. I've been there. Shoot, I'm still there. When you're done we'll toss your things in the big dryer—they'll be done in no time. Just don't tell nobody, okay?"

"Oh, thank you," Sarah said into the plastic shower curtain.

"Take your time, dear. When you get your things together, I'll be right next door in the locker room."

The shower and clean clothes gave Sarah a fresh outlook on things. Floretta, the owner of the booming voice, was kind and helpful without judgment or pity. Coming downstairs, Sarah felt more confident with her long red hair clean, peeking out in ringlets from her yellow scarf. She walked over to the bulletin board next to the information desk, where a boy her age looked over at her and smiled. Surprised but pleased, she gave a quick smile back.

"What ya looking for?" the Smile said.

"I don't know . . . just looking."

"Well, if I see an ad for a beauty contest I'll let you know. You would win for sure."

Sarah tilted her head and narrowed her eyes, recalling words of warning from her mother. The boy's smile turned to a sneer.

Sarah turned back to the bulletin board.

The Smile laughed as two of his friends ran up, bumping him into Sarah.

"Hey, man . . . she's too much for you," one said, grabbing the Smile around the shoulders.

"Yeah, Red, forget him. I'm more your type," the other added, peering at her.

A brush of anger came over her. She glared into the faces of all three punks. "Look," she said, "just leave me alone."

The trio pulled back, sniggering, and were about to counter, when a man stepped between the wise guys and Sarah.

"Think it's time you boys move on. Can't you tell when you're not appreciated?"

Looking up at the hulk with the gym bag slung on his shoulder, the boys seemed to shrink.

"Hey . . . we were just being friendly."

"Good-bye, boys," the man said.

The three looked at each other, shrugged, and headed out.

The man shook his head and turned to Sarah. "You all right?"

She looked up. The man's eyes were kind. "They didn't mean anything. They were just being—"

"Jerks?"

"Yeah," she said. "Thank you,"

The man nodded. "Take care."

Sarah smiled and watched him head up to the gym, then turned back to the bulletin board.

Scanning a half-dozen handwritten index cards for jobs, she landed on one that caused her to stop and stare.

Teacher assistant at the Y for art therapy class, mornings, $6/hour. Call Mrs. Angie Campana: 212-323-5420

She stood back in disbelief while she chewed her lip and twirled her hair with a finger. This was something she had complete confidence in. She understood to her core the power of art to communicate emotions and stories. And she was good at it.

She couldn't wait another minute. She went to the phone booth a few feet away, excitedly dug into her shoulder bag for a dime, and called the number.

"Hello, Angie here."

Sarah caught a quick breath, "Hello, Mrs. Campana…this is Sarah Davis. I saw your ad on the Y bulletin board for an assistant art teacher."

"Yes, I'm looking to start in a few weeks. Tell me about yourself."

Sarah explained she'd had three years of art in high school, had won several awards in juried art shows, and was planning to go to college to become an art teacher.

She didn't mention her current situation or the fact that she didn't have enough cab money to get across town, never mind to pay for college.

"Well," Angie said, "sounds like this might work. Can you meet me at two next Monday, at the Y café?"

"Oh, yes," Sarah said – her heart racing as she continued to twirl her hair.

"Good," Angie said. "Bring some samples of your work."

"Yes, I'll do that. See you then." Sarah hung up, holding her breath.

Sliding open the phone booth door, she raised her hand to her mouth. *I have an interview . . . an interview for a real job.*

Heading out from the Y, Sarah sparkled with hope. A glorious shower and clean clothes, a new friend in Floretta, and, on top of that, a job interview. The YMCA would definitely be on her daily route. Now to the soup kitchen on 28th Street for a hot meal, and then find some place for the night.

3

Independence Day

Mike woke early with a pounding head, a sense of dread and visions of how an entire room ignored his playing at Johnny's. Then there was his confrontation with Rudy and the dead-end conversation with his agent.

He couldn't take another day like that.

He sat up slowly and peered across at his beloved piano in the center of the room. All would be lost without the hope it held.

Mike's fondest dream surfaced as he admired the glossy lacquered ebony. Someday he would find the key to an opus that would offer hope to a troubled world. It was possible. Music had the power to heal.

Swinging his legs out from his floor mattress, he sat for another minute trying to recall what day it was. *Oh, yeah . . . Wednesday. Good.* Wednesdays he volunteered at the local soup kitchen, something he'd grown up doing with his family in Harlem. Recalling those fond memories reminded him he needed to talk with his father about quitting NYU.

Standing up, he stretched and hobbled the few steps to the kitchen sink to get a cool glass of water. He thought briefly of adding a splash of bourbon—just a hair of the dog. *Wait, isn't that what alcoholics do?* Maybe some aspirin instead.

After putting coffee grounds and water in a stovetop percolator, he was drawn as always to the sculpted instrument of wood and metal. He scuffled to the middle of the room, sat at his piano, and reached out to the ebony shoulders and bowed for a moment.

Lifting his head he gazed out across the room at nothing particular, then started playing, letting his spirit move his fingers as the resonance of the soundboard and strings filled his soul. He drew on themes and melodies that had come to him over the past week—inspiration from, sounds, sights, smells, or watching people move about the city. If he needed a dash of sunny inspiration, he only had to look over his shoulder for his grandfather's old rod and reel standing in the corner next to the coat rack. The ancient crank reel and metal pole had been his as a kid and never failed to bring back sweet memories of fishing with his dad along the Hudson River.

If he conjured up something he liked while playing, he would make notations in his journal, keeping them as reference to draw on someday for a masterwork—a dream he batted around more for fun than anything.

Feeling a little better, he sat at the piano with his freshly brewed coffee and peanut butter toast, smiling. *I'll be okay for another day. Thank God for music.* But after another heartwarming sketch he had to man up and head to Harlem to talk to his father. On his way he would check in with Frankie, his old roommate from Cornell, whom he trusted would give him an honest perspective on his dilemma.

He took the subway up to 116th Street and Columbia University, where Franklin was now going to med school.

"Michael Monroe," Franklin said bowing regally as he opened the door then grabbed his old roomy for a man-hug. "Come on in, y'all."

"Y'all?" Mike said, curling his mouth. "So you're from the South now?"

"Yeah, I guess," Franklin said, closing the door behind Mike. "Can't help but pick up the accent now that I'm dating a Southerner."

"Oh brother," Mike said with a shake of his head. "So what ya eatin' these days—possum and parsnips?"

"Exactly," Franklin said, chuckling. "Man, I miss you. Couldn't stand staying at the frat house after you left. Besides, I had to get serious if I'm ever to finish med school."

"Probably a good idea if you're going to be cutting into people," Mike said with raised eyebrows.

Franklin's apartment was sparse, much like Mike's, minus the piano. The two of them sat at the kitchen table and bantered a bit, with jabs and counter-jabs as if they had been saving up insults for each other. But then Mike grew quiet.

Franklin just looked at his friend and waited.

"Frankie," Mike said, looking up from his hands, "I can't do it anymore. Sure, I can do the homework, even though it takes me twice as long as anybody else because I'm such a slow reader . . . and math is like trying to learn an extinct language. But really, it just isn't me, man."

Franklin shook his head. "What do you have to complain about? You have it made in the shade with Kool-Aid with a babe named…what's-her-name—"

"Forget the lame poetry, Frankie. I don't know what to do. This is serious, man."

"Okay, sorry. What's the alternative?" Franklin smirked. "I know you were a good wrestler in college, but you'd get killed as a pro."

Mike sat back in his chair and sighed. "Frankie, I love making music." Then leaning forward he looked his friend in the eye. "My music teacher in high school told me not to waste my talent, and here I am, slogging through business classes while my soul shrivels like a prune." Mike paused. "When I jammed with Allen and Morris on Saturday nights, time evaporated. There was this thing we used to do. I would lay down a series of chords on the fly or something I had worked out earlier, and they would improvise, filling in with harmonies and counterpoint—we could go on for hours. What a blast. You remember the parties we played at."

"Yeah, man, you were awesome," Franklin said. Then studying Mike a moment, he added, "Okay, this is serious. I know you felt pressure from your dad, and you struggled with classes. So . . . maybe you have to do your own thing."

"Frankie," Mike said, getting up and pacing about the room. "I've got to make a decision. I can't do both—music and the stores."

His old roommate watched him pace for a bit. "Mike, I know this is hard, but I'm always here for you, brother."

"I know, Frankie," Mike said as he went to the window and looked out at the gray fall sky. "It would practically kill my father if I quit. He's counting on me."

♪

As Mike strolled up the familiar cracked sidewalk of his Strivers Row childhood home, he once again went over what he would say. He walked up the steps, stood a moment at the top for a deep breath, and opened the door.

"Mikey, what are you doing here?" hollered his kid sister, Trina, as he caught her coming down the stairs from her bedroom. "It's Wednesday—"

"Runt," he said, cutting her off, "I missed you so much, I just couldn't wait till the weekend."

"Yeah, right," Trina said as she headed into the kitchen. He looked in the living room to his left, and then followed his sister through the dining room into the kitchen.

"Where's Mother?" he asked as his stomach churned.

"Think she's doing laundry downstairs," Trina said, setting a sandwich down at the table and pulling up a chair.

Mike tried to calm himself by getting a glass of milk, and then sat across from his sister.

"So, Brainiac, what did you learn in school this month?" she said.

"Stuff you wouldn't understand, Runt," Mike volleyed back.

"Still beating up on a bunch of scrawny white kids?" Trina returned.

"I don't wrestle at NYU. That was Cornell. But I could make an exception for a skinny little black girl." He made a quick lunge at Trina, knocking her slightly backward from her chair. Her feet kicked out for balance, and in what seemed like slow motion, he watched their mother's prized flowered vase topple sideways off the table and crash to the floor.

"Man . . . you're going to die when Mother sees this!" Trina said, sticking out her chin.

"No, you will if you say a word before I try to glue it together!"

"You don't scare me." Trina grabbed her sandwich and made a quick exit for the stairs, looking back to see if she was being chased.

Mike picked up the pieces of the vase, put them in a paper bag, and hid the remains in the broom closet for now.

He loved both his sisters, though they were polar opposites in personality. Trina was the jokester, while his older sister, Persis, was more serious and beautiful and expected to marry a college-educated man and have good-looking grandchildren for their parents.

Mike got up and walked into the living room to wait for his mother to come upstairs. Looking at the family pictures all about the room, he thought of the many times he'd taken the four-hour bus ride home from Cornell before graduating. On Sundays after church, the girls would set the table in the dining room with the "good" dishes in honor of him being home. His mother would always cook up one of his favorite Southern dishes she'd learned growing up in Georgia, and his father would say grace, ending as usual giving thanks for a prosperous business that both served the community and provided for the family. After dinner, everyone would gather at the door as his dad gave him a hearty handshake and told him how proud he was of him.

Sitting there with all the pictures of his loved ones smiling at him, his heart began to ache. Maybe this was a mistake. Just as he stood to leave, his mother came out from the stairs.

"Michael, what's wrong? What are you doing here?"

"Wow, aren't I still part of the family? Can't I surprise you once in a while?" Mike's heart started to pound as he feigned annoyance. "When will Dad be home?"

"He'll be here in a little bit. Why do you need your father?" his mother said, looking anxious.

"I want to share some news," Mike said feebly. "I'm quitting NYU."

4
Soup Kitchen

Mike moaned as he stood looking out his window onto Bleecker Street. *Now what?* He had never seen his father so angry. Mike knew he hadn't presented his case very well, but what was done was done. *Finally I'm free . . .*

Thankfully it was Wednesday—his night to volunteer at Holy Apostles Soup Kitchen on 28th Street, as he had done for the past year since transferring to NYU. He had learned to value volunteering as a kid, serving regularly at shelters around Harlem with his parents. It was hard to explain, but sometimes he felt more comfortable with the homeless than his own family.

Heading out of his apartment into streets drenched with rain, he wrapped his scarf twice around, pulled down his denim hat, and leaned into a blast of wind left over from a North Atlantic squall. He loved the coming of fall. The weather changed the city—the sounds of flapping canvas awnings, the intensified colors, people scurrying to buses and cabs, the inside-out umbrellas pointing skyward. After hustling up 8th Avenue to the old brick-and-stone entrance of Holy Apostles, he felt energized, his anxiety completely flushed out.

"Al, what's for dinner, my friend?" Mike said, bursting into the kitchen after walking through the large basement-turned-dining-hall.

Al, with the rugged looks and demeanor of a weathered cowboy, turned as he stood amid the commercial-grade appliances, counters, and sinks to acknowledge Mike.

"Ahhh, the music man. When you gonna give that up and come work for me full-time?"

Mike unwound his scarf, whipped off his black peacoat, and hung both on the corner rack before looking around for a quick snack. "Maybe I will. How much you gonna pay?"

"Pay would be the same," Al said as he returned to peeling a pile of potatoes at the counter.

"I see. So I'd be movin' in with you and your sweet mother," Mike said, trying to keep a straight face.

"Oh, I don't think so. She's not particularly fond of your kind."

"She's prejudiced?" Mike said, fighting a grin.

"Yeah, against musicians." Al threw an apron at Mike. "Time to get to work, kid. Get the hamburger out of the fridge and brown it."

"Kid? I'll be twenty-three soon. But I suppose compared to you—"

"Shut up and get cookin'," Al said with feigned authority, pointing his paring knife in the direction of the stove.

Mike chuckled as he sauntered to the huge fridge to get out the hamburger.

Shortly, the rest of the help arrived. Most had been homeless at one time and volunteered to give back. After they all got their marching orders from Al, the kitchen was filled with a half-dozen people crashing around preparing meals for two to three hundred homeless people. Soon the aroma of fresh-baked bread, sizzling hamburger and onions, and coffee brewing filled the kitchen and hall. Whenever possible, Al insisted on fresh meat and vegetables, which called for a lot of peeling, slicing, and mixing—but it tasted better and everyone enjoyed the process much more than just heating up frozen or canned food.

The doors opened from four-thirty to six-thirty, making it about a four-hour shift for Mike once cleanup was done, but he still had time to get to Johnny's before eight—a twenty-minute hustle from there.

People slowly ambled in, some relatively cheerful and clean and others ragged and street worn. All seemed in no particular hurry as they sat in chairs at folding tables around the large open room. The walls were paneled in dark wood, and featured large bulletin boards plastered with notices of services and calendars of upcoming church events.

The serving tables were soon filled with huge stainless-steel bowls of food manned by the kitchen help. Al, who had once been a cook at a dude ranch near Cody Wyoming, rang a beat-up brass dinner bell and hollered "*Cooome* and get it, my friends," which brought smiles and head wags from some of the newcomers. Folks lined up patiently, nodding to one another in recognition.

Although he sometimes had to swallow back emotion, dishing up food was Mike's favorite part. He felt an easy connection with the street people, and it never failed to bring him peace as he served them.

Standing at the serving table ladling out food, Mike saw one of the regulars ambling down the line. "'Sup, Leroy, how's the foot?"

Layered as usual in a flannel shirt, holey green sweater, and heavy wool overcoat, Leroy said, "Better, man, and you?

You makin' it okay?" Catching Mike's eye, he added, "I worry 'bout you."

"You worry about me?" Mike said, taken aback.

"Yeah. Sometimes I see sadness in you. Believe me, I know the look."

"Uh . . . you got me, man," Mike said, smiling. "Ever think of becoming a shrink?"

"Yeah, maybe. You need to see one?"

"Could be, man, could be. I'll let you know." Mike thoughtfully watched Leroy as he went on down the line. *Man, am I that transparent?*

Turning his attention to the next person in front of him, Mike was stunned. He drew in a quick breath. Standing there peering out from a rumpled raincoat and scarf was a porcelain-skinned young woman with silky red hair and lavender eyes— her face an exotic flower in a bed of thorny weeds. He was transfixed, then realized he was staring as she looked straight ahead at his apron.

"Sorry . . . I haven't seen you here before. I'm Mike," he said, ladling hamburger gravy over mashed potatoes on her plate.

"Hi," she said.

"What's your name?"

"Sarah."

"Okay, Sarah, hope you have a good dinner." Immediately he pursed his lips. *What a lame thing to say.*

After a few more stragglers came in to be served, the help went out to sit and eat with the *customers*. Looking around the crowded hall, he caught a glimpse of the girl in the yellow scarf sitting by herself in the far right corner. Plate in hand, he wove his way in her direction, stopping to chat and joke with some folks he'd missed earlier.

As he approached Sarah from behind, he noticed she was rocking slightly from side to side as a strange barely audible melody radiated from her. He stopped to take it in. He was baffled—it was like nothing he had ever heard, and he just stood there trying to make sense of it.

Suddenly, Sarah stopped and looked over her shoulder at him.

"Hi, remember me? I'm the potato-and-gravy guy." Mike slid back the folding chair next to her and plopped down, trying to recover from embarrassment. He nodded his head, speechless for a moment. "You have a nice voice, ya know?"

"Oh," she said, glancing only slightly in his direction.

Even though he was a regular volunteer at the kitchen, seeing people in all stages of down-and-out, his heart sank over this small hunched form. He had just thought of something to say, when the sound of crashing dishes and rustling came from the table behind them.

It was unusual for a fight to break out at the soup kitchen, and everyone turned from their plates in the direction of the scuffle. Mike jumped up and ran over to the ruckus. Still in pretty good shape from being on the college wrestling team, he felt confident he could calm things down. It turned out not to be much of a problem—the combatants being two weathered women who were more about shaking each other than swinging fists.

With their energy quickly spent, the squabble was soon over, and Mike headed back to his seat—hoping to pick up where he'd left off, but the girl had vanished like a vapor. Standing there, looking out over the murmuring crowd, he wondered if she had been real or if he imagined her. He cringed as her enigmatic voice wafted about in his mind. How could such a delicate flower ever survive the cruel life of the streets?

After cleaning up the kitchen, and much good-humored abuse from Al and the other staff, Mike walked out the side door to 28th Street, popped open his trusty umbrella against a chilling drizzle, and headed the ten blocks to Johnny's in Gramercy Park. Making his way through the evening bump and hustle, he thought about how the cauldron of humanity provided inspiration for his music. However, because of the recent falling out with his family, melancholy had become a dominant theme. He knew he had to make things right, but tried to put it out of mind for another day.

Reaching Johnny's a little early, Mike ducked inside, shook his umbrella, and went straight to the piano. With just a few of the regulars at the bar the place was quiet except for Rudy banging around in the storage room. Flipping on the spotlights, he slid out the bench, sat down, and reached for the keys to see what might emerge. A wistful melody appeared first as a solo voice, and then wove its way through bright sustaining chords with a playful give-and-take. Playing off each other, melody and chords danced in a joyous romp, often ending in a discordant thump, only to pop up again and run about the keyboard like children playing tag.

After five minutes, he ended his improvisation with a thread of melody trailing off like a setting sun. With his fingers sustaining the last notes, he looked up to see Rudy standing next to the piano with a drink in his hand.

Rudy appeared dazed as he handed Mike the drink. "Wow . . . that was something."

Mike just shook his head. "I don't know where that came from, man."

But that wasn't entirely true. He suspected it had something to do with the shy homeless girl from the soup kitchen.

𝄞

When the fight broke out, Sarah dropped her fork and rushed from the church basement. The angry shouts brought back the frightful memory of a bloody fight she'd witnessed while hiding behind a dumpster her first day on the streets. She couldn't stand to see something like that again.

She hadn't finished eating her dinner but put off hunger by thinking of her good day at the Y. Walking to the 31st Street shelter to check in for the night, she saw people heading into St. Francis of Assisi across the street as choir music beckoned through the open door. Raised a Methodist, she was curious what a Catholic service would be like. At least it would distract her from being hungry.

Sitting down in the last pew, she followed the sublime sound of the choir, humming quietly to herself. Music was as vital to her as oxygen. She leaned back, closed her eyes, and reminisced about singing in the children's choir at the small country church in Kentucky. She would glance over at her beloved family as she sang her heart out; their smiling faces conveying love and confidence. Then there were the picnics, the softball games, and gardening with her grandma. She became heartsick. *What will I amount to without them?*

The parish priest, seeing Sarah in the back after everyone had left, walked to the end of her pew.

"Excuse me, my dear. Can I help you?" he asked, smiling kindly.

Sarah, yanked from her dark reflection, peered over at him. "Oh, just lost in a memory."

He nodded back. "Will you be all right?"

"Oh yes," she said, forcing a smile. She stood and thanked the priest, assuring him she was fine although she really wasn't and once outside felt unsteady. Quickly she sat down in the shadow of the church colonnade, hoping to regain her strength before going across the street to the shelter.

5

Words

Walking home late Wednesday from playing at Johnny's, Mike winced recalling his father's violent reaction to leaving NYU. *"Get the hell out of here!"* The fierce words rang in his ears, stunning him speechless. Making it even worse, Runt started to cry and his mother fell into a chair with her head in her hands, rocking back and forth. There was nothing for him to do but leave. Each time he replayed the scene, it always ended with the same simmering frustration, anger, and guilt.

Walking through the murky early morning streets with an occasional siren wailing in the distance, Mike sighed as he thought of his baby sister. He ached for her flying hugs and sassy grin. Then there was his mother's cooking. Although he took it for granted at the time, she always made a special effort to cook his favorite meals. And even though he wouldn't admit it to her, he admired Persis for her strength and insight. But how could he go home without proving he could make it on his own? *But is playing at Johnny's making it?*

Cutting across the shadowy corner of Union Square Park with nostalgic thoughts of home, a rush of footsteps and a hushed voice commanded from behind, "Stop or die. Turn around, you die! Just drop your wallet so you can live."

Mike froze, and pondered what to do as his heart began to pound. *Did this guy have a gun, a knife, or what?* Then without warning something hard smashed down on his head.

Numbness spread across his skull, then a violent pain shot from his head to his shoulders. With a thud, Mike dropped to the ground and rolled onto his side catching a glimpse of the mugger's gloved hand reaching for Mike's wallet. With his head lying on the cold concrete, trying to catch a breath, he watched a dark shadow run around the side of a nearby building.

Mike lay panting. Angry he hadn't defended himself, he got to his hands and knees and was struck with an eye-squinting headache. Blood dripped down the side of his face onto the sidewalk between his hands. He had to do something quick before he passed out.

He struggled to his feet, weak and wobbly, and pressed his scarf to his wound. He stumbled along the sidewalk remembering the nearest emergency room was only a couple of blocks away. The few people that were on the streets went out of their way to avoid him.

A wave of antiseptic met Mike as he staggered into the crowded ER, where a short-tempered nurse gave him clean gauze and motioned to find a seat. It was a busy night for stab wounds, ODs, and sundry other mishaps. He found a chair between a worried-looking mother cradling her hacking child and a teenager with a towel wrapped around a bleeding hand.

Holding his head as he sat with his elbows on his knees, he heard a familiar sweet voice wafting from behind one of the drawn exam room curtains. In this woeful place of pain and suffering came a redeeming balm, displacing his anxiety with a peaceful calm.

Could this be the same shy lavender-eyed girl he'd sat next to just a few hours ago? Her voice had an indescribable quality, bringing serene smiles to all within earshot.

When the girl came out from around the curtain, Mike straightened in his seat. Sarah. *What is she doing here? Is she hurt?*

"Hey," Mike said, getting up from his chair.

"Oh . . . hello," Sarah said. Then looking anxiously at his bloodied head and scarf, "What happened? Are you okay?"

"Yeah, I'm fine . . . you remember me?" he said.

"Oh sure. You're the mashed-potatoes-and-gravy guy."

"Yes I am. How'd you like it?" he said, and immediately felt stupid.

"Impressive—the best I've ever had," Sarah said, trying to keep back a smirk.

"Okay, it's not exactly French cuisine," Mike said. Then giving Sarah a serious look, "I overheard what the doc said about eating better."

"Yeah, I should have finished my dinner, but the fight scared me. A policeman found me passed out across from the shelter."

"You're okay now?"

"As long as I'm careful to eat right."

"Sorry, it's rare people get into it at the shelter." He racked his brain for what to say next. "Mind if we sit a minute? My head's splitting," and pointed to a couple of open seats.

"You know," Mike said with a wide-eyed smile as they sat, "I could fix you one of my mother's famous Southern dishes after I get patched up. I'm actually a pretty good cook."

Sarah hesitated answering and looked at his bloodied head and coat.

"No big deal—you should see the other guy." Mike tried to sound nonchalant. Then he lowered his head. "Okay, I got mugged, but I'll be alright."

Sarah still appeared unsure.

"Look, I know what you're thinking. Why do I hang out at the soup kitchen?" Mike paused, raising his eyebrows. "What can I say? I enjoy real people and their stories. Through them I find inspiration for my music."

"Music? You play what? Chopsticks?" Sarah said with her head atilt, smiling.

"Well," he said. "You remind me of my sister, Trina. She is a bit of a smart aleck also."

Sarah gave him a half grin. "Sorry, but I don't know anything about you."

Mike nodded. "Okay then. I'm Mike Monroe. I live in the Village on Bleecker Street. I play piano at Johnny's in Gramercy Park. My aspiration in life is *not* to run a business of any kind. So I make music."

"Gee, sounds like you know what you don't want," Sarah said. "That's something, I guess. Southern cooking, huh? What part of the South?"

"The best part—Georgia."

"Oh. I was hoping you would say Kentucky," she said wistfully.

"I can do Kentucky. I'll just add more bacon fat to everything."

"Wow, you do know what you're doing." Then, as she peered deep into his eyes, a wave of peace seemed to flow over her. "Well, I suppose I could rearrange my plans."

His heart warmed from that smile. *What is it about this girl*?

"Great!" Mike said. He leaned toward Sarah. "Now you have to tell me a little about yourself while I wait to be patched up."

As the emergency doors burst open with bleeding and broken bodies, Sarah relayed how she had lost the apartment in Chelsea and been in and out of shelters after her mother died. With her poor eyesight it was a challenge to find work, but she was pretty sure of getting a job at the Y.

Mike listened. He wasn't happy with his parents, but at least they were still alive. He felt ashamed thinking he had it rough.

"What is it?" Sarah asked.

"Oh . . ." He paused. "I have to ask. Do you always sing to yourself like that?"

This seemed to embarrass her. She turned away.

"Sorry . . . it's wonderful," he said, wishing he had phrased it better.

Sarah looked back. "Guess I don't think about it . . . it just comes out."

Sarah continued to talk about how much music meant to her, which got him so excited he was ready to leave immediately and take her to his flat and play for her, but she insisted he stay and see the doctor first. Finally, after another hour, Mike's name was called, and twenty minutes later they were out the door heading into a magenta glow gathering in the east.

Leaving the ER with Sarah at his side, a bandage wrapped around his head, looking like a Civil War casualty, Mike was both relieved at finding her and a little apprehensive. Right away he picked up on her uneven gait, something he hadn't noticed at the kitchen. Looking over at her he wondered what he was in for, but had learned to trust his gut, and this felt right without knowing why. The early morning streets were empty except for a few delivery trucks and a couple of people hustling to open breakfast delis and coffee shops. Almost to his apartment, he was going nuts for a cup of coffee and pulled Sarah into Leo's Bakery, a small hole-in-the-wall joint with a green awning he knew opened at five a.m.

The heavenly smell of freshly brewed coffee and baking pastry hit them as he pushed open the glass door with the tinkling bell.

"Sarah, have a seat. I'm going to bring you the most unbelievable pastry the world has ever known," Mike said with a gigantic grin, happy he could introduce her to something he really loved.

Sarah looked at the huge curved glass display case with trays of all kinds of bakery delights and smiled at Leo, who stood behind with his slicked back hair and kind face peering over the top.

"Hey, Mike, haven't seen you for a while—you up early or up late?" Leo said, then looking closer at him, added, "And what's with the bandage?"

"Well, Leo, you could say I'm up early and late. As for the bandage—I got mugged, but it was the price I had to pay to find my friend Sarah."

Looking at Sarah, Leo said, "Gee, you must be special. What will you two have?"

"The mugger got my cash, so could you float me a couple of donuts until I get some money?" Mike pleaded.

"Sure. What would you like?"

Mike turned to Sarah. "They're all amazing. What do you think?"

Sarah appeared like she was making a life and death decision from the look on her face.

"I better go with the plain old fashioned," she said.

Mike was thinking of a bismarck slathered with chocolate icing but said, "make it two."

"And coffee?"

"Yes, coffees." Then smiling at Sarah, "I'll drink yours if you don't want it."

"Think I would like some," Sarah said with gusto.

Leo handed Mike the donuts, each in its own waxed paper bag, then the two mugs of steaming coffee, and said, "Because this seems like a special day, this one's on me."

Mike grinned. "Thanks, man, you're the greatest." Then he glanced at Sarah. "It is special."

6
Greenwhich Village

The freight elevator whined to a stop and clanked open on Mike's floor. The fourth-floor loft was divided into four small studio apartments housing a newly wed couple down on the left—both working in the financial district, an artist/sculptor first door on the right—only seen hauling up raw materials or hauling down various works of art, a vacant apartment further down on the right, and Mike's door immediately on the left— the apartment of the business school dropout from Harlem. But after a year in the Village, even though the flat was cramped – his grand piano taking up much of the room – he couldn't imagine living anywhere else.

"So, what do you think?" he asked Sarah as he led her through the door.

"Great, I guess. Can hardly tell," she said, squinting. "Don't see well in low light."

"Oh, sorry. I'll fix that." Mike reached for a panel with a half-dozen light switches. Flipping them all, the room took on a kaleidoscopic glow.

"I use the lighting to set different moods when I'm composing."

"Wow, is this the land of OZ or what!" Sarah said, grinning like a kid opening Christmas presents as she gazed about the rainbow-spattered room.

With a twinge of embarrassment he watched Sarah scan the sparse furnishings. An old four-drawer dresser and box springs and mattress staked claim in the far right corner. Straight ahead, a large blue vinyl beanbag chair with wooden apple crates on each side, one full of music review magazines and the other holding an orange ceramic lamp with an aqua shade. Next were heavy dark-green curtains covering a window overlooking Bleecker Street bordered by a floor-to-ceiling bookshelf made of scrap lumber filled with sheet music, notebooks, and a reel-to-reel tape-recorder. In the middle of the room sat Mike's imposing grand piano with the lid yawning up.

Immediately to the right in an alcove, a small table and two chairs sat in front of a classic 1940's kitchenette with a rounded porcelain sink and a sloping countertop for draining dishes. Then a two-burner gas stove with a minuscule oven – possibly large enough to roast a pigeon. Next to that sat an early Frigidaire with an odd assortment of pots, pans, and cooking utensils teetering on the top. A small shelf over the sink held several bottles of liquor, boxes of cereal, and canisters for coffee, sugar, and flour.

"Wow, who did your decorating? You must have spent a fortune," joked Sarah.

"You know," Mike said, smiling, as he reached to pull out a chair for her, "I would be offended if that hadn't come from a scrawny street urchin."

Sarah suddenly stiffened and whirled around and faced him appearing hurt. She seemed to lose her balance momentarily, looking for a way out. He hadn't meant anything by his joke and stood trying to think what to do.

"So that's it—I'm your good deed for the day?" Sarah blurted as she pushed past him. He reached for her arm, but she yanked it away.

"Wait!" Mike shouted.

Sarah crashed to the door, but the dead bolt and sliding hasp stopped her momentarily. Just then the phone sitting on the corner of the piano, rang.

"Please . . . wait a minute," Mike begged. "Let me answer this."

Sarah stamped her foot, turned around and crossed her arms.

He wanted to explain that he'd been joking, but the jangling of the phone unnerved him.

"Hello," he said, looking over at Sarah.

"Michael," his mother said sharply, "your father's in the hospital. Get here as soon as possible."

"What? Hospital . . . what hospital?" he said.

"Columbia. He's had a stroke. We're not sure how bad it is." She began to cry.

"Oh no . . . I'm on my way." He groaned and slammed down the receiver.

Mike looked at Sarah with his mouth open. Her eyes widened and stared back.

"Crap! I can't believe it," he said, breaking into a sweat.

He snatched his coat and some change from a money jar on the dresser, and turned to Sarah. "I need to go. My father's in the hospital. Stay here if you want."

"No," she said. "I'm fine. I can take care of myself."

He wasn't so sure, but he had to get going.

Taking the elevator down in silence, Sarah followed him out to the street. He could hardly think straight as thoughts of what to say to his dad swirled.

He started to run but turned back to Sarah. "I'm sorry. Please forgive me."

Sarah reached out for his arm. "Mike, just go. See your family."

He was torn. He feared he would lose track of her. "Could you meet me here at six tonight? I'll find out what's going on and come back."

"Sure . . . go," she said, waving him away.

With his heart threatening to leap out of his chest, Mike spun around and rushed to the 14th Street subway station, weaving through the flowing river of people heading to work.

Double-stepping down the stairs of the subway entrance to the turnstile, he fished in his pocket for a token and jammed it in the slot. He ran to the edge of the platform, turned and peered into the dark abyss trying to will the next train to arrive. Finally, after pacing for five minutes, Mike shoved his way onto the A Train heading to the 168th Street station in Washington Heights. He endured the twenty-minute trip going over what he would say to his father. He hated disappointing him and hoped he could better explain why he had quit NYU.

Persis met him as he ran up the subway stairs. She appeared frantic - holding an umbrella against a drizzle. He hadn't seen much of her since moving to the Village and knew she was upset with him but buried the thought and reached out to give her a hug.

Persis gasped at seeing his bandages. "What happened?"

"It's nothing. How's Dad?"

"I don't know, Mike," she said as her lip started to quiver. "It's bad—we have to hurry."

As they raced the few blocks to the Columbia Medical Center, Persis filled him in on what happened.

"Father has been killing himself trying to get the third store up and running. Sorry, bad choice of words, but you know how driven he is!" she said, catching her breath.

"Even though he got home after midnight, he was up again at five. Then Mother heard a crash in the bathroom. He had collapsed and hit his head on the sink. Blood everywhere . . . Mike!" She stopped and grabbed his arm. "What would we do without him?"

"Hey, I'm here," Mike said, trying to keep his cool while his gut churned and his shoulders stiffened. "We'll get through this."

Rushing into the hospital, Persis led him to the elevator and up to the third floor.

"Mother and Trina can't wait to see you. They're here with Dad," Persis said, hustling down the hall.

When they burst into their father's room, the bed was empty.

"I know this is right!" Persis said. "What did they do with him?"

Persis grabbed Mike's hand and rushed out of the room and down the hall to the nurses' station.

"Where did they take him?" Persis demanded.

"Who dear?" the nurse said.

"Our father—Lewis Monroe."

The nurse turned grim. "They took him to the OR—he's gotten worse."

Mike stared at his sister and started to tremble as a chill come over him.

𝄞

Sarah felt bad for Mike as she watched him run to the subway with his coattails flying. Without much thought, she slung her bag on her shoulder and headed in the general direction of the YMCA. Going over all that happened in the past few hours, she questioned why she reacted so violently when he was only trying to help. She struggled with accepting charity and ached for her family.

To ward off the despair welling up, she started to sing softly as she walked, trying to envision what her job interview might be like. She would show her sketchbooks and explain how she taught the neighbor kids to draw when she lived at the Chelsea Apartments. Her spirits began to lift with thoughts of teaching and getting paid for it. Then, thinking of Mike, someone she felt she could trust, she couldn't wait to meet him back at his place and tell him the news.

So with renewed optimism, when stopping at Samson's grocery on the way to the Y, she bought the strawberry Twizzlers along with a sandwich and milk.

7

Passing

It all seemed unreal as the family stood around the gravesite. Mike had sat beside his comatose father late into the night, hoping for one last conversation but it was not meant to be.

The doctors did everything they could, but too many campaigns on and off the battlefield had taken its toll. His father had lived his life as a person on a mission, and that mission had been to go as far as fast as possible, striving for new goals and always planning ahead. Once when home from college, his father, a career soldier, had told Mike he didn't want to be buried at Arlington but in the small cemetery in Harlem to be near his family. Mike had no idea it would happen so soon.

Looking at the casket as it was lowered into the ground, his thoughts wandered to when he was a kid and his dad was his hero, his everything.

Michael, you know what?

No, what, Dad?

You are amazing to me. You are so like your mother, I wonder if you have any of my genes in you at all. You are filled to the brim with your mother.

Is that bad, Dad?

No, it's wonderful. But I hope there won't be a war for you to fight when you grow up. I don't think you should be a soldier.

What should I be, Dad?

We'll have to wait and see, Michael. God has a plan—we'll just have to wait and see.

A faint smile came to Mike as he thought of his dad and the many good times they'd had, going to ballgames, fishing on the Hudson River, taking road trips in their old station wagon. But with the mournful call of taps and the first shovel of dirt striking the casket, his heart clutched with anguish, knowing how much he had disappointed his father. He could never fix that now.

After the service at the Harlem Baptist Church, family, relatives, and friends decided to walk the four blocks back to the Monroe family home, sending the black limousines on their way. As they strolled, all the neighbor folks came out on their stoops to express their sorrow and condolences. Seeing this outpouring of love and how much his father meant to the community, Mike suffered a full frontal attack of guilt. He couldn't wait to get a drink.

As the living room, dining room, and kitchen filled with relatives and friends holding plates of food and drink, Mike, somewhat sedated after a long pull from a flask of bourbon, ambled about making polite conversation. He was able to keep his feelings in check until his uncle Luther cornered him, penetrating Mike's protective veneer.

"Michael," he said warmly, pulling him in for a hug. "It's been such a long time."

His uncle held Mike out to study him. "How are you, son?"

"I'm okay, Uncle." Mike tried to smile.

"Man," his uncle said, "I think it's been five years. What ya been up to?"

Mike brightened a little. "I'm playing at a club in Gramercy Park and doing some composing."

"You always loved music. Guess business wasn't for you," his uncle said with a searching look.

"Well . . ." Mike wasn't sure how honest to be. "I tried—"

"I know you did, Mike," his uncle said. "Your mother has kept me up to date. I'm sure you did the right thing."

"Yeah . . . I think so." Mike looked past his uncle in hopes of finding an excuse to move on, maybe even to hide out in his bedroom, but before he could think of something his uncle continued.

"Mike, now with your father gone, I want you to know I'm just a phone call away."

"Thanks—might take you up on that," he said as his uncle wrapped his arms around him again.

There was no mention of family business until all the relatives had left. With everyone gone, Mike knew he needed to bring up the stores, especially with a new one opening soon. The past year had convinced him that leaving NYU was the right decision, yet he couldn't ignore his family's need for help, so he anxiously gathered everyone to the dining room table for a meeting.

"Michael," probed his mother, "what is this all about?"

"I don't know what to do. I want to help with the stores, but I—"

"Michael," his mother said, putting up her hand, "what are you worried about? Persis has been helping your father for the past year, waiting for you to finish with your MBA." She leaned back in her chair and crossed her arms. "Even though she had other plans, she proved to be an amazing manager and businesswoman. Your father was so proud."

"I didn't know he was going to die," Mike said, straightening in his chair. "I was hoping to show him I could make it in music."

His mother stiffened. "And how well is that going?"

Mike swore under his breath, but loud enough for his mother to hear.

"Michael, you may use that language with your friends but not in my house!"

"Sorry." Then taking a deep breath and letting it out slowly, he turned to Persis.

"Is there anything I can do?"

"Wish you had called once in a while. Father was so demanding, I could have used some moral support," she said and turned away.

He peered at his baby sister, who looked as if she was about to cry.

Mike's throat tightened. "I don't know what to do. I want to help but I—"

"When you were needed most, you weren't available," his mother said sharply. "Your father shouldn't have let you play in those vile smoky bars."

"But Johnny's is a famous club," he said.

"I don't want to hear about it. Just go back to wherever you're hiding. I think we'll manage."

"But, Mother—"

Once again her hand went up, along with the eyebrows. Mike looked over at Trina. Red-eyed, she sprang from her chair and ran off to her bedroom while Persis, looking straight ahead, appeared stoic.

Mike stood from the table and went up to his bedroom. Standing in the doorway, he looked around at the wrestling trophies, music posters, and old clothes hanging in the closet.

He went in, pulled out a few things from dresser drawers, threw them into a duffle, and headed down the stairs and out the front door without a word.

Riding the subway back to the Village, he was conflicted—a little relieved yet humiliated. *If I had helped with the stores, Father would still be alive.* He went numb as he stared out the window of the train.

8

Rescue

The wind whipped at Sarah's coat and scarf as she stepped out Monday morning from the 31st Street shelter. Thinking back on Thursday, she wondered what could have happened to Mike. She had gone to meet him that evening after he rushed off, but not hearing from him after four days she figured she might not see him again. He was nice, but she had to focus on getting a job and taking better care of herself.

As she walked, eating a peanut butter sandwich, she fretted over her interview for the art assistant job. Attempting to calm her anxiety, she considered what to enter in her sketch journal. Making her way to Madison Square, the autumn winds seemed angry as they funneled through the stone and glass canyons of the city. People no longer escaped from their offices for a break of fresh air and a glimpse of some blue and green but hustled about with a definite purpose.

Sitting down in the park, although chilled, she was fascinated by the colorful mix of leaves and watched as some lost their grip from the swaying branches and swirled about her bench. She got out her sketchbook and, closing her eyes, tried to envision the art room at the Y. Then it came to her.

She would draw a child sitting at an easel painting a picture. It was a loose sketch, but it captured her vision and only took half an hour to draw. Somehow it gave her a boost of confidence. She knew she could draw well, and the position was only for an assistant, so she felt confident. Things would be easier with a little money, and she would be on her way to getting off the streets. But what if she didn't get the job? Her nervousness returned with a vengeance.

Pushing through the large metal doors of the Y, she headed to the information desk, paid her two fifty and went up to the showers. The first person she saw as she entered the locker room was Floretta.

"There you are, girl. Gonna do some laundry today?" Floretta said, putting her hands on her hips.

Sarah laughed. "No, no. I want to get cleaned up for a job interview."

"Oh, sweetie, that's great. What is it?"

"Teaching art to kids who've had some trauma in their lives. It's just an assistant position, but it's been a dream of mine to teach," she said brightly.

"Well, go get 'em, child. I got faith in ya," Floretta said.

"Thank you. I can't wait," Sarah said as she began to dig in her bag.

Her interview wasn't until two, so she decided to have a good lunch at the Y café while she waited, dipping into her dwindling reserve. But this was special, and she had to appear as healthy as possible. After a large bowl of steaming soup, she got out her sketchbook and tried to relax.

A half hour later a tall middle-aged woman with a caring smile walked in and looked about. Sarah stood and waved. The woman caught Sarah's eye and walked over to her table.

"Sarah," she said reaching out her hand, "I'm Mrs. Campana. I'm so glad to meet you."

"I feel the same. It's been a dream of mine to teach art," she said, quivering with excitement.

"Oh, my, " Mrs. Campana said, motioning for her to sit. "Well, tell me a little about yourself."

Sarah fumbled a bit, trying to talk while she tunneled into her bag to get out her sketchbooks. Hoisting them onto the table, she explained how she had gotten straight A's in art in high school and wanted to take art in college as soon as she could. She had loved working with the children that came to her impromptu Saturday art classes she held in her parents' apartment.

When she had finished recounting her art experience, she was practically out of breath.

"That all sounds great, Sarah," said Mrs. Campana.

Sarah grinned in anticipation.

"But I'm so sorry. I hired someone this morning for the position." Mrs. Campana looked pained. "I assure you, if something else opens up, you'll be the first person I call. Your drawings are wonderful."

Sarah sat dazed. She wasn't sure how to react.

"Sure . . . that would be great," Sarah said, sagging in her seat.

"Sarah," Mrs. Campana said with a nod, "you're going to be great someday. Please give me a call once in a while to keep in touch."

By the time Sarah left the Y, it was late. She stayed in the library studying sketching techniques of Da Vinci and other classical artists until it closed at eight, then went back and sat working on her drawings in the café for another two hours until it closed.

When the lights around her dimmed, she couldn't bring herself to head to the shelter right away, so before leaving she went in the bathroom and put on a sweatshirt and pants under her coat and headed out the door.

"Sorry, Sarah, but I hired someone this morning."

Thinking back on those words, she wanted to cry as she scuffled the few blocks back to the park.

Numb with despair, she didn't have the will or strength to go on to the shelter. Instead, with the wind moaning in the trees, she lay down on her bench using her shoulder bag as a pillow and clutched the handmade silver cross. Pulling her yellow scarf down over her forehead and drawing her feet up inside her mother's raincoat, she fell asleep, waking briefly in the early morning to a cold drizzling rain.

Trembling, with her energy spent, she fell back into a dream. She was laughing and singing—sitting with her mom, dad, brother, and Grandma Mae on the sun-drenched porch of their Kentucky farmhouse, each doing some light chore: mending socks, shucking peas, cleaning a gun, and sharpening a knife. She was looking into her beloved parents' faces, when she heard someone calling her name.

$\natural$

Guilt-ridden for offending Sarah and knowing she was back on the streets and alone, Mike searched everywhere he could think of after coming back from the funeral. He was encouraged when Al and Leo mentioned Sarah had been looking for him, but not finding her after walking the streets and checking in the local shelters, he went back to the ER at one in the morning as a last resort.

With a sense of dread, he walked through the automatic doors and stood with his hands in his pockets, waiting his turn at the ER reception desk. After describing Sarah to the night nurse, he was told she was in fact there and was directed to the side hall, where she lay on a gurney with an IV stuck in her arm. Not knowing what to expect, he walked up to her side with his hand to his face.

"Sarah it's me—Mike."

Sarah slowly turned her head and opened her eyes, "Oh . . . Mike." She smiled and took in a long slow breath. "I was having the nicest dream."

He just looked at her, shaking his head. "Crap. You can't keep ending up here like this."

At first he was greatly relieved at finding her, then angered. Although exasperated, he applied every ounce of charm he possessed to convince her after being released to come with him to get some much-needed rest at his flat.

Even though it was within walking distance, he hailed a cab, and within minutes they were at his place. He made hot tea and had her lie down, covering her with a pile of blankets. He went about preparing a hearty soup for her, but she soon fell asleep. After getting the soup started, he went to his piano to continue working on a composition he had started earlier. Soon he heard Sarah stirring and saw her peeking at him from under the covers.

"Dammit, Sarah, you trying to kill yourself lying out in the rain like that?" he said, glaring over at her, trying to control himself.

She gazed over the top of the covers, appearing wan and bleary-eyed and whispered, "I didn't get the job."

This shook Mike. He understood disappointment. His anger melted away as he thought about what to do.

"I'm so sorry—can we just start over?" he said, dropping his shoulders. "Could you please forgive me for my stupid street urchin comment?" He paused, waiting for her to respond. "This is where you say you forgive me."

Nothing. She had fallen back into a deep sleep.

Later, while gently playing the piano, he heard a sweet harmony coming from across the room.

"You okay over there?" he asked, looking over his shoulder.

"So, you like my singing?"

Being a little careful, he said, "Yeah, it's nice."

"Is that all? Nice?"

"That's it," he said, slamming down an ugly discord on the piano. "If you're going to be sarcastic, expect to get it back. Don't dish it out if you can't take it!"

"I can take it, and I forgive you." She paused, and then sat up with the covers tucked under her chin. "Feel better?"

"Oh boy, you are something." He smiled, shaking his head. "Alright," he said, getting her attention as she made rustling sounds as if she was going back to sleep. "I need to know a few things."

"What?"

"Who are you?"

She propped herself up. "You know—Sarah. The one you kidnapped from the ER."

"Come on. Tell me more about yourself. What's your family like? What was it like living in Kentucky? Stuff like that."

She filled in more details about moving to New York with her parents, where they lived in Chelsea, and her time in Kentucky living on a peaceful farm that supplied all they needed.

He was intrigued by how she learned to sing so beautifully, but was careful not to appear probing.

"You do have an incredible voice." He said it in a way he hoped would be an opening for her to fill in more details.

However, this seemed to embarrass her. She said she never thought much about her singing. It was something she and her mother had done together just for the fun of it.

"I guess my mom and Grandma Mae encouraged me the most."

"Can you read music?" he asked.

"No."

She explained she never had a reason to read music; she just sang what came to her depending on how she felt.

Her voice was unlike anything he had ever heard. Was it like a flute, or an oboe, or maybe a violin? Actually, it seemed like all three at once. It struck him in a profound way, inspiring new possibilities—melodies, harmonies, chords, all fresh yet poignant. He had to understand it.

He was hoping to get some hot soup into her and coax her to sing, but she had fallen back asleep. He got up from the piano, went over to the bed, and gazed down on her soft innocent face. He had to know more about this girl and that amazing voice.

$$\text{𝄞}$$

When it looked as if she would sleep through the night, he got out the heavy quilt, blankets, and a pillow and made a pallet on the floor in the corner opposite his bed. He had this setup for friends who couldn't make it home after a late night of drinking.

With little sleep from tossing about and adjusting blankets, Mike woke up at nine—early for him. After a quick trip to the bathroom he started cooking breakfast, wanting to have it ready when Sarah woke up. With the comforting aroma of sizzling bacon, eggs, and toast filling the room, Mike went over to his bed and nudged the heaping pile of blankets.

"Hey, Sleeping Beauty, I think you should eat something."

A moan floated up.

"Come on now. I've been slaving in the kitchen for hours."

"No you haven't. It's been about ten minutes. Just waiting for you to finish."

"Okay . . . how you feeling?"

"Starved."

He was beginning to like the idea of a roommate. She was a bit of a pain, but appreciated her tough, independent spirit. After breakfast and a nice long shower, Sarah came out all perky and smiley.

"You know," he said, looking over his shoulder as he cleaned up in the kitchen, "you could stay here until you find a job and hopefully stay out of the ER while you're looking."

She walked over and sat at the piano and plunked a few keys. "Would you teach me to play sometime?"

"Of course," he said, turning and facing her.

"Your playing is incredible, you know."

"Really?" he said, pleased. "Often I play without knowing what will turn up."

"I understand."

She then got up and gathered her things into her bag and went to the door as he watched.

"Thank you for taking me in," she said, smiling. "I'll never forget your kindness."

"Wait a minute," Mike pleaded and went up to her. "Where you going?"

"I need to keep checking at the Y and the unemployment office for work."

He turned so she wouldn't see his grimace and got his coat. "Hang on. I'll walk you down."

𝄞

Wednesday presented a sparkling autumn day after the cold front and rain had moved through. As they stepped out the front entrance of the apartment, they saw a U-Haul van parked in front with someone reaching in the side door for something.

"Sarah, wait a minute," Mike said and walked up to the van.

"Hey, man, moving into the Palace?" Mike said with a hand out as the young man turned around with a duffle.

"So that's what they call it," the guy said, reaching for a Mike's hand.

"Our little joke. What floor you on?"

"Oh, uh . . . the fourth floor."

"Fantastic! You're just down from me, at the end of the hall on the right, right?"

"Right." he said, noticing Sarah coming over.

"And here she is, sensational Sarah, who you will be reading about someday in the music reviews, and I'm Mike." Mike stopped and looked at Sarah. "And what am I?" he said, smirking.

"You're something else," she said, red-faced but grinning.

"Yeah, I'm something else." Turning back to the man, he asked, "And who are you?"

"I'm Jesse—from Minnesota."

"Minnesota? Is that . . . where is that?"

"Well"—Jesse chuckled—"you go to Chicago, then drive about six hours northwest into a strong icy headwind."

"Sounds lovely. Say, need any help? Sarah here, despite her frail appearance, is quite strong," Mike said.

Sarah narrowed her eyes and punched Mike. He groaned loudly, exaggerating his pain.

"No, this is the last of it," Jesse said, holding up his duffle bag, "but thanks,".

"Get settled and come on over. We'll have a few beers. I'm the first door on the left off the elevator. You do drink beer?"

"Oh yeah, but only if it's Grain Belt." Jesse snickered.

"Grain Belt? Oh, I get it—that's a joke."

"Not really, but whatever you have is fine. See you soon then," Jesse said and headed for the entrance.

Mike liked him instantly, thinking it was great having another single guy on the floor, and chuckled at the coy look Sarah had given him. But when he turned to tease her about the look, Sarah was already swept into the lunchtime crowd flowing down the sidewalk.

"Alright," he shouted, trying to catch up with her, "I'm going to give you one last chance to change your mind."

Sarah peered back and hollered over her shoulder as she weaved her way through the masses.

"Really, I'll be fine at the shelter, but I'll see you later at Holy Apostles."

He rushed up to grab her arm but stopped within reach. *Crap, her independence is going to get her in trouble.*

Then calling back to Mike as she joined the crowd crossing the street, "What're you serving tonight?"

"How do I know?" he yelled back. Then, waving his hand in frustration at her, turned back to his apartment.

"I can't believe it. New York City. I'm living in New York City!" Jesse rushed to the window to check out the view as Charlie, his yellow lab, looked up, trying to make out what he was saying. He had just gotten here and already met two fascinating people, especially Sarah—what a beautiful girl. The fourth-floor flat in Manhattan was exactly what he needed—within walking distance of the city's assets that were most important to him: his publisher, Washington Square Park for Charlie, the great historic Carnegie Library, and the coffee houses of Greenwich Village he was hoping would render a fresh perspective and help get him past a tenacious writer's block.

He had moved east from a small town in Minnesota after being listed as a finalist in the National Book Awards with his first novel. New York, to him, was where someone serious about writing lived. That, and he needed some space from his fiancée's parents. The plan was to set up residence and finish the draft for his next book. He would then return home to marry Becky, his college sweetheart, when she graduated in three months, and bring her back to New York to live happily ever after. However, the publisher of his debut best seller,

The Boy Who Found Life, was becoming impatient, with him taking longer than he had planned on the draft for the next book. On top of that he was having some doubts if Becky, a small-town girl at heart, could adjust to the chaotic pace of big city life. With more than a little panic collecting in his chest, he wasn't sleeping well. And even Charlie, who normally was pretty low-keyed, was becoming anxious.

Charlie danced back and forth when Jesse opened the door after returning the U-Haul. Dropping to his knees, he gave Charlie a big hug as they sat on the floor facing each other. This would be quite an adjustment, but his editor assured him there were lots of people in New York with dogs, and sitters and kennels were available if Jesse needed to leave town, but Jesse couldn't imagine leaving his sidekick for very long.

His studio apartment had a simple layout—long and narrow except for the kitchenette that receded in an alcove to the right. A closet and bathroom were through a door on the left at the end of the room. It took less than a half hour for him to arrange the single bed, an old upholstered reading chair, an end table and lamp, a card table and two folding chairs, his typewriter, a hi-fi (his pride and joy), and some clothes. He'd made sure to bring Charlie's tattered braided rug that he placed alongside his bed just like back home. With the meager furnishings in place, he stood at the door and admired the simple arrangement.

"Okay, dog," he said grabbing a leash and a plastic baggy in case Charlie needed it, "Let's see what this town is all about." He wanted to check out the route to the library and Washington Square and then get a bite to eat.

Walking down the hall, a lyrical thrumming met them as they approached his neighbor's door. It stopped them both. Charlie cocked his head, and Jesse stood there to let the sound wash over him. There was a quality about the music that touched him in a profound melancholy way. *Wow, this guy is good*. He was *really* looking forward to meeting Mike now.

While exploring on their first venture, Jesse scoped out some of the cheaper basement-level restaurants. Cradling a large slice of pepperoni pizza in one hand—from a real Italian pizzeria—and hanging on to a tugging Charlie with the other, he smiled to himself as the new smells of the city, bustle on the sidewalks, and rumble of traffic assaulted his senses. Jesse picked up a few things from a small local market, amazed how fresh the fruit and vegetables looked sitting in bins under the store awning. As he unlocked the door coming in from his first trip out for groceries, it struck him that he was actually becoming a resident of this magical place. After putting his food away, he reassured Charlie he'd be back soon and headed down the hall, primed with anticipation.

"Come on in, man," came a shout after his knock.

As soon as he got in the door, a beer was thrust into his hand. Mike already had a mixed drink started.

"I didn't expect New York to be so welcoming. You get these impressions about New Yorkers . . . who knows from where," Jesse said, checking out the place.

"How we treat people is important, man. If we don't care for each other, what is there—right?"

"Yeah, of course." Then, pointing to the piano, he said, "How in the world did you get that monster in here?"

"Oh, this baby? It's the reason I moved here. This floor used to be a dance studio, and it had been left behind when it was divided into apartments." Mike grinned. "I got it for a song . . . get it?"

"Yeah, I . . . I guess."

"Say, talk about stereotypes. You aren't one of those stoic Midwesterners, are you?"

"Uh . . . I don't think I'm very stoic."

"Sorry, man, I'm just messin' with you. Tell me why someone from the great state of Minnesota would leave the beautiful land of ten thousand lakes."

"Okay, so you do know a little about the state," Jesse said with a grin.

"Yeah, *Giants in the Earth* was required reading in prep school."

"Uh, that was South Dakota. Prep school?" he questioned.

"Yup, prep school."

"Sorry. You just don't look the type," Jesse said, a little embarrassed.

"Yeah, I know. I wasn't the type, but my folks thought I was. Okay, back to why you moved to the greatest city on earth," Mike said, pouring himself another drink.

"I'm a writer. It's possibly unfortunate that my first novel was a best seller, so now my publisher expects more of the same. So I've come here to get a fresh perspective and hopefully some inspiration."

"Wow, sounds intimidating."

"Maybe a little, but I've got some ideas. What about you? Do something in music?"

"Playing at a club in Gramercy Park for now, but looking to spread out some."

"Great. I'll have to stop by some night." He hesitated a moment, "Say, tell me about Sarah. What's her story?"

"Sarah." Mike said looking off. "Like no one I've ever met. I'm thinking she might be an angel. I'm not kidding. There's something going on there I can't quite comprehend, but it's wonderful."

"How did you get to know her?"

"It's a bit of a story. Once a week I serve at a soup kitchen, where I met her the first time, then twice in the emergency room. She has diabetes, and being homeless, she doesn't always take good care of herself, but the most interesting thing is her incredible voice. I've heard her sing a couple of times, and it's amazing. Somehow I would like to help her, but I'm not sure how to go about it."

"Poor kid. She seems really sweet."

Mike nodded. "Sweet maybe, but tough. I tried to get her to stay here until she got a job, but she wouldn't have it."

After sharing more family background, Mike had to get to the soup kitchen so Jesse headed back to his room to take Charlie for his evening walk.

Heading down to Bleecker Playground to see if Charlie might meet some new friends, Jesse thought how fortunate he was to have Mike as a neighbor. He admired Mike's artistry at the piano, but his curiosity was piqued by Mike's overly confident exterior that seemed to mask something entirely different. Then as he took in the exotic cityscape with stone and glass columns jetting into the evening sky, he felt strangely at home and was finally able to relax with the thought that moving to New York had been the right decision, at least for now.

10
Sarah

It bothered Sarah that Mike was upset with her after they left meeting Jesse. She tried to think of a way to thank him. When she got to the Y and saw nothing of interest on the bulletin board, she got an idea for a drawing and found a seat in the Y café, ordered tea, and dug out her sketchbook. Gazing up, she envisioned a scene with Mike standing in the crowded street yelling at her. She giggled, as she drew Mike with a frown shaking his finger at her. She then added a caption at the bottom: "Thank you for caring." Finally, happy with the composition she got out her colored pencils to finish it off.

After an hour and two cups of tea she was satisfied and slipped the sketchbook into her bag and headed to Holy Apostles. She could hardly wait to give it to him.

When she reached the dining hall, she made her way to the serving line and tried hard to keep a straight face as she stood in front of Mike, who was serving meatloaf.

"Hey, Miss Independent, how was your afternoon?" he said with his head atilt.

"Fine. I have something for you if you would like to join me for dinner," she said.

"Really? I'll check my calendar." Mike looked skyward for a moment. "Looks like I'm free—see you in a few."

Sarah found a table in the back corner and sat eating her dinner waiting for Mike. She pulled out her journal, feeling anxious and unsure of herself. She had never given anyone a drawing before—at least someone other than a teacher or her mom and dad—she suddenly felt embarrassed.

Mike finally came up and flopped down in his usual fashion and asked, "Well, what y' got? Hope you didn't spend too much."

She couldn't look at him.

"Sarah, what is it?" he said, looking concerned.

"I . . . uh . . . did a drawing,"

"You can draw?"

"Well . . ."

"Let me see it," he said, holding out his hands.

She reached in her bag, rooted around a bit, and came up with her sketchbook. When she gently tore out the drawing and handed it to him, she looked away.

"Wow, you did this?"

She flushed and tried to change the subject, but he went on and on about how amazing it was and how he wanted to see more of her work. Then suddenly Mike looked alarmed.

"Oh, I have to go. I've an audition for a singer at Johnny's. When will I see you again?" he asked, picking up his picture and admiring it again.

"What are you doing next Wednesday about this time?" she said softly.

Mike sighed and rubbed his forehead. "Yeah, see you next week—and please stay out of the ER."

"I'll do my best." Then putting her hand to her lips, she pressed her hand to his cheek. "Thank you—see you around."

He gave a little smile, stood up and headed to the kitchen. When he got to the door he stopped, looked back at her for a moment, then went inside.

She watched as he disappeared into the kitchen, then got up and headed out into the cool evening, pulling her coat collar up around her neck and buttoning the top button. She liked seeing him again and wondered what it would be like to date someone like Mike—or Jesse, for that matter. She then fell into a sweet daydream of a boy she had dated in high school. The one who took her to the movies on their first date and gave her a kiss in the last row of the theater. They had just started going steady, when his family moved out of the country. Then, with the scream of a police siren, her daydream was chased away. How could she have a boyfriend now? She needed a job and a place to live.

Walking as her mind wandered, she once again found herself outside St. Francis. Hearing the organ throbbing and the choir singing, she decided to slip in and listen to them practice before heading across the street to the shelter. As she sat in the last pew under the choir loft, she couldn't help but follow along, singing softly to herself. As the music transported her, she closed her eyes in the shadowy light of the voluminous domed interior and soon was lost in a reverie. She didn't notice the choir had stopped singing until a warm voice spoke from beside her.

"Hello, I'm John Matthews, the choir director. I heard you singing while we were on break," he said as he sat down at the end of her pew.

"Oh, I'm sorry, I . . ." she stammered, looking over at him.

"Don't be sorry—you have a beautiful voice. What's your name? Are you new to St. Francis?"

"Sarah Davis," she said, turning to him. "I've been here a couple of times."

"Then you live nearby?"

She thought a moment. "Yes, fairly close by."

"Good. Would you consider singing with us? We could sure use some help in the soprano section."

"Oh I don't know. I don't read music very well."

"I don't think that will be a problem." Then, leaning toward her, he cupped his hand to his face to whisper, "Some of the others don't read either, but after going over the material a few times, they pick it up. I have a feeling you'll do just fine."

She was unsure, but with a little more encouragement along with a welcoming smile, she relented. As she followed him up the stairs to the choir loft, her nerves jangled. At the top of the steps, the whole choir of about fifty men and women turned toward her. The director reached for her hand and led her to the front of the group.

"Choir, this is Sarah Davis. I'm thinking she would be a great addition. She sings soprano," the director said, looking over at her.

She held her breath and tried not to look scared, feeling terribly self-conscious in her old coat and scarf as the entire choir broke into applause and a welcoming cheer.

"For now you can sit between Beatrice and Lena. They'll take good care of you."

She stepped up a couple of rows, slid to the right and sat between the ladies making room for her. Lena smiled and held up "Ave Maria" for her to see.

She had never sung in such a large group before. But braced by the beautiful resonance of their voices she gradually gained confidence and instinctively blended in with the others. After practice the choir members greeted and complimented her, which embarrassed her. But she found she rather liked the attention and immediately thought of bringing Mike sometime.

The next couple of days dragged as she went about her new routine on the streets: going to the park to sketch if weather permitted, checking the Y bulletin board and the unemployment office for jobs. She finally mustered the courage to stop at Mike's apartment and ask him to come with her on Saturday evening to church. Not finding him home, she dug out her sketchbook and did a simple drawing of St. Francis, tore it out of her journal, and wrote: *Come to St Francis on 31st for 6 o'clock Saturday evening Mass—if you dare. Yours truly, Street Urchin.*

She felt a little foolish sliding it under his door, but at the same time hoped he would come.

After auditioning yet another good-looking but lackluster talent, Mike grumbled as he made his way back to his flat before heading to Johnny's. This made three thumbs down in one week. He was depressed. He'd quit NYU not only because he wasn't cut out for business but to have more time to compose and develop a unique sound. Crap, maybe he was just a piano man with a "microphone that smells like a beer."

He opened his apartment door and stepped inside. Noticing something between his feet, he bent down and picked up a drawing. A wave of joy swept over him as he read the note and admired the sketch. *That girl has made my day.* Yes, he would stop at the church on his way to work and see what Street Urchin was up to.

All manner of people flowed up the granite steps and through the huge oak and bronze doors of St Francis of Assisi. He was moved to see so many different faces of those both well dressed and shabby. However, once inside the packed sanctuary he immediately felt out of place. It wasn't at all like the small Harlem Baptist Church he grew up in. Not wanting to be disrespectful, he wasn't sure about dipping his fingers in the bowl of water to cross himself like the others. After deciding against it, he slid into the first pew he came to and looked around for Sarah. Trying to relax he scanned the lofty ceiling and multiple alcoves with statues of various saints. Paintings and stained-glass windows depicting biblical scenes filled the immense space with color and light. But where was Sarah? He thought she'd meet him on the steps, or was this one of her little jokes?

Annoyed, he was about to leave, when a priest came up the center aisle with a robed altar boy carrying a tall golden cross, followed by a choir. Mike's chest seemed to vibrate as the massive pipe organ thundered a brief interlude announcing evening Mass. The choir floated by in flowing robes, humming a familiar song he couldn't quite place. Reaching the front of the sanctuary the choir turned, faced the congregation, and starting singing. This was really different from the rocking gospel singers in his church—formal sounding but nice.

Wait—was that Sarah in the front row? How had he missed seeing her come up the aisle? He couldn't take his eyes off her as the voices filled the high vaulted church in four-part resonance, giving him chills. As he sat wide-eyed with his hand to his face, a sound entered the hallowed space like the zing of a crystalline arrow shot high above the others. It struck his heart like a blow, bringing tears to his eyes. He knew at once it had to be Sarah.

After the choir walked out the side aisles and up to the loft in back of the sanctuary, he sat in reflective silence for the rest of the service trying to comprehend what he just experienced.

It was truly heavenly. Yes "Ave Maria" was a masterful composition, but what made it transcendent was that voice.

Not sure when Sarah would reappear, he stayed in his seat after the service ended, gazing at the massive mosaic mural behind the white alabaster altar. Suddenly a small pair of hands reached around and covered his eyes, as if he had to guess who it was.

"Street Urchin, is that you?" he said with feigned surprise.

"None other. Wasn't sure you'd show up," she said, coming around from the back of the pew.

"Why wouldn't I? It's not often I get asked on a date to go to church."

"This wasn't a date, it was an invitation," she said, screwing up her mouth.

"Okay, whatever. So how long you been doing this behind my back?"

"I don't have to tell you everything," she said with a sassy look.

"No, really, it was great, and your solo—amazing," he said, fighting back his emotions.

"I've been to a couple of practices. Most of the music I pretty much knew, except 'Ave Maria,'" she said. Then bobbing her head up and down, she added, "I think I can do this."

"Yes, I'd say you did alright," Mike said and indicated he wanted to leave.

Mike fell silent as they descended the church steps into the cool evening air.

"What's wrong? I know the music is formal, but I thought you would like it, being a musician and all," she said, ending with a smirk.

"Sarah, you can't go back to the shelter."

"I'm fine now. Thanks to you for letting me rest up at your place." She smiled as she turned to cross the street.

"No, wait," he said, reaching for her arm. "You want a job?"

She stopped. "Well, I certainly need one. I've been checking at the Y—"

"Stop, listen to me. You can stay at my place for a week or two. We can work out some music together so you can sing with me at Johnny's." He grew animated as he envisioned the great things they could do together. "I'll set up another bed in the alcove with a curtain. You trust me, don't you?"

"I don't think my mother would approve," she said, then paused a moment. "I'd get paid for singing?"

"Of course you would," he said, shaking his head. "We just have to sell my boss on it."

Sarah looked down. "I don't know. Singing in a group is one thing. But—"

"Sarah."

"What?" She peered up at him.

"Wouldn't it be worth a try?"

"Well . . . I suppose. But I'll stay at the shelter and come over in the afternoons—if I'm not too busy." She flashed a broad grin.

"Already a diva," he said, smiling back.

When Sarah didn't show up Monday afternoon as planned, Mike fell into a funk and began pacing, thinking something happened to her before they'd even gotten started. As he passed by the window on one of his laps around the room, he looked out at the dark rain clouds rolling in from the Hudson and saw her standing across the street gazing up at his building. *How long has she been there?*

Busting out the door, he saw the elevator was busy, so double-stepped down the stairs, knifed through a crowd on the sidewalk and dodged cars as he jaywalked across the street. He ran up to her panting. "What the hell are you doing?"

"You swear a lot, you know," she said, looking at him askance.

He paused to catch his breath. "What's going on Sarah?"

"I was just thinking about my life and what I should be doing."

He took a step back and hunched his shoulders. "What to do? How about getting off the streets," he said, his voice raising. "I might be able to help if you just give me a chance."

Her eyebrows squished together. "I don't understand how this is going to work."

"It's really not complicated," he said, through tightly drawn lips. "I play and you sing."

Sarah peered from the corner of her eye. "Do you really think I can sing professionally?"

"Yes I do. Rudy's willing to give you a try tomorrow night. You'll just have to trust me on this. Can you do that?"

She looked down the street, and then up at him. "Yes . . . I suppose I can," and she picked up her bag, took his arm, and they crossed the street to his apartment.

♪

When they stepped inside his flat Mike couldn't wait another minute so went straight to the piano and had Sarah sit on a stool next to him. He coaxed her to sing a couple of her favorite songs, as he backed her up in her chosen key. His chest swelled hardly believing what he was hearing. Am I dreaming this?

"How do you know what to play?" Sarah questioned when she had finished her second number.

"How do you know what to draw, when you draw?"

"Yeah, but this is different."

"Not so different, I think."

Then reaching into a pile of sheet music stacked high on the corner of the piano, he got out a song and handed it to her. "Now it's my turn. Here are the words to 'Somewhere over the Rainbow.' I'll do a little intro, and then you come in when it feels right. I'll follow your tempo."

"Okay, I'll do my best," she said, looking anxious as she twirled a tuft of her hair.

He practically passed out hearing her sing the old standard in an incredibly fresh way. Gazing at her as she held the last note, he pondered what had gone into the making of this fabulous instrument. It was way more than a talent or a gift; it was unique because of who she was.

The session was going so well he couldn't help himself. He had to try something new to see how she would handle it.

"Well," he said, grinning wildly. "I think 'Somewhere' will definitely be on our play list." He feigned searching for something to gather his emotions before going on.

"One more thing." He paused and reached for Sarah's hand to get her full attention. "I would like you to join me on a number you've never heard before. It's an improvisation. With this one you just go with what comes to you, trusting your gut. I'll start with a few bars to set the mood, then you come in anytime you feel comfortable."

Her eyes widened, "I do whatever I want?"

"Whatever you feel like."

She nodded. "I can do that."

She stood from the stool, heaved a breath – her face aglow with anticipation.

Mike had just started an intro, when the phone rang. Scowling, he let it ring, hoping it might quit, but it persisted. Searching through piles of papers, under the piano, and around on the floor, he finally found his phone and answered.

"Mike here."

"Hello, Michael. It's your mother."

He frowned as his throat tightened. "Is everything alright?"

"Yes, everything's fine. Could you come home? I have something I need to discuss with you."

He squeezed his eyes shut and grimaced. Then scanning the room, he said, "Sure, what is it?"

"Your father left you some money. I want to go over that with you."

"Money?" he said as his pulse spiked. "Why would he leave me money?"

"Just come home, Michael. We'll go over it then."

He knew it was his mother's dream that he take over the business, get married and have kids, but he would gladly give up any money if he didn't have to think about those blessed stores again.

"Alright," he said as a wave of anxiety gripped him, "I'll come tomorrow afternoon before I go to work."

"Good. See you then," his mother said and hung up.

He put the receiver down and sat a moment staring at the phone. Would she try to change his mind about school? He wasn't sure he could take another confrontation.

"Sorry, I need to run home tomorrow," he said. "I'm not sure how long it will take, so I'll have to meet you at Johnny's at eight, if that's okay."

"Sure," she said. "I'll go after I stop at the Y; it's only a few blocks from there."

He was determined to continue their practice. He wanted to make sure Sarah was comfortable with the music for their debut. But everything he threw at her she knocked out of the park. He was more concerned about his nerves—so much was riding on this. He knew Rudy hasn't been happy with him and was probably looking for a replacement.

That night he had trouble sleeping. His thoughts alternated between thinking about going home and worrying how he would introduce Sarah at Johnny's. To make things worse, memories of the good times with Miranda bubbled up, causing him more heartache. His whole family had loved her.

♩

Visions of his childhood came to him as he passed by the Strivers Row townhouses. There was something comforting about the linden-shaded streets and backyards that slowed him down. As he approached the three-story brownstone he used to call home, a crackled voice called out to him.

"Michael, is that you?"

Looking over his shoulder, he saw old Mrs. Johnston in her usual spot, sitting in that ancient straight-backed chair so she could survey the street and maintain order in the neighborhood. Mike noticed her hair was mostly gray now as she worked at something in her lap.

"Mrs. Johnston, how are you?"

"I'm good, son. Say, sorry I missed your daddy's funeral. I was laid up."

"Yes . . . sorry you couldn't make it, ma'am."

"You must be sick, missin him?"

He winced. "I do, ma'am. Terribly." He waited patiently, knowing there was more coming.

"Say, you married yet to that beautiful Miss Miranda?"

What warmth he was feeling vanished entirely. "No. That didn't work out."

"Oh, sorry, my boy. I'm sure you'll find somebody nice."

"Yes, ma'am," he said, offering the best smile he could muster. "I must be going. So see you later."

"Say hi to your mom for me," Mrs. Johnston said with a big smile, showing off her gold-capped front tooth.

He waved and moved on down the sidewalk, and tried to get past the unintentional double whammy. Maybe he should just turn around now. He was about to puke, and he wasn't even in the door yet.

Walking up the familiar stone steps of his childhood home, he took in a deep breath as he opened the big six-paneled oak door. Immediately he was met with a flying hug from his kid sister, who had just gotten home from school. He hadn't realized how much he missed her.

"Runt," he said, smiling, "have you missed me?'

"Not hardly, just buttering you up so you will teach me how to drive."

"Drive?" he teased. "Surely you must mean ride a bicycle."

"You don't know how old I am, do you?"

"Sure I do—fourteen, maybe fifteen."

"Man oh man, how old are *you*? I think your memory is starting to go," Trina said, pouting.

"Runt, I would do anything for you." He closed his eyes as he tried to envision his baby sister driving. "I don't know if I'm qualified."

"Mother said to ask you, but I see how it is. You don't have time for me. Fine!" Trina spun around and stomped from the room.

"Michael, could you come in here, please," his mother called from the kitchen.

"Crap," he muttered, "What's next?"

He rubbed the back of his neck and braced himself for the next skirmish. When he walked in, his mother was sitting at the kitchen table with a serious look mixed with a bit of sadness.

"Sit down, Michael, I want to get this over with." She hesitated for a moment with a check in her hand. "Your father left you a little money." She paused again. "Its ten thousand dollars. He figured it would pay off your college loans so that wouldn't hang over you. He was very upset with you . . . as you know."

"Yes, Mother," he said as beads of sweat started to form on his forehead. "You know—why don't you keep it for the business."

His mother leaned forward. "Why would I do that? He left it for you. It has nothing to do with the business. He loved you, Michael."

He laced his fingers behind his head and tried not to lose it. "Fine, Mother . . . thank you," he said and reached for the check.

"I'm sorry. I'm trying to understand how you feel." She sat back in her chair. "If it wasn't your calling to go into business, I guess you did the right thing. I just wish you could have handled it better."

"I know, I know," he said. "I've replayed it a hundred times, and I know I should have presented the idea better to Father, but I didn't, and I can't change that."

Great, he thought, *can't wait to see Persis and get an earful of how I dumped the stores on her and left for the high life downtown.*

"Where's Persis?" he asked cautiously.

"At the store. They're setting up a new produce department. She's there twelve hours a day."

He snorted to himself. "Just like Father."

His mother remained silent for a moment. "It feels like I don't know you anymore. Please tell me what you're doing these days. Are you still serious about Miranda?"

"That's over with and not something I want to talk about."

He felt bad for being short with his mother, so without much else to say he told her about Sarah and having her join him at Johnny's, but left out that she was homeless and a pain in the butt.

"Please bring her by to meet us sometime—that is, if you still feel part of the family."

"Mother"—he paused catching her pensive gaze—"I assure you I still feel part of the family, and I promise to bring her up sometime, and yes, I will teach Trina how to drive."

He stood and grabbed his duffle. "I have to get to work. How old is Runt, anyway?"

"Trina is sixteen," his mother said sadly.

Damn, how did I not know that?

He stopped at the door, stepped back briefly to hug his mother, and headed out.

On the subway back to the Village, he tried to stuff his guilt over his father's death and neglecting his family. Only now with his father gone did he think of a way to explain his decision. He could have asked him to come downtown, show him the flat, and explain his creative process in coming up with new compositions. He could have taken him to Johnny's, introduce him to Rudy and the evening crowd and shared a beer. Why hadn't he done that? It would have been so easy.

Not able to dam up the guilt flooding in, hopelessness sank in. By the time he got to his apartment, his heart was pounding and he could barely breathe. He thought he was losing his mind or maybe having a stroke. His hands were beginning to shake. He fumbled for his keys and struggled with the lock. *Man, what's goin on? I'm losing it—big-time!*

After swinging the door open with a bang, he looked for the bourbon over the sink and saw it was almost empty. Lightheaded with panic, he slammed the door shut and went for the bottle. He quickly downed what was left, closed his eyes and waited for the liquor to take effect.

"This is bad, very bad," he called out to the room.

He went over to the piano and dropped down onto the bench. He tried to play something, but the keyboard was a blur.

"Crap, man, you got nothing!" he yelled.

He stood and kicked back the bench, knocking it down with a thud. Grabbing his keys and some money, he charged out the door and down the stairs to the street then turned for the liquor store on the corner.

12
Abyss

Jesse was having some success and smiled as he worked on the sequel to his first novel. The mantra "write about what you know" kept coming to mind. But he wasn't sitting in his parents' basement anymore, writing about the Midwest. No. What he needed was to expand the world of his characters with some inspiration from this amazing city.

"Charlie," he said, nudging his napping friend, "let's hit the pavement, find a park for you, and people-watch in the theater district."

Charlie peered up, stood, and shook himself awake.

As they headed out the front of the apartment they saw Mike coming toward them from the corner. Jesse always enjoyed his upbeat salutations and was ready for their usual banter, when Mike rushed past them, head down, without a word. Jesse spun around.

"Hey, Mike, what's up?"

Mike turned. "Oh, hey, man."

"You okay?"

"Oh . . . yeah, I was just working out something. You and Charlie out for some air?"

"We're heading for Times Square."

"Watch your wallet. You should be okay with Charlie though. See ya."

"Yeah, see ya," he said, then headed back down the street puzzling over Mike's behavior.

§

Jesse had learned to simply take in the world in front him when looking for inspiration—open not filtering. Strolling up Broadway to the theater district, the luminous marquees were muted by a soupy drizzle that had just begun. He'd forgotten his umbrella but decided to enjoy himself anyway, dodging splatter from the Yellow Cabs while running from marquee to marquee. Charlie, with his ears pinned back and squinting, not enjoying it quite as much. The misty rain put Jesse in a melancholy mood, which he would draw on later for inspiration. He had devised a productive schedule in his new home that pleased him: writing first thing in the morning till noon, then again in the evening when he had a different perspective on things.

Dripping wet after their walk, he and Charlie dashed to the entrance of the apartment, taking the stairs for a bit more of a workout. As he reached the fourth floor, he didn't hear the soft thrumming of piano as they walked past Mike's door—only a curious silence. He shrugged and continued down the hall looking forward to a nice hot shower.

After sharing a dinner of leftover stew with Charlie, he sat down at the typewriter. An hour or so into his draft, the protagonist was about to meet with some serious trouble, but Jesse wasn't sure how to develop it. About then Charlie stirred and let out a jaw-dropping yawn, causing Jesse to think about lying down for a little break. It wasn't long before both were asleep with a soft patter of rain against the window and ledge.

𝄞

"Jesse!" came a scream from the hall along with the pounding of fists on the door. "Please help me!"

Disoriented, Jesse lurched up in bed, his eyes wide. He stumbled over Charlie getting to the door and swung it open to Sarah's panicked face.

"I smell smoke! I think Mike's in there, but he's not answering!"

He pushed past Sarah with Charlie hot on his heels barking frantically. He broke into a run and hit Mike's door hard with his shoulder as he desperately cranked the knob. The door didn't budge.

With no time to call the apartment manager, he ran to the stairway, yanked out the fire extinguisher, and ran back to the door and slammed the doorknob. Charlie was really going crazy now. Sarah stood back with her hands to her face while Jesse slammed again and again, finally breaking the knob off. Then, standing back, he kicked as hard as he could, splintering the wooden doorframe. The door swung open with smoke billowing out like an evil genie.

Sarah shrieked as Charlie raced up and down the hall barking, not knowing how to help his master.

Jesse yelled to Sarah, "Find the fire alarm—check on the other apartments!"

Smoke continued to billow out as flames raced up the curtains, setting the bookshelf on fire. "Dammit, Mike—where are you?" he roared as he stumbled in coughing with his arm across his nose and mouth.

He found Mike with his head back, sprawled out in the beanbag chair. Tripping over bottles and dishes, Jesse grabbed him by the shoulders, dragged him out the door, and over to the stairway. Sarah met up with him after pounding on the other doors and finding no one home. He revived Mike enough to get him to his feet so Sarah could direct him down the stairs. Then he went back into the apartment with the fire extinguisher.

Crossing the room, his lungs burned and his eyes filled with tears. The fire extinguisher was barely adequate to keep up with the flames spreading from the curtains to the rug and bedspread. Overwhelmed with smoke, he was about to give up, when he heard yelling and the clomping of boots coming up the stairs. As he turned to the door, firemen poured in and yelled for him to get out.

Gasping, he stumbled out and down the stairs, stopping on the landing to catch his breath. A fireman at the entrance checked him out to see if he was all right. Jesse assured him he was okay and wove his way through the commotion on the street to Mike and Sarah sitting on the curb. Thankful but angry, Jesse stood looking down on them beneath the streetlight, huddled under blankets from the firemen.

"What's going on, Mike? You nearly burned the place down!" he hollered over the sounds of roaring engines and sirens.

"Sorry, man, I . . ." stammered Mike, shoeless and looking dazed.

Dropping down next to them, Jesse said, "If it wasn't for Sarah, you'd be dead."

Mike hung his head between his knees, mute, trying to collect himself. Then turning to Sarah, he said, "What can I say? Thank you for checking on me. The last I remember I was lighting a cigarette and . . . I don't know."

The fire chief came over to check on Mike and thank Jesse for his quick thinking in trying to put out the fire. They had gone over everything, and it was safe to go back up. The damage was mostly smoke from the curtains and rug.

After heartfelt thanks all around and a few more questions from the chief, the trucks roared off, leaving Jesse, Sarah, and Mike sitting on the curb with a small group from the apartment talking among themselves as they looked over at them.

Sarah reached for Mike's arm.

"I went to Johnny's, but Rudy said you hadn't shown up or called, so I knew something was really wrong," she said, then pulled the blanket up under her chin.

"Not just something—everything. My family, my career," he said, looking off down the street. "Crap. I've even hosed up your life."

They sat a few moments in silence as scraps of paper whirled around them, whipped up by an oncoming cold front.

"Mike, you can stay at my place. I've got an air mattress and sleeping bag for special guests," Jesse said with a crooked smile as he stood up.

Sarah nodded at Mike and got up to leave, shouldering her bag.

"Sarah, please stay. I need a friend tonight," Mike said, reaching up to grab her hand.

She winced at his grip. "I need to get to the shelter. Besides, you have a good friend who pulled you out of the fire."

Mike dropped her hand and slumped at the curb.

Sarah, appearing resolute, crouched, and gave them each a quick hug and headed down the street. As Jesse watched her, he was struck by the strength of this young woman. Not only was she lovely, she possessed a calm assurance. He had to know more about her.

𝄞

Nauseous, Mike trudged behind Jesse up the stairs. Reaching the fourth floor, he saw his door hanging open, and it occurred to him there might be some damage to his beloved piano. Not wanting to look but needing to, he told Jesse to go ahead, he'd be down shortly. Mike clenched his jaw and peered into the room still reeking of smoke. The curtains, bedspread, and rug were charred and could be replaced, but the bookshelf he'd made from two-by-fours and a scrap pallet had burned and fallen onto the piano, badly scorching the ebony lid.

"No!" he pleaded as he rushed to his cherished instrument. He couldn't take anymore. His dad was dead, his mother incensed, and he's probably lost his job. Now this. He gingerly lifted a charred piece of bookshelf off the piano and tossed it across the room. Rubbing his fingers along the deep ugly gouge, he groaned; then slowly sunk to the floor and rocked back and forth.

13

Epiphany

"**M**orning, Sunshine," Jesse said, as he typed away on his Smith Corona. "It's almost noon."

Charlie looked up, thinking Jesse was talking to him.

"Not you, hound," he said, leaning back in his chair. "How about some eggs and bacon, Mike?"

"No, no, no," Mike said, peering at Jesse from the sleeping bag on the floor. "How about a beer?"

Jesse got up from his desk and headed for the kitchenette. Charlie got up and followed, looking for a little snack.

"A beer . . . hmm," he said, opening the fridge. "I don't think so. Seems the last time you had some drinks you tried to burn down the city."

"Oh yeah—the fire! Crap! Is everybody okay?" He sat up with a gasp.

"Yes, yes," Jesse said, talking over his shoulder as he got breakfast started. "Figured you might have some missing pieces about last night."

"How bad is it?"

"Could have been a lot worse.'"

Mike pulled his knees to his chest and bowed his head. "Man, I know. Not cool."

"Yeah, looks like your piano will be scarred for life."

"Okay, I get it. Enough already," Mike said, unzipping the sleeping bag.

"I've seen this before. I don't know you very well, but I recognize a drunk when I see one. Boozers run in my family," Jesse said, bending down to give Charlie something to eat.

"Oh, so that makes you an expert," Mike said, groaning as he stood up.

"Yeah, I guess it does."

"Well, I don't think I have a problem. Last night was just an accident."

Jesse arched his eyebrows, dug in his pocket, and tossed Mike a key ring. "Here are some keys. Go down and check out your place and see how much you remember. Your door hinges are okay, but I put hasps and padlocks inside and out, to hold until the super can replace the frame, doorknob, and latch."

Mike looked at the keys and moaned. "Thanks for taking care of that. I owe you, man."

"You're welcome," Jesse said and walked over with two cups of coffee and handed him one. Then he went back to his typing and sat down, appearing like something was on his mind.

"Don't know what your feelings are about Sarah, but I can't stop thinking about her."

Mike blew in the cup and took a long sip. "Thought you were getting married soon."

"Yeah . . . that's the plan," Jesse said, puckering his lips.

Mike took another long drink. "You don't sound so sure."

"I'm sure," Jesse said. "Just never met anyone like Sarah."

Mike studied Jesse a moment, set his cup down on the table and went for the door. He stopped with his hand on the knob and peered back. "Well…she's just a friend," he said, and let himself out.

Standing in the doorway of his apartment, Mike surveyed the damage in the light of day. He saw his old metal fishing pole, bent in half, lying on the floor against the far wall. He remembered grabbing it last night in a fit of hopelessness, and trying to break it over his knee. *What was I thinking?*

He went over to pick it up and thought he would chuck it. But holding it for a moment, he cranked the reel, and with the clicking of the gears he was snapped back in time. He couldn't do it. Carefully gripping both ends of the bowed metal, he straightened it as best he could, but couldn't quite get the kink out of it. *Great, I'll never forget this night.*

Turning back to the room, he hung his head and tried to think. Somehow he had to move on. He had to get this mess cleaned up and hauled down to the dumpster. And, he was supposed to meet Sarah at Holy Apostles. So no matter how lousy he felt, he was determined to see her.

$$\oint$$

Mike didn't care for Jesse needling him about his drinking but went back to thank him for the lock and to let him know he was feeling better after hauling out the debris, cleaning up the floor, and taking a shower.

"Okay then. But if you want to know any more about alcohol abuse, you know where to come. After all, I am an expert," he said with a wink.

"Yeah, man, I get it," Mike said, cringing from the jab, heading for the door. "See you around"

Now to Johnny's, hoping to set things straight. But he wasn't sure Rudy would even speak to him. He paused under Johnny's faded blue awning and considered his options. He had none. Taking a long deep breath he entered the dark cavernous club and sat at the bar waiting for Rudy to come out from the storage room.

"Hey, man—I want to apologize for last night," he blurted as soon as he saw Rudy. "Something came up at the last minute that I had to take care of."

Rudy shook his head as he lugged in a case of beer and set it down. "You could have called," he said over his shoulder. Then moving to face Mike, he added, "This is it. If you screw up one…more…time…you're out of here. You can't be yelling at customers. And not showing up without a word!"

A couple of hunched customers sat up on their stools and peered over at them from the end of the bar.

"Really, it won't happen again."

"Seems I've heard that before," Rudy barked.

"Hang with me, man. I've just hit a rough patch."

Rudy turned to dry glasses that had been soaking. "What about the new singer?"

"We can start tomorrow night if it's okay. I know you won't be disappointed."

"Yeah . . . alright," Rudy said finally. "I wish I didn't like you so much. It would be easier to fire your ass."

"Thanks, man." Relieved, Mike spun around for the door.

"Hey, you have a name for this duo?" Rudy called out.

"I'll have one by tomorrow." He stopped and graciously bowed. "You're the greatest, man!"

"Sure I am," Ruby said, shaking his head. "This better be good."

Mike walked out of Johnny's feeling a lot lighter. Now he had to get right with Sarah.

There was something comforting about the soup kitchen at Holy Apostles. It was uncomplicated, honest, and real. There was no pretense—people just trying to get by, like himself. He needed that, especially the way he'd been feeling lately.

Upon entering the dining hall through the side door, he searched the room for Sarah. She stood in the corner to the right and waved to him. Her sad smile caused him to choke up as he started toward her with his head down.

"Hi," was all he could get out as he stood in front of her.

"You okay?" she asked, looking stressed.

"I'll be okay if you'll forgive me," he said.

"I'll forgive you . . . if I can trust you won't do something like that again. I can't lose another person I care about."

He was shaken. *She really cares about me.* His chest swelled as he reached out to her, and they embraced like they were the last two people on earth. Sarah's tender spirit awakened something in him. It made him realize, what he did with his life really mattered to someone other than himself.

14
The Moment

Mike was yanked from the abyss by Sarah's soul-saving forgiveness and was grateful he'd been given one last chance with Rudy, but waited till after dinner to talk to Sarah about Johnny's.

After cleaning up the dining hall when everyone had left, he went back to the kitchen to say good-bye to the staff. Al turned from the pots and pans he was washing when Mike came through the door. "Say, something going on between you and that pretty little redhead?"

"Gee, Al, doesn't anything get past you?"

"Not much," he said, arching his eyebrows.

"Man, she's just a friend—a good friend," Mike said, looking back at Al as he pushed back out through the kitchen door.

Sarah gave him a shy smile as he crossed the room.

Stopping in front of her, he announced, "Rudy can't wait to hear our new duo."

"Oh—so he didn't fire you after all." she said with a little smirk.

"Ouch. No, I promised to behave." He dropped his head. "Sarah, I know I'm a mess right now. God knows I need help sorting things out."

She waited a moment to catch his eye. "Mike, I'm here. I know how it feels to be lost."

"Thank you," he gasped. *I thought I was helping* her.

He pulled out a chair and filled her in on his conversation with Rudy. "We need a name for the duo. Any thoughts?"

Her face turned thoughtful and gazed up for awhile. Then she said, "*The Moment*. It would be a tribute to my Grandma Mae, who always told me to live in the moment and not fret over the past or be anxious about the future."

Perfect. He smiled, taking in her sweet aura.

"I like it," he said. "We are now known as *The Moment*."

He noticed that anytime Sarah talked about her family she became reflective and serene. The more she disclosed about herself, the more he realized how much her extraordinary life of struggle and survival contributed to the richness of her voice. That voice and that life were an enigma, yet more and more were inspiration for his late-evening compositions.

After straightening up their table and heading for the door, Sarah stopped and reached for his arm.

"You should check with Jesse. See if he could come with us to Johnny's."

He frowned. "Oh, I don't know."

"You don't know? He saved your life!" Sarah said, scrunching up her face. "He's a good guy and could use a friend."

Mike thought a bit but couldn't come up with a reason why not. "Yeah, I suppose. He could see you get to the shelter after your number."

"Why do you think I can't take care of myself?" she asked, looking hurt.

"Of course you can, tough guy." He said holding up his hands. "Alright, I'll check with him when I get home."

By the time they got to Johnny's the next evening, Mike could hardly contain himself. He introduced Sarah and Jesse to Rudy and explained the plan for Sarah's number. Jesse made small talk with Rudy as Mike found Sarah a seat at the far end of the bar. "Now don't be nervous. You'll do fine."

"I'm fine. How about you?" she said.

"Okay, I'm a little nervous. Remember—I'll do one warm-up song, and then we'll do 'Somewhere over the Rainbow' together. Start singing from the bar, then walk over to me." He glanced over at Rudy for a thumbs-up but only got a furrowed glare. *Oh boy, I recognize that look: "This better be good."*

Mike sat down at the piano and began with a familiar ballad that caused the clientele to relax and chatter with their tablemates. He held his breath as he slid into the next number, hoping Sarah got the cue. Nothing. Horror struck him. But then from the far end of the bar came that ethereal voice, falling into an improvisational harmony that stopped all conversation. He began breathing again.

Sarah seemed as confident as if she were singing just for him. She looked out over the audience, making connection like a pro. But even better—she exuded a sincerity that reached all hearts.

He motioned with his head for her to join him. Carefully she slipped off the bar stool as she sang. Then reaching for the backs of chairs while making eye contact with the customers, she made her way to the piano as all eyes followed her. She was wearing her old rumpled raincoat and scarf, which made her voice even more poignant. People sat with mouths agape.

The sight and sound caused some to tear up and others to marvel, shaking their heads in disbelief.

As she approached the piano he smiled to give her confidence, but she seemed not to need it. Looking down on him, she pulled *him* into her magic. He was swept to the mountaintop, mesmerized.

With everything riding on this one number, Mike froze as he sustained the last chord, waiting for the audience reaction. However, when the crowd erupted into spontaneous applause with Sarah disappearing out the front door as planned, there was no doubt she was a hit. Mike's face exploded with joy as he motioned for Jesse to hustle Sarah back for an encore. Adding to the euphoria of the moment, he caught Rudy smiling—something he hadn't seen from him for a long time.

When Sarah came back in the door, the crowd grew even louder. Mike bowed to her, held out his hand, and beckoned her to the piano. She appeared in shock as she made her way back to him. All he could do was grin.

"Well, it appears we need to do another number," he said when she reached him.

She just hunched her shoulders, looking uncertain.

"How about an improvisation. Something like we did at my place?"

She smiled. "Oh yeah. I could do that all night."

As he sat back down at the piano, the audience quieted, giving them their full attention.

He reached out for the keys, closed his eyes, and tried to imagine something that would be meaningful to her. He remembered Sarah telling him about the sweet dream she had sitting with her family on the porch of their Kentucky farmhouse as the morning sun warmed them.

With that vision in mind, he conjured up what that might sound like put to music.

Opening with that theme as an interlude, it seemed to resonate with Sarah as her face slowly brightened. Then, looking off over the room, she hummed and sang an enchanting wordless song, completely original. Mike soon realized he needed to follow her lead and backfill with harmonies and riffs. *My God, I can't believe this is happening.* He was rapturous.

Time stood still as he looked upon Sarah, who stood glowing, an alabaster face with a flaming red halo of hair. He thought his heart would stop.

He slowly floated back to earth as their journey came to an end. The roar of the crowd was barely audible to him as he leaned back to take a breath. When the audience finally settled down and returned to their conversations, Sarah leaned down and gave him a big hug.

"I guess they liked it okay," she said.

He gazed up at her. *She has no idea how good she is.*

"Yeah, you could say that," he said, still in shock.

"You think Rudy will hire me?"

"I'll talk to him after the next set." Mike's mind whirled with possibilities. "But he better."

Sarah's eyes sparkled as she smiled. "This was really fun. Thank you."

Jesse walked up and stood between them. "Wow, wish that had been recorded. I think you two should be golden with Rudy." He reached and gave Sarah a hug.

"Thanks," Mike said as he watched Jesse embrace her.

"Mind if I see Sarah home? Think that was the plan," Jesse said, looking at each of them.

Mike frowned. "Don't ask me."

Jesse turned to her. "Sarah, what do you think? We want you safe."

She cocked her head. "Sure, why not? It's on your way."

Jesse glanced at Mike and grinned. "See you later. Thanks for the invite."

He nodded to Jesse, glad Sarah would be safe, but questioned Jesse's intentions. Thankfully it wouldn't be long before she could afford her own place—and he would be married.

As Mike watched them head out the door, Rudy suddenly appeared with a fresh bourbon and water, looking as pleased as a cranky retired NYPD detective could look.

"You know, if this hadn't worked, you were out of here," he said flatly.

Mike tilted his head. "I kind a guessed that."

"Should I call the agent and tell him to forget sending someone?"

Mike smirked. "Probably a good idea."

"You pulled it off, kid. You were really amazing."

"Thanks, man, but I'm afraid it was all Sarah."

Before Mike left for home after his last set, Rudy called him over to the bar. In the past this would not have been a good thing. But instead of confronting Mike from behind the bar, Rudy poured himself a small nightcap of brandy, which was his custom, and came around and pulled up a stool next to him.

"So," Rudy began, "thinking of bringing Sarah on full-time?"

"Yeah, that's the plan, if that's cool with you."

"I assume you have more than two numbers?"

Mike put on his best poker face. "Of course. We've got a couple dozen, and we're just getting started."

"If it goes as well for the rest of the week, I'll want you to sign a six-month contract," Rudy said, looking hard at him.

Mike managed to look serious, although he wanted to get up and do cartwheels around the room. "Well, there's two of us now." His brain shifted into overdrive to come up with something Rudy would go for.

"Yeah, I get that," Rudy said, reaching for his drink.

"Well . . ." Mike paused in thought, and then decided to go for it. "How about the two of us get the same pay I get now, plus twenty-five percent of increased sales from an average for the week." Mike sat back, brought his fingertips together like he'd seen in the movies, and waited for Rudy's response.

Rudy turned his attention to his drink then set it down. He brought his hand up and rubbed his chin as he looked off down the bar.

"Okay," he said, turning to Mike. "We'll try that for two months and then renegotiate depending on how it goes."

Mike paused for dramatic effect, trying to tamp down his excitement, and then put out his hand to Rudy. But he couldn't help himself and practically giggled. "Rudy, you have a deal."

"Mike," Rudy said, holding his hand firmly, "I hope you'll buy that girl some better clothes."

"No problem. She did that for the effect it would have on the customers. Think it worked, don't you?"

Rudy angled his head to the side and peered at Mike through his massive eyebrows. "Yeah, okay, whatever. Son, don't forget—I was a cop for twenty-five years."

Mike puffed out his cheeks. "Yeah, man, I know *that* for sure."

Rudy returned to his drink with a snort and tossed down the last of his brandy.

Mike stepped out from Johnny's into a whole new world—like he'd escaped from a bottomless pit into glowing sunlight – even though it was one in the morning. He was giddy. He'd never been giddy before. He liked it. His first reaction was to find Sarah and give her the good news about the deal with Rudy, but he needed some time to think so headed to the nearest subway station to ride for a while until he had things sorted out.

Getting home at three a.m. and up again at six, he grabbed a quick shower and a coffee and was on his way to Sarah's shelter, wanting to be there first thing to surprise her with the news. After sitting for a half hour in a coffee shop across the street, he saw her emerge from the entrance lugging her shoulder bag. He watched to see which direction she would head so he could sneak up and surprise her. She appeared with a smile, turned to face the morning sun for a moment, did an about–face and headed west on 31st Street.

He hustled up his side of the street, crossed over way ahead of her, and hid by slipping into a doorway of a bookstore.

"Miss Davis, is that you, child?" he said in his best Southern drawl as she walked past.

Not recognizing his voice at first, she spun around with eyes wide. "Oh, you," she said, charging into him with all her one hundred and four pounds. "You gave me a fright."

Mike tried not to give away his excitement by appearing nonchalant.

"Guess what I have?"

"Cirrhosis of the liver?" she said. "Not surprised though, the way you throw down those bourbons."

"Besides that."

"Give me a hint"

"It's made of paper."

"An expensive roll of toilet paper so I don't have to use the cheap stuff at Penn Station."

"Okay, that's it. You don't get to guess anymore. I just won't tell you," Mike said, turning away trying to look hurt.

"Yes, you will. I'll just wait here until you can't stand it—then you'll tell me." She leaned close and stared up at him with a goofy smile.

"Arrrgh," he snarled. He reached in his pocket and handed her a check for four hundred dollars.

"What's this?"

"That's your first check as a pro."

Sarah looked up after staring at the check. "I don't understand. We haven't started yet."

He was fairly confident they would go to contract and estimated together they'd make about eight hundred a week. So he wrote a check from the account he'd opened with the money from his father. He felt it only fair to split fifty-fifty because without her none of this was possible.

"It's an advance. Rudy wants us under contract with him."

"But, why would he do that?"

"Because he doesn't want to lose us. He's afraid we'll go somewhere else."

She pressed her lips together and looked as if she was about to cry.

Mike pulled her over to a bus stop seat. They sat down and he held her.

"So . . . what ya gonna do with all that cash, Miss Davis?"

She thought a moment, "Well . . . I think it's time for some new clothes."

"And a place to live." he said. "I'm thinking you'll make that much every week."

"Mike—my own place." She looked as if she was imagining her dream home.

"Yes. How about we start looking tomorrow? I've heard of a couple of apartments we can check on."

"Really?" she said with eyes twinkling.

"I love it when you're happy. I never want to see you sad again," he said, grinning.

𝄞

Mike was concerned that Sarah find a safe apartment, so he searched for something affordable that was near him. He had set up two appointments in Chelsea for the next afternoon and met Sarah at Leo's Donuts to surprise her with the good news.

"The usual for you two?" Leo shouted from behind the counter as they walked in.

"You bet, man," Mike said as they sat down facing each other.

With his eyes rolled back and inhaling deeply, he said, "Isn't this the best smell in all the world?"

"It is," Sarah said. "Reminds me of when my mom would bake bread."

"Didn't you live in Chelsea when you moved here from Kentucky?" He smiled as he thought about the appointments he had lined up.

"Yes we did."

"Did you like it there?"

"It was a bittersweet time," she said, looking down at her coffee. "It was wonderful for a while. I loved school, especially art, and I had a good doctor who was helping me deal with my diabetes."

He hesitated but sensed an opening to ask about her past. "What were your parents like?"

She turned away with a far-off look.

He wished he hadn't asked. Recalling the pain of his father's death.

Sarah sighed and looked over at him. "I haven't talked about them . . ." she said, closing her eyes and squeezing back tears. Then, bowing her head into her hands, she cried silently as her shoulders shook. Mike scooted his chair around the table and sat next to her and pulled her to his chest.

"Sorry…I'm so sorry," he said as he looked over Sarah's shoulder at Leo, who stood behind the counter looking back at them with eyes watering. Mike sat and held on to her until her sobbing stopped and her breathing slowed.

Pulling back in her seat, she took a deep breath. "Thank you for asking. I haven't talked to anyone about them since they died."

He sat patiently to see what she wanted to do.

She reached in her pocket for a tissue and wiped her eyes. "Mom had a job at Macy's, and Dad worked road construction on FDR Drive. On weekends we did everything together— went to museums or Breezy Point on picnics and on special occasions to Little Italy for Sunday dinner." She paused and looked away. "Within six months I lost them both. First Dad was killed in a crane accident at the job site, then Mom just months later from a stroke. She had a hard life—sick with TB in Kentucky after losing her mother. We were barely making it in the Chelsea apartment when she died in her sleep. I think her heart just gave out."

Mike winced. "I'm so sorry. I didn't mean for you to dig all that up."

"It's okay, Mike. Thank you for caring," she said, giving him a little smile.

He thought a moment while he fiddled with his coffee cup. "So . . . would you like to check out some apartments?"

She nodded, "I would like that."

"Where would you like to look?"

She gave him a big grin. "Chelsea—it feels most like home to me."

"Great," he said, heaving a sigh. "I'm so glad, 'cause I found a couple nice apartments near 18th and 6th Avenue. Not far from the Y, Madison Park, and most importantly—me."

"Mike, really?"

"Yes. You can afford it now. And I think this is just the beginning," he said with a flourish.

Sarah's eyes brightened and gazed on him; a dreamy look, as if she was recalling something sweet. Catching her eye, he asked what she was thinking.

"I was thinking of how much you remind me of my big brother."

"You have a brother? He must be very handsome if I remind you of him."

"Yes, of course," she said, smiling. She paused a moment. "Okay, now it's your turn. You don't talk much about your family. All I know is that you went to college and didn't like it. And playing at Johnny's…didn't care for that much either."

Mike cleared his throat and thought a moment. "Sorry, I'm not in a good place with my family right now. Would rather not talk about it."

"Okay then," she said, sitting up. "That's all I got too. Say, how about those Giants? Think they might have a chance this year?"

He rolled his eyes. "Alright smart aleck, why don't we go check on some apartments? Or would you rather sleep under the stars all winter?"

"Yeah," she said, "it is getting a little nippy out."

They met Saturday morning to check out apartments in Chelsea that were within walking distance of his place. It became obvious which was the best choice for her—the second floor walk-up with a south-facing window for sunshine and furnished with all the basics: bed and dresser, couch with end table and lamp, small table and chairs, and a kitchen that even had a set of dishes and assorted pots and pans. The best part though was she could move in immediately.

Sarah trembled as she sat at the small wooden table to sign the lease. She then smiled up at him as she set down the pen giving him jolt of joy that nourished his soul.

Mike hated shopping with women—having been dragged as a kid on endless buying excursions with his mother and sisters. But he was no match for Sarah when she set her mind to something. She doggedly coerced him into a trip to the Greenwich Village Goodwill to get his opinion on an outfit for their one-night gig Mike had landed at The Caribbean in Midtown. It wasn't that he was a snob—shopping at Goodwill just never occurred to him. Standing in the middle of rows and rows of clothes, Sarah turned to him with an expression he hadn't seen before.

"Mike, I don't know what to wear at a fancy club like The Caribbean."

"Do you know how much I loathe shopping?"

"You don't care what I wear?"

"Nope. You can go naked, as far as I'm concerned."

Sarah pulled her head back and raised her eyebrows. "Boy, I thought this would be fun. You aren't fun at all. Actually, you are being rather contrary."

"Contrary? I haven't heard that word in years."

"I bet you heard it a lot when you were growing up," she said, frowning.

He sighed and looked at her with his hands pressing against his temples. "Sorry. I'll try to be helpful."

"Good," she said, turning with a broad smile. "I'll be back in a few minutes. Find a seat."

Mike knew the drill, so he wandered over to the men's aisle as he waited. *Okay*, he thought, *she wants to have fun?* He searched through the suits, grabbed a three-piece English herringbone with a hunter-green velvet vest, and headed for the men's changing room. Picking up a fedora, sunglasses, and an umbrella as he came out, he posed as a mannequin and waited for her to emerge from the dressing room.

Sarah appeared from the far end of the store and walked up and down the aisles picking up an armload of clothes. She then walked over to Mike and dumped the clothes in his outstretched arm.

"Would you please hold these, sir, while I look for my poor old uncle Michael."

"Argh, how d'ya know?" he said, whipping off the sunglasses.

Sarah giggled. "Oh, let's see. Maybe it was the Afro sticking out from under that hat or the Nike herringbone combination." She paused, looking at him a little closer. "Say, that's not a bad look for you."

"See, I can be fun," he said, going to the mirror. "Hey, you're right. This isn't bad." He studied himself. "I'm going to get it. Man, wait till Rudy sees this!"

Sarah bought a number of ensembles ranging from Laura Ashley to Gypsy Rose Lee. She was fearless when it came to mixing colors, textures, and styles, developing a unique look all her own. She left the store wearing one of her new composite outfits, with Mike in his three-piece suit. Out on the street, he noticed people gazing at her, not out of pity as before in her old raincoat and scarf but with admiration. With her striking red hair, newfound confidence, and fearless blending of colors and fashions, it was as if he were witnessing a butterfly breaking free of its cocoon.

On their way back to Sarah's new apartment, they walked past the Pippin Vintage Jewelry store. She gave him a tug back to the window to point out something that caught her eye.

"Isn't it beautiful?" she said.

"What?"

"That purple ring."

"Oh . . . yeah, I guess so," Mike said, looking closer at the amethyst stone simply set in a thin gold band. After briefly taking it in, he looked back into Sarah's lavender eyes. "You know, I bet the whole world has a purple tint to you?"

"Huh?"

"You do know I'm black, don't you?"

She screwed up her mouth and rolled her eyes with a "what an idiot" look on her face.

"Sorry, I thought it was funny," he said, pursing his lips and looking skyward. "Anyway, when I become rich and famous, I'll come back and buy that for you."

Sarah just stood there with a coy smile as he puzzled over her expression.

𝄞

Although she rarely spoke to anyone at the soup kitchen when homeless, Sarah now wanted to volunteer serving meals. She had heard about the Covenant House soup kitchen on 41st and asked Mike to go with her before their practice session. Mike liked the idea—he was curious how it would compare to Holy Apostles.

With winter settling in to stay, snow swept in from the northwest as they hustled up 10th Avenue to Covenant House.

By the time they reached the soup kitchen with flakes sticking to them like Velcro, they were caked with a layer of icy-white frosting. Warmth and nourishing smells greeted them as they brushed and stamped the snow off after entering the basement-level kitchen and dining hall. While Mike was getting information from the evening supervisor about food preparation and serving, he caught a glimpse of someone disappearing into the pantry.

Turning to Sarah, he said, "Did you see her?"

"Who?"

"I think that's my sister!" Mike said just as Persis returned from the pantry carrying a large can of tomato sauce. They paused for a moment upon seeing each other, then asked in unison, "What are you doing here?"

Persis, even wearing a simple beige smock, looked like she'd just stepped out of a fashion magazine.

"I come downtown on Tuesdays," she said, "to meet with financial people and work here in the evenings."

Floundering a bit, Mike finally got out, "I've worked in Holy Apostles' kitchen for the past year." Then remembering Sarah, he introduced her. "We met there a couple of months ago." He decided to leave it at that.

With her head to one side, Persis held out her hand, looking puzzled. "Pleased to meet you, Sarah."

"Same here," Sarah said, looking to him for what to do next.

He didn't quite know where to begin. "How's Mother and Runt?"

"Mother seems lost without Father. I'm not sure how to help her with that. And Trina misses you, of course, but don't worry—Uncle Luther is there for her and is teaching her how to drive." Persis's words crackled with hostility. She then turned her back and continued working.

He had let Runt down again. He couldn't stand it—he had to fix this. Without thinking it through, he said, "We'll come up next weekend so Mother can meet Sarah and I can spend some time with Trina."

"Fine. Do what you want. I'll be at the stores," Persis said over her shoulder.

Sarah peered at him with a sideways glance. He looked back and hunched with resignation. This little interlude was forcing him to do something he'd hoped to put off indefinitely. But what could he do?

He made an excuse why they couldn't stay, something about needing to practice. He'd had his fill of guilt and wanted to avoid explaining any more about Sarah.

Riding the subway back to the Village, he realized he hadn't even asked Persis how the stores were going. Inside his apartment, Sarah sat at the old chrome-and-Formica kitchen table to sketch as he sank into the beanbag chair. Trying to get his mind off the stores, he asked Sarah more about her family.

"You mentioned you have a brother. Where is he now?"

"I had an older brother, Adam. He was tall and strong, taking after our grandpa, I guess." Sarah paused.

Mike jumped in. "You had . . . ?"

"He drowned," she said, looking straight at him with a softening expression. "When we lived in Kentucky, he borrowed a boat to take me for a ride and a picnic for my twelfth birthday. On our way to a sand bar island we hit something that knocked me out of the boat and put a huge hole in it. Even though he couldn't swim well he didn't hesitate jumping in to save me with the only life vest, but when he tried to swim back to the boat he went under. They found him downriver the next day." She paused. "He was my idol, my best friend, my hero. I think of him every day and pray I will see him again."

She said this in a way that shook him – without a note of sadness but with a sense that Adam was still with her in some way.

"Sarah, how did you manage?" Mike asked, tearing up.

"Grandma Mae said we couldn't change what happens. We're not in control of everything. Neither can we understand what keeps the stars up in the sky. We are only responsible for how we react to things that happen."

He wasn't sure he could accept what Sarah was saying, but asked, "Your grandma meant a lot to you."

"I think she saved my life also," she said, brightening. "She was my world when Mom was in the sanatorium and Dad worked in the mines. I think Mom got TB because she was so depressed and weak from losing my brother. Dad was away for weeks at a time, so it was Grandma Mae and me. She taught me everything: how to cook, sew, milk a cow, grow vegetables, and how to be happy with what you have and live in the moment—not in yesterday or tomorrow." She paused and looked off as if summoning a vision.

"Whenever I would get low, she would quote something from the Bible. Like, 'Child, you're not to worry about a thing. Aren't you more valuable than the birds of the air, which God cares for?' or 'Don't go borrowing trouble from tomorrow; it has enough trouble of its own. Get your Bible now and see if I'm not right. Hard times bring you closer to God, and sunny days are your reward for hanging tough. You and me are tough, right, Sarie?' She would call me Sarie and pull me close, hugging me hard."

Mike went silent as he thought how he would feel with so much tragedy. "I don't think I could have survived what you've gone through."

"You could. I would help you," she said with a smile that clutched his heart.

Sarah's story transported Mike into her world of loss, hardship, and enduring love. Reflecting on the death of his own father, his heart ached for her. However, he worried her simplistic view of life made her vulnerable to sleazy opportunists. How could she possibly survive? You had to go after life with a stick and beat your way through.

As he pondered Sarah's soulful narrative and how he might translate it into music, a greater challenge pushed its way into his mind. Taking Sarah to meet the family.

17

Becky

Becky looked like a dream as she came down the jet way. With her long blond hair, baby-blue eyes, and curvaceous stride, she garnered approving looks from most of the men and even some women. Jesse felt a little smug as he went up to greet her with a hug and a kiss.

"You look great," he said. "How was your flight?"

"Not bad, except for the whiny kid behind me and the man next to me who fell asleep and snored."

"I'm sorry," Jesse said.

"I'll get over it. So what are we going to do now that you've got me here?"

"Oh, there is so much to see, but first I want to show you our cozy apartment in Greenwich Village. It's got so much character," he said, giving her a hopeful smile.

It had been over a month since he'd seen her, and for whatever reason he was nervous. He had fallen in love with New York and feared she wouldn't feel the same. And then there was Sarah, who had crept more and more into his mind.

Grabbing Becky's suitcase, the size of a small steamer trunk, Jesse hailed a cab for the Village. After a heart-stopping ride, weaving through Midtown traffic with Becky practically drawing blood with her hand on his knee, they were dropped off in front of the Bleecker Street apartments. Jesse grew uneasy sensing Becky's anxiety as they rode the clunking freight elevator up to the fourth floor.

"Well, dear, what do you think?" he asked hopefully, as he swung the door open to the studio apartment.

"It's cozy, alright," Becky said, winkling her nose as she scanned the tight quarters.

"Here—sit in my reading chair," he said, then sat on the bed facing her.

Becky hesitated a moment as she squirmed in her seat. Jesse braced himself. "I still don't know why you had to move here. Minneapolis is a big city and only a half hour away from my parents. Besides, you've only been in New York a month. How do you know this is right?"

He'd already thought out the answer. "This is the cultural center of America. It's the great melting pot of ideas, art, and commerce. When you are out among the crowd, you can feel the energy surging through the streets. I need that. I'm sure you'll like it if you just give it a chance."

"I don't know. What I feel is scared. I don't think I could ever ride the subway, from what I've heard."

"They have cops on board," he said confidently.

"Oh, that makes me feel a lot better. And what about Charlie? Surely he won't be staying in our apartment."

"Can we *not* get into all that right now?" Jesse pleaded. "Let's head out; I want to show you some things."

Although they were engaged and had known each other for more than three years, he began to question if she really knew him. And had she forgotten their plan? He was to take a couple of months and settle into the apartment, and after

Becky finished school they'd get married and return to New York. Ignoring what his gut was telling him, he put on a big smile and coaxed Becky out of her seat for a hug.

When they embraced, she was rigid and unyielding. He decided to move on and led her to the door. "Let's go. I want you to meet someone. I think you'll really like 'em."

When Jesse said good-bye to Charlie, the lab didn't budge, just lifted his eyebrows to watch them leave.

On their way down the hall, they faintly heard Mike and Sarah practicing.

"They're fantastic. They would be great playing at our wedding," Jesse said, stopping at Mike's door.

Becky tugged on Jesse's arm to get his attention. "You know my mother has everything planned."

Everything planned, all right. But where do I fit in? His pulse spiked, and he could feel his face getting hot.

"Rebecca, I would like to choose at least one thing for our wedding. They wouldn't charge much, I'm sure."

"Money's not an issue, you know that." Becky stood with her hands on her hips.

"Please…just give them a listen," he said and knocked on the door.

Mike opened up with a big grin. "Come on in, you two."

Jesse stumbled a bit, then said, "Mike, Sarah—I would like you to meet my fiancée, Becky."

Sarah shot Jesse a quick look and stepped up to greet Becky as Mike bowed in mock formality. "So nice to finally meet you. Wow, Jesse, you have a real prize here," Mike said, stepping back and eyeing Becky up and down.

Becky presented a tense smile. "I've heard so much about you. Your playing is lovely."

"Lovely . . . thank you," Mike said with raised eyebrows as he looked over at Sarah. "Please have a seat." He gestured with a sweeping arm toward the big blue beanbag chair.

Becky walked over, studied it a moment, and then decided to back into it. However, the back of her ankles hit the vinyl and stopped her short, causing her to plunge backward with her arms flailing. Reaching back to break her fall, her hands sank into the sides of the beanbag, which, being filled with Styrofoam, offered little support. After a loud screech, everyone was immediately flashed by Becky's pale-pink underwear as she tried to gain her balance before rolling onto the floor with her rear end in the air.

Sarah gasped. Mike ran to assist her, and Jesse just closed his eyes in embarrassment. Getting Becky to her feet, Mike apologized profusely. He kicked the beanbag as if it had done something wrong, then dragged over the chrome chair from the kitchenette, where Becky sat with her shoulders back and her hands in her lap.

"Sorry about that. I've got to get a real chair and throw that thing out," Mike said, looking as if he was holding back a snicker. "Anyway, can I get you a drink or something?"

"A Tab would be fine," Becky said, brushing her hair back and smoothing out her skirt.

"A Tab? Let's see . . . I have Coke, beer, or bourbon."

"A Coke with lots of ice and a straw will be fine," Becky said.

"Okay, a Coke on ice. And you, Jesse?"

"Make it two."

"Okay, two Cokes on ice coming up."

Sarah sat on the piano bench with a steady smile, her eyes revealing unreadable thoughts. She shook her head, no thank you, when Mike asked if she wanted anything.

Jesse was anxious the whole time, and Mike was overly polite trying to get Becky to relax. And Becky—she was a round peg in a square hole, as Jesse's Norwegian grandma might have said. After some stilted conversation and a Coke, Becky made it clear she wanted to get some rest.

Trying to include them in their plans for the evening, Mike invited them to *The Moments'* debut at The Caribbean.

"Oh, that sounds lovely, but Jesse says we have a lot to do before I leave," Becky said, turning to Jesse with a tight smile.

As they stood at the door Sarah reached out her hand, but then gave Becky an awkward hug good-bye.

"It was nice meeting you, Becky," Mike said with a gracious smile. Then looking at Jesse, he turned serious. "Sarah and I are headed to Harlem tomorrow to spend time with my family, so we'll see you in a few days."

Jesse fought back a laugh, knowing Mike was stressing about the introduction. "Have fun with that."

Mike narrowed his eyes at Jesse, apparently not finding it funny.

𝄞

Heading out the next morning, Jesse was determined to show his fiancé a good time, in spite of her skepticism of returning to New York after the wedding. First to the major sights: the Empire State Building, Rockefeller Center, and the Statue of Liberty. Then there was shopping at Macy's and Saks Fifth Avenue. As they walked and talked, she seemed to relax as long as they could take cabs everywhere and eat in those nice cozy—and expensive—restaurants.

By the time he dropped Becky off at the airport, after their day of sightseeing and shopping, he was looking forward to his time alone—to write and go for walks with

Charlie. He was troubled, knowing this wasn't how he should feel. He needed to talk this over with someone and soon. Maybe when Mike got back from Harlem he could help with an honest perspective.

18

Strivers Row

A repairman showed up at Mike's apartment, shortly after Jesse and Becky left, to paint the room and fix his door. If Mike would leave, the guy could get started right away and be finished in a couple of days.

"Well," Sarah said as she was about to head out, "looks like you'll have to stay at my place tonight."

"That would work," Mike said, nodding to the repairman, who headed down to get his tools. "I need to find a sub for Johnny's and run some errands first."

"Good, make it there by five and I'll have a *real* Southern meal waiting for you," she said as she left.

He hurried to pack a duffle and set out for Johnny's and then a flower shop. After meeting with Rudy and getting his approval for a sub, he found himself standing in front of a florist cooler and a colorful bank of flowers wondering what Sarah would like. His imagination surged as he played out various scenarios of what Sarah's offer to stay over could mean. As he scanned the many shades and shapes, it became clear to him: Van Gogh's lavender irises would suit her fine.

He tried to keep a sober face, holding the bouquet behind his back as Sarah opened the door of her apartment. He knew immediately he had made the right choice when her eyes lit up, seeing the flowers.

"Oh . . . thank you," she said, burying her face in them. "They're beautiful—and you are very sweet."

Just when his ego was taking flight, bound for great heights, Sarah added, attempting to keep a straight face, "You know what my Grandma Mae would say if you tried something with her sweet Sarie?"

Mike closed his eyes, screwed up his mouth, and said, "I bet I can guess." Then as he stepped in with a goofy grin, he added, "I would like to have met her and thank her for . . . uh . . . making you who you are."

"You would have loved her. She could see something good in anyone—I suspect even you." Sarah snickered and pointed to the kitchen table. "Now sit down. I've got some good Kentucky cook'n' for you."

"Okay," he said, pulling up a chair. "Let's see how it compares to my mother's. By the way, we're having one of my favorite dinners tomorrow, so you might want to pack like you're moving in 'cause mother's cook'n's so good you won't wanna leave."

"We'll see about that," she said as she dished up her specialty of grits, pork belly, and sweet-tater pancakes.

𝄞

As they were leaving Sarah's flat in the morning with their bags, a couple neighbors met them in the hall. Their incriminating looks didn't seem to bother Sarah in the least. They obviously didn't know this girl very well. Sarah just smiled, wished them a good morning, and turned for the stairs arm and arm with him.

Heading out onto the street and down to the subway station, Mike began to fret about the introduction he couldn't put off any longer. Then he looked over at that lovely sweet face and thought, *how could they not love this girl?*

Walking up 138th Street in Strivers Row with Sarah at his side, he recalled how happy his father had been to move the family here after living in a cramped two-bedroom apartment where Mike had to sleep in a curtained alcove off the dining room. He was so proud of his dad then. Even though city corruption and a poor economy plagued those days, his father managed to buy their home at a price that was right, having saved money from three tours in Vietnam. He had shared all this with Mike in the hopes of interesting him in business.

Mike suddenly felt a fresh stab of regret remembering how badly he had disappointed his dad – once again he tried to stuff the guilt.

After walking up the familiar front steps, Mike unlocked the door and motioned for Sarah to be quiet as they gently set their bags down. Peeking into the living room and dining room, he whispered for Sarah to follow him up the stairs as he searched for his baby sister. It was their little game whenever he came home to try to sneak up and scare her without her seeing him. But if she knew when he was coming, she sometimes hid and got the drop on him.

As he tiptoed across the upstairs landing to search in Trina's bedroom, Sarah, wearing one of her eclectic layered outfits, was left at the top of the stairs studying the rich mahogany-trimmed banister and the crystal chandelier. Just as he headed into Trina's room, his mother walked in from the kitchen.

"Good heavens, can I help you?" she said, looking up at Sarah.

Shocked by his mother's sharp reply, Mike stepped back from his sister's bedroom, catching her searing look.

"Mother, this is Sarah," he said, frowning.

"Hi," Sarah said, weakly, peering down.

"Sarah?" his mother repeated. "I'm sorry. I'm Rose. It's nice to finally meet you." She paused to recover. "Please make yourself at home. Supper will be ready soon."

Just then Persis walked in from a back porch and greeted Sarah as they came down the stairs and asked if she would like a tour of the house. Sarah seemed pleased to see Persis, and Mike was happy they were leaving the room so he could have a word with his mother.

"What was that about?" he said, following her back into the kitchen. "I told you I was bringing her with me."

"Mike," she said with a hushed tone, "surely there are a number of lovely black girls you could be dating. Or is this the result of your new bohemian lifestyle?"

"I don't know where you got the idea we're dating," Mike fired back. "I'm surprised Persis didn't fill you in after we ran into her downtown."

"Persis?" she said. "You mean you introduced her to your sister and didn't bother to tell me anything about this?"

He was about to return fire, when his beloved Runt rushed into the kitchen, slamming into him with a huge hug.

"Taking a break from your world tour to bless us with your presence? I feel so honored," she said in her sassiest of tones as she bowed. "And Mother said you were bringing a friend. A girlfriend."

"Okay, you guys," he said, holding up his hands. "Sarah's just a friend."

"A friend," mimicked Trina. "I seeee."

Just then Sarah came into the kitchen behind Persis. Seeing Sarah, all Trina could say was "Oh."

Catching Trina's reaction, his mother quickly suggested they go to the living room and show Sarah some family photo albums.

Mike was steamed by his family's response to Sarah, but looking at the old picture albums helped him lighten up.

"Here we are at Grandma Monroe's playing in the fire hydrant. With Dad in Vietnam we spent a lot of time there," he said, starting to relax. "We didn't have much, but we still had fun."

He caught Sarah looking at him. She seemed to say with her eyes, that she was fine and understood this was difficult for him.

After a half hour of Mike and his sisters laughing and snorting at old photos, his mother called them to dinner.

As usual she fixed one of his favorite Southern-style dinners. This time it was fried chicken, mashed potatoes, gravy, and okra—which Sarah couldn't get enough of. Table talk varied widely, but with many touchy subjects, Mike steered the conversation so not to make anyone uncomfortable – something that occasionally got him *the look* from his mother. Upon finishing, Sarah gushed about the meal and thanked his mother for serving her all-time favorite dessert: pecan pie. Mike noticed anytime Sarah talked, his mother studied her intently. He wasn't sure what that was about.

After the dishes were cleared, Mother suggested they move to the living room, where the ancient Monroe upright piano made its home.

"Michael," his mother said, getting right to the point as they walked in, "play us something. I'd like to hear what you're performing at that club."

He was suddenly more nervous than he had been in years.

"Well," he said, stepping over to the piano and sliding onto the seat, "I could play the piece I wrote for Sarah. She has inspired me in so many ways."

"Sure," his mother said, looking at Persis, puzzled. "Whatever you want."

He motioned for Sarah to sit next to him, and closing his eyes started in with an interlude that allowed her to join him when she felt ready. He never quite knew what to expect, but it was always wonderful. As piano and voice entwined, they communicated in a way that went beyond words, blanketing the room with a lush resonance.

When he finished the final chord with Sarah smiling sweetly, he slid around to incredulous looks of wonder and delight on all three attentive faces.

"Lord, child," Mother said, "where did you get those pipes?"

Sarah shyly looked at her. "Oh . . . your son is so talented. He wrote the music. I just sing what comes to me."

"Michael, that was beautiful. That's *your* composition?"

When he assured her it was, all she could do was shake her head. "My, my—you do have a gift."

Persis sat back on the couch with a softened look. "Michael, that was amazing."

"Yeah," Runt said, standing and pumping her fist. "And when you *do* go on your world tour, I'm going with ya."

Mike beamed. He couldn't have been happier if he had just won a Grammy.

𝄞

The Monroe household had formed many traditions over the years, but the one that had remained, whenever the kids got together, was the Saturday night game of Monopoly, accompanied by a large bowl of popcorn and homemade fudge. There were the official rules and then there were house rules, which had a way of morphing depending on whose turn it was. No blood had ever been spilled, but an occasional heated argument or a stomping off could abruptly end a game.

Mike's mother moved to her favorite chair to read but still within earshot when the game was retrieved from the hall closet and set up on the dining room table. Even before they got started a dispute broke out over who got what token and who would be banker. After a half hour, with the game in full swing, the volume ebbed and flowed, with Mike teasing Trina mercilessly, Trina whining and sputtering, threatening to quit, and Persis attempting to maintain order—something she thought her duty, being the oldest. However, when Sarah's turn came up she would quietly roll the dice, move her piece, and lean back in her chair smiling, seemingly enjoying the banter but staying out of the fray.

After two hours with the game looking as if it could go all night, Mike noticed Sarah was looking tired and tried to claim he was the winner because he had the most money. This didn't sit well with the others—no surprise—so the game was set aside to be finished the next day. However, Mike couldn't remember a time when they actually finished the game the next day.

His mother emerged from the living room with an affectionate smile as she watched her children and guest head up the stairs to the bedrooms.

Mike turned and went back down to give his mother a hug good night. "Isn't she something?"

His mother considered his words. "She is special. What are you thinking?"

"I don't know what to think," Mike said. "Miranda left me pretty dinged up."

"I know, dear," she said.

"But Sarah is different."

His mother clasped her hands in front of her. "Give it time, Michael. It'll unfold the way it's supposed to."

He thought a moment. "Mother, forgive me for being a bad son and not coming home sooner."

Tears came to her eyes as she reached for his face and kissed him on the forehead. Then, holding her hand to her heart, she motioned for him to head up the stairs.

When he walked past his sister's bedroom, he heard murmuring and giggles wafting from behind the door. He was glad they were hitting it off so well, but was afraid he might have some explaining to do when Sarah got him alone.

As was customary, all members of the Monroe family, including guests, were expected to go to the nine thirty Sunday morning service at Harlem Baptist Church, something that was never questioned. But that didn't mean there wasn't much prodding in the morning to get everyone together at the front door to walk the four blocks to church. Not used to raising much before noon, Mike groaned at being hounded every five minutes to get up, by Runt's annoying cackle, and of course there was the usual logjam at the bathroom, causing much debate and hollering.

Finally getting her brood out the door, his mother occasionally stopped the procession to say hello and introduce her prodigal son's friend to neighbors who were out and about, enjoying the fifty-degree weather of a sunny January thaw. He smiled to himself knowing he could not rush his mother, for this was her time.

Once in church, as they made their way to the "Monroe Pew," his mother continued to greet and kibitz with her friends and introduce Sarah with glowing comments. When the choir came up the aisle, Sarah sat up in her seat and turned to watch them sway to the beat, humming to herself in sweet harmony, causing nods of appreciation from those around them.

It was a challenge, but Mike got his family out the door in record time at the end of the service so he could catch the noon kickoff of the Giants game. After fifteen long years it finally appeared they might have a chance at the NFL playoffs. Leading the four women felt like plowing through thick mud. He looked back with a grimace and a nod every block they strolled to get them to speed up.

With home coming into view, Mike noticed someone huddled on the front stoop looking toward him. With a couple more steps, his chest suddenly felt crushed under a massive weight. The bright sunny day turned dark as he recognized the tall mahogany-skinned beauty with the Angela Davis–style Afro.

Miranda stood flashing her trademark million-dollar smile, but when she started to walk toward him, her face dropped and she ran to him sobbing. As she threw her arms around him in a clutch, he stood there in shock, his arms pinned to his side and his heart pounding.

"Mike . . . please say . . . you'll forgive me," she said between sobs.

His mother gasped and quickly gathered a staring Trina and hustled her into the house, followed by Sarah, and then Persis, who peered back at Mike with disgust.

19.
Jesse

"**W**hat should I do, Charlie?" Jesse moaned as he threw himself on his bed. "I'm trapped in a box canyon with no way out."

The yellow lab just raised his eyebrows and looked at him as if to say, "I could have told you. And by the way, there's only one way out of a box canyon."

Dazed by Becky's visit, Jesse thrashed about, hoping to get a little nap. He thought he had it all worked out, but from their last conversation it was apparent Becky thought he would get New York out of his system and they would settle back in Minnesota—but the opposite actually happened. He had fallen hopelessly in love with the city.

Just as he rolled over to face the wall, there was a quiet knock at the door.

"Jesse . . . it's Sarah."

Jesse couldn't believe it; her timing couldn't have been better. He leapt up and opened the door, then reached out to give her a hug and usher her in.

"Am I glad to see you but weren't you going to stay in Harlem a couple of days?"

"Something came up. I needed to come back."

He studied her face as she sat on the floor with Charlie. "What is it? Didn't you get along with his family?"

Sarah gazed up at him. "That's not it—they're great."

Turning her attention back to Charlie, she said, "Did Mike ever talk to you about Miranda?"

"No. Who's that?" Jesse asked, sitting down on the edge of his bed.

"According to Persis, Mike was crazy about her until she dropped him to go on tour with a rock band."

"So?"

"She showed up unexpectedly after church this morning. She was looking for reconciliation." Sarah leaned in to give Charlie a hug. "I needed to leave."

He wasn't sure how to feel—sad for Sarah or happy for himself.

"How are you doing?" he said.

"I'm okay. Why wouldn't I be?"

"Besides looking exhausted," he said, "I wasn't sure how you felt about Mike. Seems you two have a connection."

Sarah thought a minute. "I love working on music and playing with him at clubs, but he's too complicated. We always talk surface stuff, never about how he feels. It's a one-way conversation with things of the heart. Besides, Miranda is so beautiful. Looks like she wants him back."

Jesse didn't think she was totally honest about her feelings but let it go, deciding to change the subject.

"Would you like to go for a walk," Jesse asked. "I'm feeling rather stressed."

"Sure. It's nice out. I'll bet Charlie could use some exercise."

Charlie's ears immediately perked up and went to get his leash. He loved it when Sarah was around, and Jesse felt the same.

The afternoon was sunny with a false hint of spring. As they walked in the direction of Washington Park, Jesse poured out his soul in cathartic fashion.

"How did I get this far without knowing we're so different?" he moaned.

"Maybe you've changed."

"When we were at college we did everything together. Even the summers we spent time together at her parents' lake house or Christmas break at their winter condo in Aspen. We had a great time no matter what we did."

As they continued to walk and talk, with Charlie happily prancing alongside scanning the sidewalk with his nose, Jesse finally was able to relax. But he noticed Sarah was slowing down.

"Sorry, I'm wearing you out with all my problems," he said.

"I'm fine—just had a long day. But if you come over first thing in the morning, I'll fix you a breakfast of biscuits with sausage gravy and a side of sweet-tater pancakes."

Jesse brightened. "That sounds great, but I'll have to cancel the pity party I had planned," he said with a sideways grin. "Is Mike coming?"

"He's still in Harlem with Miranda. I don't know when he'll be back," she said and fell silent the rest of the way to her apartment.

Standing at her door Jesse hated to leave.

"Thank you for listening to me. It really helped," he said, and pulled Sarah in for a quick hug.

Sarah smiled as Jesse held her out at arm's length. Then, as if seeing her for the first time, he was struck by how beautiful she was. Something stirred in him. He felt helpless and pulled her back in and kissed her. She didn't resist.

Plunged into a pool of liquid sunshine, his heart raced and his face flushed. However, the warmth didn't last, as a chill of guilt swept in.

"What's wrong, Jesse?" Sarah asked.

"Sorry . . . I wasn't thinking."

"It's okay—it was just a kiss."

Jesse's chest heaved. "I should go."

"Okay. See you in the morning . . . 'bout eight?"

"Oh yes," he said.

Looking back, before heading down the stairs, Sarah was still standing at her door, with a warm sweet smile that could melt an iceberg. Jesse turned, double-stepped down the stairs, and burst out of the entrance of Sarah's building feeling panicky. What just happened? He was supposed to be sorting things out.

Back from Sarah's, he sat down to type but just stared at the blank page. Less than a week ago he was set to marry his college sweetheart and live happily ever after, now this. His world was shifting beneath him.

As he thought about what to do next, the phone rang. He answered it with "hello".

"Jesse, dear," Becky's mother said in her usual affected tone, "I need your tux size so we can get it ordered. You have less than four weeks, you know."

"Yes, of course, Mother Olson. Uh . . . I'm a forty-two long and pants, thirty-two waist and length." He paused and stiffened. "Did Becky mention my friends playing at the wedding?"

"Jesse, we committed to the orchestra a month ago, so I think we're all set for music."

Jesse fell back into his chair. "Fine. Can I speak to Becky, please?"

"Oh, she didn't come home this weekend. Her sorority is having a party."

With that little slap, he bid Mother Olson a good night, hung up the phone, and once again pleaded with Charlie for help, but all he got was the eyebrow lift again. At least he had breakfast with Sarah to look forward to.

♩

Did he actually kiss her? The vision of Sarah tugged at his heart when he first woke up. Then Mrs. Olson's voice wormed its way into his daydream, hitting the Fast Forward button with him standing at the altar in a tux. Then that kiss came back in view. Was he just lonely? His thoughts whirled. *What should I to do?* Hundreds of people have been invited.

Going with his heart, he jumped up, showered and dressed in record time, then hustled the six blocks to Sarah's with Charlie strutting alongside.

Charlie's tail wagged excitedly as Jesse knocked at her door.

"Come in, you two—the door to Sarah's Kitchen is unlocked," she sang in operatic fashion.

He let Charlie go in first to greet her. *Not only does she look like an angel, she sings like one*. Even though he hadn't slept well, Sarah's presence energized him. Looking around, he noticed her passion for color was expressed in the sparse furnishings from Goodwill. The smell of her cooking was amazing, and his mouth began to water with anticipation.

Sarah had dog food in a bowl ready for Charlie, and a place set for Jesse with steaming coffee, biscuits, and meat gravy. When he cleaned his plate, she piled it up for a second round—with golden pancakes, butter, and maple syrup, along with a glass of milk.

"This is incredible," he said, stuffing his face with another helping of sweet-potato pancakes. "It's the ultimate comfort food."

"Thank you," Sarah said. "Glad you like it. So maybe now I can ask you a favor?"

"Shoot—up to half my kingdom."

"Could we go to the Metropolitan Museum? I haven't been in a long time and there's a picture I would like to show you."

"Sure. We can drop Charlie off on the way." Jesse smiled; pleased she wanted to share something that was important to her.

After taking the subway to 77th Street and walking a few blocks, they reached the great-pillared entrance. Sarah knew just where to go. Up a couple of floors and through several galleries, Jesse found himself surrounded by the sublime radiance of the Impressionists.

"Here it is," Sarah said, walking over and stopping in front of Claude Monet's "Four Trees."

Standing next to her, he was drawn into the exquisite shades of purple, golden-yellow, blue, and green. It wasn't the dark purple of the foreground that drew his attention, but the lavender off in the distance that pulled him through the dark trees, into the air. He understood immediately why Sarah loved this painting. He was amazed at her knowledge of art, and as they walked through the other galleries, she talked about her dream of becoming an art teacher. Jesse was sure she could become anything she set her mind to.

After being sated by the lush liquid colors of the Impressionists, they headed to the street, stopping in front of the museum at a food cart to buy hot dogs with sauerkraut and mustard—she told Jesse that had been one of her dad's favorite things to do with her. Even though he was still stuffed from breakfast, he managed to get a hot dog down, smiling the whole time.

After his last bite Jesse moaned and said, "Okay, now it's my turn to share a passion of mine. Let's stop at my place so I can play you some music from my vast collection."

"Vast huh?" Sarah questioned. "I'd like to see just how vast."

After taking the subway to his apartment and a frisky hello from Charlie, he went to his record cabinet as Sarah flopped down in his easy chair.

"What would you like to hear? I've got classical, jazz, show tunes, rock—you name it."

"Just about anything by Mozart, Miles Davis, or Mancini," Sarah said.

"You're kidding."

"I thought you had a collection."

"I get it—you're testing me."

"You don't have any of them, do you?"

"Of course. Which will it be—'Serenade in B Flat Minor,' 'So What?,' or 'Moon River'?" Jesse said smugly.

"I was kidding. Play anything by Billy Joel, but don't tell Mike. He might get upset."

"I thought you were a poor farm girl from Kentucky?"

She straightened and crossed her arms, "They got radios in Kentucky."

"Sure they do," he said, throwing up his hands. "All right, here's 'New York State of Mind,' one of my favorites."

With Billy Joel singing his heart out, Sarah smiled, turned to the window, and looked out on the city. Shortly she began to move to the music and sang along in her enchanting style. As he watched her silhouetted by the late afternoon light, he was struck by how little he really knew about life—if a former homeless girl from the hills of Kentucky could have such an impact on him.

When the song ended, Sarah turned back to him. "I should probably go."

Jesse sat up from where he was lounging on his bed. "Okay if I walk you home? We can leave Charlie here."

She thought for a second. "Sure, why not."

He was quiet as they started for her place, with the temperature dropping and a few snowflakes starting to flutter about them.

"Penny for your thoughts," she said, looking over at him as they strolled.

"Sorry." Taking a few more steps, he stopped to look in the window of a men's clothing store. "To be honest, I can't say."

"Is it that bad?" she said, stepping up beside him.

His shoulders dropped. "I'm supposed to be getting married in a few weeks." He looked at her reflection in the window. "But all I can think about is you."

"Oh my," Sarah said, turning away and covering her mouth. "I'm sorry. That kiss *was* a mistake."

He closed his eyes and rubbed his forehead. "Maybe it was," he said. Then looking over at her, he whispered, "And maybe it wasn't."

"Jesse," Sarah said, pulling back. "I can't be part of breaking up a marriage."

"But—"

"I have to leave," she said, and hurried off down the street.

Jesse stood with his hand out trying to think of something to say, but nothing came. He was suddenly nauseated as he watched Sarah disappear into a crowd pouring up from the subway.

Mike was a mess. He'd wanted to escape with Sarah when Miranda showed up, but after reining in his emotions, he knew he should stay and hear her out. Even though he was devastated when she left him, seeing her again rekindled a feeling he thought was dead. Sitting on the front stoop, in the afternoon sun, he listened as Miranda pleaded forgiveness.

"I never stopped loving you," she said with tears flowing. "Leaving was a mistake."

He looked down the street at nothing in particular, thinking. "You put that band before us. You have no idea how that hurt."

She reached for his face so he would look at her. "It was an opportunity I thought I needed. I was wrong, Michael."

He turned away and tried to shake the sorrow stewing in his gut. "So what's next?"

She clutched her hands to her chest. "Can we just get back to where we were? Jimmy had some great venues lined up."

Mike stood, stepped down to the sidewalk, and stuffed his hands in his pockets. He looked out onto the street, closed his eyes, and clenched his jaw.

"Michael," Miranda pleaded, "look at me."

He turned and looked at the most beautiful woman he had ever seen, but it wasn't enough. Things had changed.

"I'm sorry. I can't go back," he said.

Visibly shaken, Miranda stood with her hands to her face. "You have to give us another chance."

He looked deep into her chestnut-brown eyes and slowly shook his head. "I'll get you a cab."

Miranda seemed to lose her balance and stumbled into his arms, weeping.

𝄞

Mike closed the door of the taxi and gave a half wave to Miranda. He had always been confident in his relationships, but he was now headed into uncharted territory with Sarah. Spending the rest of the day and Monday with his mother at home, Persis at the stores and teaching Trina to drive, he needed to get back downtown. After getting his new keys from the apartment manager, he stopped at Leo's for "healthy" donuts and coffee, and then went straight to Sarah's without bothering to check out his apartment.

Standing at her door, Mike knocked loudly and shouted, "Special delivery, ma'am." Then hid his face behind the donut bag.

Sarah cracked the door open and peeked out. After a second, she closed the door and said, "Sorry, no one's home."

Mike held the bag of donuts aside and bellowed, "Saraaah" in the style of Brando in *Streetcar Named Desire.*

Sarah flung the door open and reached out and grabbed him by the shirt. "For Pete's sake, get in here before someone calls the police."

She closed the door, leaned against it, and scrutinized the madman. "Where's Miranda?"

"May I sit down first?"

"Be my guest." Sarah gestured toward the table.

"First off," Mike said as he sat down, "I'm so sorry about Miranda breaking in on our time. That relationship was over and done with six months ago. I don't know what she was thinking, but I needed to be kind and make sure she understood how I felt."

Sarah looked dubious. "Wow. She's stunning. Sure you know what you're doing?"

Mike sat up with a sour look "Yes, I know what I'm doing."

"Okay," Sarah said, pulling back.

"So, are you ready to get back to work?" he said.

"Sure. How about first thing in the morning?"

He wanted to get started immediately, but not seeing her for a few days, was struck by how weary she looked. It scared him. What was going on with her?

"Yeah . . . we can do that." He hesitated as he studied her. "You worry me—"

"I know," Sarah interrupted. She fussed with her coffee cup and sighed. "I let my medication run out, but I'm okay now—just a little tired."

Mike settled in like he wasn't going anywhere and looked hard at her. "Sarah, I really need to know more about you if we are going to be a team."

Sarah got up and cleared the plates, then stopped and stood at the kitchen sink. "Okay," she said and returned to the table. "Maybe it's time to tell you the whole story."

Mike nodded and leaned back in his chair. "I'd like that very much."

Only an occasional cab disturbed the frigid late-night streets of Chelsea as Mike stepped out from Sarah's apartment building. He was dazed by conflicting emotions. He tried to make sense of Sarah's extraordinary life as he hustled back to his flat. Not only was she an exotic flower but able to bloom against impossible odds.

His mind raced as he opened the door to his apartment. Full of emotion and ideas, he went straight to the piano, more concerned about tapping into Sarah's inspirational narrative than noticing the freshly painted room. After a thankful prayer, he became immersed in a creative frenzy with fragments of melodies and counterpoint forming in his head. With all that he had just learned he would be able to piece together her whole story.

He scooted to the kitchen table and grabbed his notebook. As fast as he could write, he organized a rough outline for a composition portraying the significant events of her life—to be transposed later into various movements.

It would be an expansive composition, capturing the full range of human emotion. He would work at keeping the theme pure, weaving it throughout the entire piece. It had to show that no matter how arduous the journey, faith, hope, and love could see you through.

He envisioned it might take eight, maybe nine, movements to fully tell the story with an overture and postlude to bookend the narrative. Four movements: one for each family member who contributed to her life yet tragically lost to her. The beloved Kentucky farm that nurtured their bodies while the forty acres of stump and stone tested every fiber of their will. And finally, survival on the streets: her triumph over homelessness where

Sarah's song found its way to be heard, nourishing all who have ears to hear.

As each movement took form in his mind, he began to envision the ensemble needed to perform such a composition: standup bass, cello, violin, woodwind, percussion, guitar, horn, him on piano, and, of course, Sarah. He figured they could gather at his flat on Saturdays, each player contributing ideas and their unique talent. He went over his notes again and again to see if he had captured everything.

Setting his pen down, he suddenly became aware of his breathing—his chest rising and falling. He sat back in his chair and looked around the room, feeling like he just woke up from a dream. A yellow haze of morning sunlight poured in through the Bleecker Street window along with the bustling street noise of Greenwich Village. The clock over the sink read nine thirty. He hadn't eaten, and had only drunk a coffee or two. He looked down at his notebook. The pages were filled with ideas and music notations of themes and instrumentation of an opus roughly outlined into movements for *The Girl in the Yellow Scarf.*

A mysterious force had entered him, leading him charging without hesitation into the unknown. He never doubted it was for good. At first the composition seemed a sad tale of hardship and suffering, but it gradually unfolded into a stunning story of grace and love he thought would have lasting relevance. He marveled at the creative process of making art—like assembling a puzzle, each step leading to the next. When he realized that composing an opus of Sarah's life story is what he was destined to do, his heart became so full he thought it would burst.

21

Washout

"So what's the big occasion?" Sarah asked as she took in the checkered tablecloth, candles, and the heavenly smell of roasting garlic and tomato sauce at Mama Rosa's. Mike had called Sarah after his all-night creative explosion and asked her to dinner at his favorite restaurant in Little Italy. The birth of his opus was like a heavenly gift dropped in his lap, but he wanted to get her permission and thoughts on what to do next.

"Can't I treat you to something nice once in a while?"

She studied his face a moment, and then snickered. "Okay, what's up? If you just wanted Italian, we could have gone to Gino's down the street for your favorite slice of pizza."

"Right, we could have done that." He paused in thought. "Sarah, I couldn't sleep last night thinking about your life." He hesitated again. "Anyway, it inspired me to begin a composition about your story, as you told it to me."

"I inspired you?"

"Yes," Mike said, sitting up in his chair, "but I need to know if it's okay to do this. It's your story."

"I don't understand what you want to do."

"Well . . . this is what I thought so far. But I really need your input."

She nodded.

"Right now I have an eight-movement composition sketched out," he said, hardly able to sit still. "I'm thinking we would need a seven-piece band along with you and me. We can rehearse on Saturdays in my apartment and in about three months we should be ready to perform. It's that simple."

Sarah smiled and shook her head. "Simple? Where are you going to find these people and how would you pay them?"

"I have a couple of musician friends at Cornell, and maybe I can find some students at NYU." Mike paused as he looked across the restaurant. "I got some money from my father's will that should get us through."

She folded her arms and sat back. "Sounds like you know what you are doing. What do you need me for?"

He snorted. "What do you mean? You're the centerpiece. Without your voice we have nothing. And I also need your help with the music and lyrics."

Sarah seemed pained. "But I don't know how to do that."

He laughed. "Don't tell anyone, but I don't know what I'm doin' either. We'll figure it out."

Sarah's expression slowly changed from a look of worry into a contented smile as he waited for a response.

"So?" he said "What do you think?"

"I think you're crazy," she said. Her eyes wide, she leaned toward him. "But wonderful. If you think we can do this, then so do I."

Mike reached across the checkered tablecloth for her hands. "Really—you think it's possible?"

"Sure, no sweat," she said.

Then, looking into each other's eyes, they broke out laughing until their sides ached and tears streamed down their faces. His spirit soared, so thankful for this unfathomable force in his life.

As other diners looked on, they were finally able to control themselves enough for him to share his plan. Gazing at her as he presented his notes, he felt like the captain of a great sailing vessel with Sarah the compass, sun, moon, and stars. Together, anything was possible.

$$\text{\textflat}$$

Before they had to be back to Johnny's, Mike wanted to drive to Cornell and see if his musician buddies would be up to working on his composition. He got permission from his mother for Trina to drive the family car, which would give her a nice long stretch to hone her driving skills, and he had Sarah come along so she could see the campus and help convince his friends by singing for them.

With the roads cleared from a cold front that had dropped six inches of snow, he assured his mother Trina would be fine as they packed the car for the five-hour trip north to Ithaca and the campus of Cornell. The day was optimistic, bright with a cloudless blue sky, and as per the Monroe family tradition, a cooler was packed with drinks and plenty of snacks to eat along the way. While driving through the small towns of upstate New York, Sarah exclaimed how the fresh fallen snow looked like marshmallow frosting covering buildings, trees, and the rolling mountains of the Catskills. He and Trina had to agree, with wide smiles. The time they spent together was priceless—singing old gospel songs passed on to Sarah from Grandma Mae, laughing at lame knock-knock jokes, and playing several rounds of the alphabet game. The trip was empowering for Trina, with Mike flashing a confident smile anytime she checked his face for reassurance.

"You did good, kid," he said as they drove in the east entrance of the college where students scurried about in brightly colored parkas among the massive trees and old stone and red brick buildings. "Don't think, though, that Mother will be giving you the keys to cruise all over Manhattan."

"Why not? Bet you did."

"Never mind that," he said, peering at his beloved kid sister. "Besides I would like to see you safely out of the city, going to school here."

"Think they would let another Monroe kid in?" Trina said with a smirk.

He rolled his eyes and gave her the big-brother look. "Just decide what you want to do now, so you don't waste time like I did," he said, stabbing his finger in the air to emphasize each word.

$$\large\oint$$

Mike had arranged to meet his musician friends Allen, Morris, and Roy at the Cornell Music Center. Sarah followed Mike and Trina down a hall, practice room doors on both sides, as he reminisced how he first found his passion here. He smiled as they entered the small room – acoustical tiles on the walls and ceiling and a piano and drum set in the corner. A lanky young black man with a Lionel Richie haircut set his standup bass down, walked over, and grabbed Mike for a hug; picking him off the floor and shaking him.

"My brother, I was afraid I'd never see you again."

"Good to see you too," Mike said, gasping for air.

"And who are these delightful ladies?" Morris said, setting Mike down.

"Well," Mike said, pulling down on his rumpled sweater, "this is Sarah, and it's been a while, but you've met my sister."

"Sarah," Morris said, reaching for Sarah's hand as he turned to Mike with a wink. Then extending his hand to Trina, he added, "And good to see you again."

Trina nodded, grinning up at Morris. He then looked back at Mike. "And how is your kid sister these days? I always thought she was the smart one in the family."

"Oh, man—this *is* my kid sister," Mike said, shaking his head as Trina beamed.

"No way," Morris replied, winking again at Mike.

"Always the ladies' man. Girls, be careful around this dude—he's dangerous."

As they were catching up Roy sauntered in, Allen trailing behind. Mike's friends couldn't have been more different. Roy, short and skinny with long dreadlocks, and Allen, who could easily be a stunt double for BB King.

It had been over a year since he'd jammed with his friends, but it didn't take long for them to pick up where they'd left off, warming up with a few familiar numbers. Mike then had them sit back while he played and Sarah sang one of their new compositions. The trio listened briefly, occasionally glancing at each other. However, halfway into the number they couldn't stand it any longer. Roy slipped over behind the drum set as Morris picked up his bass viol and Allen strapped on his guitar, quietly filling in with rhythm, bass, and countermelody as if they already knew the number.

𝄞

Sarah chortled, watching Mike's friends groove and sway to the beat as they looked at each other, grinning wildly. She responded to the fuller sound with greater confidence, flourish, and resonance in her voice. The added instrumentation was like a whirlwind of tones that picked her up and spun her around the room, threatening to carry her out into the air.

"Oh my," she gasped with the final note, "you guys are amazing."

"Yes . . . yes, yes," was all Mike could say as the last chord faded into silence.

Morris looked over at Roy and Allen and shouted, "I don't know about you guys, but I'm in up to here!" He waved his hand back and forth high over his head.

"That makes two of us," Roy said, flipping his drumsticks in the air. "How about it, Allen?"

"I can dig it, wouldn't miss it," Allen said, looking over at Mike. "Where in the world did this come from?"

Mike gazed at Sarah. "It's that voice and behind it a profound story of survival and love. It wrote itself—I just held the pen." Sarah felt her face redden as she looked down at her hands.

"Well, we still have time on the room, so why don't we try more of this thing?" Morris said.

"Man…hoping you'd say that," Mike answered.

Mike dug in his satchel and handed out copies of the music he'd brought, and for the next couple of hours they jammed, experimented, and improvised. Sarah and Trina listened for a while then went out to explore the campus and bring back drinks and snacks from the car.

With their time up, Mike laid out his plan for rehearsals. It'd be tight, but practices would be at his place on Saturdays between noon and six. Anyone commuting to the city could crash at his place if needed. Morris and Roy were graduating in March so would be closer after starting their jobs in Manhattan. And Allen would make it as often as possible.

After packing up and a rowdy farewell from his old band, Mike, Trina, and Sarah drove off as daylight faded in the west. Mike was nervous about Trina driving at night, but she insisted, with Sarah's support, saying if she didn't practice now, when would she?

"Well, what do you think, Sarah?" Mike asked, leaning over the front seat to look back at her as they left campus.

"Roy is really cute the way he tosses his hair around. I love Allen's brilliant smile, so charming and warm, and Morris, well . . ." she said, holding back a smile.

"Alright. Besides cute, charming, and whatever."

"I don't know, Mike. It's exciting, but scary."

"I know," he said with a deep sigh. Then peering over at Trina, "You okay, there?"

"I got this, Mikie," Trina said with confidence as she gripped the steering wheel.

Gradually all three sank into their own thoughts as a stream of headlights flashed by them as they returned to the city. Sarah had loved spending time with Trina and meeting Mike's friends, but sensed a growing anxiety in him. Yes, he had quit smoking after the fire in his apartment, but she noticed he still relied on a "little" bourbon to calm his nerves. She worried about that and hoped she could help him handle the stress.

𝄞

Mike woke the next morning questioning his sanity. Most of his buddies would be graduating and launching their careers, while his future held little more than living from paycheck to paycheck. His only salvation would be completing and performing his opus in a variety of venues and maybe landing a record deal. A lot was riding on this, so the pressure was on.

Some of the musicians he knew had graduated from NYU, so he posted a notice on the campus bulletin boards at Steinhardt Music Center; then walked the halls handing out information to anyone he ran into. Surprisingly, he received a dozen responses, and within days got commitments from everyone to start the following weekend.

Mike was flying high by the time the musicians showed up on Saturday. He had to move the mattress out into the hall, and pile the table, chairs, and storage crates into the alcove in the corner to make room for all eight of them.

Katie the violinist and Mellissa the cellist, students at NYU, arrived together; then Carl, a first year student at Manhattan School of Music. Morris, Roy, and Allen rolled in a half hour late but ready to jam. A good-looking bunch, Mike thought—especially Katie. He knew his Cornell buddies could cut it, but the other three were unknown. Yet, he was optimistic.

Mike went to the window after six hours of agonizing practice and gazed down at the happy couples on the street heading out for the evening. *What just happened?* Trying his best not to betray his feelings, he turned and searched for Sarah. Catching her eye she relayed through an empathetic smile that she understood. But his three Cornell friends avoided eye contact, looking away with blank expressions. Mike was sick with disappointment.

After a quick dinner of pizza and beer, his Cornell buddies headed back to school. The other three lingered for a while until Mike politely brought up that he and Sarah had to leave for work. Katie stopped at the door as they were heading out and turned with a seductive smile. "Mike, this is so wonderful. I have a few ideas on the music if you're interested."

"Sure," he said as he went to the kitchenette to pour himself a bourbon and water. "I'm open to anything."

"Here's my number," Katie said, penning it on a scrap of paper. "Call me anytime."

Mike forced a smile, thanked them all and said he was looking forward to next Saturday. Sarah then helped him drag the table and chairs back to the kitchenette. Mike started pacing.

"She's not a nice girl, you know," Sarah said leaning against the table with her arms crossed.

He stopped and peered at her. "What are you talking about?"

She crinkled her forehead. "You know what—the blonde violinist."

"First of all, what do you know about anything? You're only nineteen, and—"

"You deserve better. I saw the way she fawned over you. It's disgusting," Sarah said, wrinkling her nose.

"What do you mean?" he said, flustered. "What can you see anyway? Dammit, Sarah, you have no say who I see and what I do!"

"I see good enough to read good character," she said, looking aside.

"Maybe I don't want character," he said, "Wait! Why am I even having this discussion with you—"

"Whatever, but you know I'm right." Sarah turned her back to him, walked over and flumped into the beanbag chair.

♪

The week melted away with Mike and Sarah working on the opus in the afternoons and playing at Johnny's in the evening. There was no mention of the blonde violinist; although it irked him that Sarah made him feel guilty about thinking of dating Katie.

By the time Sarah got to Mike's for Saturday's practice, the mattress and box springs were already in the hall to make room for the group.

Sarah let herself in, stopped abruptly and sniffed the air. "Wow, that's some powerful aftershave. Expecting someone special?"

Mike was *not* in the mood for this but couldn't let it go. "Hope we're not going to have a problem here," he said, and walked over and looked her in the eye.

She just stared back expressionless, holding his gaze. He wasn't about to flinch, but then the door burst open. Morris lugged his bass into the room and stopped as he caught sight of the toe-to-toe confrontation.

"Helllooo?" Shall I come back later?"

Trying to cool himself, Mike joked, "Yeah, haul that monster downstairs and come back in five minutes." He paused. "Just kidding, man. You're right on time, Morris. We're done here, aren't we, Sarah?"

Sarah kept her gaze, forcing Mike to turn away.

Morris couldn't help snorting as he went to set up. The remaining musicians sauntered in except for the contentious one who called to say she would be late. She asked if the two of them could work on some of her ideas after the others left. Sarah seemed to sense what was going on and stared at Mike as he hung up the phone.

The second practice started out even rougher than the first. He knew the students were uncomfortable with improvisation, the violinist hadn't shown up, and without Allen, who decided to move back to Detroit, the instrumentation was thin and out of balance. Mike was stuck. He cut the rehearsal short after only an hour. He walked over to the old Frigidaire, got out beers for everyone and suggested they take a break. With everyone gathered around, Mike tried to compose himself.

"First I want to apologize for putting you through this experiment. I'll pay you for a full rehearsal, but I think you would agree this isn't working. I'm sorry," he said, trying hard not to lose it.

Most of the group nodded in agreement, quietly finished their beers and packed up to leave. Sarah sat out of the way in the beanbag chair looking out the window. Morris and Roy hung back after the others left, to have a word with him.

"Roy and I have talked a lot about this," Morris said, standing at the door. "We feel you've got a nugget here and would like to see it through if you want to give it another shot."

Mike looked up from studying his beer label. "Really. You're still interested?"

"All you need are the right people. We're in whenever you're ready," Roy, said.

Mike shook his head as if trying to regain consciousness from being knocked out. "Oh, man, I really needed to hear that."

He got up and went to the door to give them each a hearty man hug and thank them for hanging with him. After they left he heaved a sigh and gazed over at Sarah.

"Did you hear that? They believe in it."

Sarah smiled. "Of course they do, because it's wonderful."

Mike started to pace as he thought about what to do next. After his second lap around the room, a knock came from the door along with a syrupy voice. "Mike, it's Katie. You home?"

Sarah's sweet empathetic smile curdled into a tightlipped scowl as she got up to leave.

Mike wasn't sure he wanted to answer the door as Sarah brushed by him.

"I'll get the door. I'm sure she wants to be alone with you, but I doubt if she needs any more practice."

Sarah opened the door and cordially invited Katie in without a hint of contention. She was as good an actress as she was a singer.

"I'll pick you up at seven for The Caribbean. Try to be ready," Mike called out as he stood looking at the shapely blonde with the pouty lips.

Sarah flung a wave over her shoulder as she left and closed the door with a little extra tug.

𝄞

After a standing ovation from a packed house at The Caribbean, Mike's joy was brief; he needed some time alone with Sarah. Arriving back at his flat, Mike plopped down at his piano in silence. Sarah sat at the table looking over at him.

"Well, how did the practice go after I left?" she asked flatly.

"If you're referring to Katie, I fired her too."

Sarah frowned. "Sorry, maybe I was out of line," she said in a whisper.

"Let's drop it," Mike said, rubbing his forehead. "We have to practically start over. Where am I going to find who I need?"

Sarah raised her hands. "Hey, let's not panic. Know what my grandma would say?"

"No, but I bet you're going to tell me."

"For this situation she would probably quote Proverbs—something like 'Trust in the Lord and lean not on your own understanding. In whatever you do acknowledge Him and He will direct your path.' That's not exactly right, but you get the point."

"Ooookay, but how is that going to help me?"

"Make a plan. Where can we find the people you need?" she said.

"The good ones are all over the city, playing in clubs, concert halls, even on the streets."

"Right, so let's go get 'em," she said.

He couldn't help but smile, fascinated by her confidence. He wished he had a spoonful of her faith.

"Right. Why didn't I think of that?" he said wagging his head.

Sarah sat up and leaned on the table. "You have a passion that is contagious because you believe in your music with all your heart. I feel it, and others will too. So…go get the people you *need* using your passion, your heart, and your story. They will believe in it when they see you believe in it."

"Really?" he said, tilting his head as if trying to hear something off in the distance.

"Oh, man, its just common sense," she said looking skyward, "maybe you *did* spend too much time with your head in the books."

22

New Day

In spite of a freezing February day, Mike's mood matched the bright morning sun – Sarah's optimistic view turning bewilderment into promise. He practically strutted down Greenwich Avenue to the Bagel and Bean coffee shop, where he was meeting her to brainstorm a plan to search for musicians. Sarah wanted to try something different than donuts at Leo's, and Mike said he would go along with it—once. His first impression wasn't good. It seemed a little uppity and bright for him. The dozen or so tables were all in neat little rows, with a waitress scurrying about taking orders. No heavenly smell of *freshly* baked bread. No aroma of *freshly* ground coffee. No yelling your order to the owner who was at the ovens taking out *freshly* baked pastry. Oh well, he was starting to think he would do anything to please the smiling redhead sitting at the table by the window. Even eat a stale bagel. However, when he sat down and looked into her adorable face, the first thing she said squelched his good mood.

"Mike, we should have Jesse join us in our search."

He frowned. "I don't know. He's busy with his novel. Besides, I like spending time just with you."

"He loves your music. I think it inspires him."

The waitress suddenly appeared wearing a frilly pink and white apron.

Mike looked up at her. "Coffee, plain bagel, and cream cheese for me."

"Same for me," Sarah said.

The waitress smiled, wrote their order and scurried off.

Sarah peered back at Mike. "Well?"

He hesitated, agonizing over what to say. Suddenly he had an idea. "Okay, why not have Persis come along too?"

"You think she would?"

"It would be good for her to get away from the stores. Anyway, she finds you interesting."

"Interesting?"

"Yeah. I'm not the only one who thinks so. You seem to fascinate my whole family."

Sarah looked puzzled. "That's a compliment . . . I guess?"

"Of course it is," he said. "Alright, back to the plan. I'll check with Jesse and Persis this afternoon, search the music reviews and newspapers, and put together a list of musicians. It's best to contact them in person, so it'll mean a lot of running around. I know it's a needle-in-the-haystack approach, but we have to start somewhere."

Sarah gazed at him for a moment. "It's good to see you so happy."

"I am. Can't wait to see what turns up," he said, leaning back, almost relaxing.

Sarah straightened. "Great! Let's meet at my place at eight, and I'll fix y'all some breakfast!"

Mike snickered. "Really—y'all? Come on, you're a New Yorker now. It's youse guys.'"

"Holy cow," Sarah said, standing up. "Maybe if you don't like the way I talk, all y'all will be uninvited," she said with a slight smirk, turning for the door.

"Now, ma'am, don't get your knickers in a knot. I's just joshin wif ya," Mike said, jumping up to catch up with her.

Sarah stopped so suddenly that Mike bumped into her. She turned to face him, looking dead serious. "Shush! I think I hear your brain rattling. Sounds to me like . . . a BB bouncing in a boxcar."

"Ouch. Now you're getting nasty."

"Don't get me started," Sarah said in her best Southern drawl. "I learnt a ton from my Grandma Mae." She then spun around for the door muttering something about a Kentucky stump having a higher IQ.

Mike totally cracked up and ran after her, racking his brain for a comeback.

𝄞

Walking up to his floor after dropping off Sarah at her place, Mike thought about the good day they'd had. The crowd at Johnny's was exceptional with a line out the door and Rudy slinging drinks as fast as he could, probably needing to hire another waitress.

Finding it hard to sleep, thinking about the challenge ahead, Mike got up to look out at the night lights on Bleecker Street, and rather than pour a nightcap of bourbon and water, he drank from the reviving spring of hope and thanked God for the girl in the yellow scarf.

𝄞

The two night owls were slow getting started the next morning. Mike showered, made some coffee, and walked down the hall with two cups in hand. As usual, Charlie greeted him with a quiet woof just as Jesse opened the door, blurry-eyed.

"Sure you're up for this?" Mike asked.

"Give me five—I'll be right out," Jesse said, stumbling to the bathroom.

"Take your time. Charlie and I can catch up."

As they headed out from "The Palace" and up to Sarah's, Mike sensed something bothering Jesse.

"You're awfully quiet, man. What's up?"

Jesse kept walking with his head down. "It didn't go well when Becky was here."

Mike tried to be kind. "Honestly, she did seem out of her element. But, it's all new to her. How was it when you first got here?"

"I loved it from the first day."

They walked another block when Jesse broke the silence. "I didn't date a lot until Becky. I guess I was a bit of a nerd. I think she liked that I was the editor of the college paper and got recognized for my writing. Actually we kind of grew up together. It was easy." He looked away. "I never realized there were people like Sarah, uncomplicated yet profound. She sings like an angel, draws like Da Vinci, and cooks like a five-star chef."

"Wow!" Mike said, wondering how Jesse would know about her cooking. "You've been going with Becky for how many years, and you're just figuring this out now?"

Jesse shrugged. "Wish I'd met someone like Sarah earlier."

Mike grimaced. "You sound confused, man. Have you talked this over with your dad?"

"No, he would be so disappointed. I couldn't do that."

"From what you've told me about him, I would trust his perspective on this."

Jesse slowed down and hung his head as he walked. "Sorry, I don't mean to be a downer."

Mike hadn't experienced such a jab of jealousy before. It wasn't a good feeling. "Come on, I've got a surprise for you at Sarah's."

After waiting a half hour for Persis, they decided to go ahead and eat, figuring something must have come up. But just as they were finishing, Sarah got up to answer a knock at the door.

"Hello, everyone," Persis said, frowning apologetically as she breezed in. "I'm so sorry, it took longer at the store than I thought."

Jesse seemed to be holding his breath as he looked at Persis with a slight goofy grin. Mike smiled, catching Jesse's reaction. Persis was wearing a crimson beret, safari jacket with a paisley scarf, and coffee-brown bell-bottoms. He knew he could count on her to look like a million bucks.

After introducing Jesse, Mike went on to explain his plan.

"Sarah has convinced me we can find who we need. She seems to have insight that is beyond me." He paused to take a deep breath. "So here's how it will work. Rehearsals will be at my place, noon to six each Saturday for ten weeks, a hundred dollars per practice session. A venue hasn't been decided, but performance pay would be split evenly between all players. I'm looking for guitar, trumpet, violin, and cello and will follow up with a call to set up auditions at my place starting next week."

He split up the list of musicians, clubs, and agencies to check on.

"Sarah and I will take everything above 34th Street and you two take everything below. Then we'll meet in Gramercy Park for a late dinner." Pleased with his plan Mike began to relax a little as he watched Jesse and his sister interact.

♪

The search led them from Lower Manhattan to Washington Heights – hopping cabs and buses, or hoofing it to contacts during the day, then hitting a few clubs at night. When they met for a late dinner it was obvious Jesse and Persis were having a good time, his sister showing a side Mike hadn't seen before. Sitting at a corner booth at the Gramercy Park restaurant, they compared notes.

"Okay, I'm sorry you two had such a lousy time," Mike joked. "But I would like to hear if you actually did any good."

"Just one more story," Persis said, laughing. "I can't believe it. I almost lost this guy. He ran and jumped on a bus thinking I was right behind him, but I had darted to get a paper from the newsstand. When I turned around, I saw the bus had taken off with him as he pounded on the window to get my attention. I quickly hopped a cab and told the driver, "Follow that bus!" I was killing myself laughing, with him gaping out the rear window while I frantically waved for him to get off at the next stop."

Both were now holding their sides as they leaned against each other. Their guffaws were contagious, and Mike and Sarah helplessly laughed along with them.

They were finally able to eat a little dinner and share notes on the contacts they'd made. Then, with hugs and smiles all around, Persis caught a cab home, Jesse walked Sarah to her apartment, and Mike reluctantly headed for a late solo set at Johnny's.

𝄞

Mike and Sarah continued their search into the week. Often before going to work they would listen to Frankie "the Love Man" Crocker on radio WBLS, to find who was playing and where in the city. Mike's ears perked up when he heard Garrett Jordan was performing at a small club in Midtown.

"This guy is amazing on the guitar," he said. "We really need someone like him who can play cool and hot, pop and jazz. He's about the best there is."

"Let's check him out after Johnny's. What do we have to lose?" her voice sparkling.

Mike convinced Rudy to let them off early so they could get across town to catch Garrett's last set. The Black Diamond in Midtown had a reputation for carrying only the top performers and as usual was crowded. Mike and Sarah entered the club and wove their way through the dense pack of tables, past the small stage, to grab the last seats available along the back wall. All eyes were on Garrett, who was flailing at a solo as the red, yellow, and blue spots gave the smoky club an extraterrestrial glow. At the end of the number, the crowd erupted. Mike hadn't heard anything like it. At first he was enraptured with the thought of getting someone of this caliber, but then pessimism sank in. At the end of the set Mike got up to leave.

"Where you going?" Sarah said.

"I can't ask him. He's out of our league."

Sarah wouldn't budge. "So you don't deserve the best?"

Mike just shook his head and turned for the door. Sarah got up and walked over and onto the small stage, getting Garrett's attention. Smiling, she asked him something Mike couldn't hear. Mike stood in disbelief as he watched her move to center stage. When she took the microphone and began singing, she reached out her hand beckoning Mike to join her. As her song floated over the crowd, it stopped everyone heading for the door. Momentarily embarrassed, he put his head down, but his feet lead him to the stage and the piano.

The house band stopped their packing and found chairs to sit and listen. Sarah moved next to the upright piano, empowering Mike with her voice and that smile. Garrett looked on with stunned amazement and, seemingly unable to help himself, jumped back up on stage with his guitar to add elaborate riffs and a consolation of improvisations that in turn drew Mike, with eyes closed, into extemporaneous themes he himself had never imagined. This give-and-take with Sarah adding vocal harmonics and spirited countermelodies went on for over fifteen minutes, ending with the three practically gasping for breath and the crowd going crazy with shouts and applause.

As the three bowed to the crowd, Garrett turned to Mike and asked who they were and where they were playing. Then, taking the microphone, he addressed the crowd.

"It's rare that the Black Diamond has a walk-on as extraordinary at these two. I would like to introduce them to you. Mike, here on piano, and Sarah, vocals, known as *The Moment*, now playing at Johnny's in Gramercy Park."

Once again the crowd went wild with some coming to the stage to thank the three. When the audience settled down, Garrett asked Mike and Sarah to join him in his dressing room.

"Well, you guys sure got my attention. What did you want to talk about?" Garrett said as he went to the cooler for a couple of beers.

"Thank you so much for letting us play," Sarah said. "You are amazing and, well . . . Mike has a proposal for you."

Mike tried to gather his thoughts. "Isn't she something?" he said, shaking his head. "Well, I'm putting together an ensemble to work on an eight-movement opus…a composition I've written that was inspired by the incredible voice and story of this young lady. I have the core sections written out, but I'm looking for musicians to augment the main themes and suggestions on expanding the orchestration. My hope is after ten weeks or so of rehearsals to have it performance ready. Honestly, I have a limited budget but enough to pay everyone for ten weeks of rehearsals—"

"Mike," Garrett said, holding up his hand. "I do want to see the music, but I have a good feeling about this. I'm in for the first rehearsal, then we'll go from there."

Mike was hoping he heard Garrett right as he stared at him for a moment. "Great," he finally said. "We start next Saturday at noon, my place. Here's my address and phone number." Mike handed Garrett his card, grinning like a kid. "Cool man, see you then."

In total they handed out more than twenty simple business cards that gave Mike's address and phone number. He marveled at the energy that sustained him day after day with only a few hours of sleep a night. It all felt so right. This is what he was born to do—write and perform his own music. But none of it would be possible without Sarah. Her fresh perspective was critical in keeping his opus dream alive. He still couldn't fathom how this sweet girl with failing sight could be so pragmatic and clear-eyed. In a world with so many shades of gray, what you see is what you get with her.

By the end of another week Mike had auditioned fourteen musicians. It became obvious who were the best fit—those with both musical and collaborative abilities. He was so stoked he could hardly stand it. And, to top it off, the ever-resourceful

Morris had found them a great venue for the premiere performance. The Naumburg band shell in Central Park had a summer concert series open to new groups throughout the month of June. Many notable performers had been featured there in years past, from John Philip Sousa to Simon and Garfunkel. Morris, possibly stretching the truth a little about their experience, got them on the schedule - Tuesday evening at six o'clock, the third of June, giving them less than ten weeks.

Finally Mike had all the pieces. Now he had to assemble them into a beautiful work of art.

The Moment was getting reviewed regularly, but most centered on the "out of this world" voice of its vocalist and rarely mentioned the pianist. The latest review was a bit negative, noting it doubtful the twosome would find their way out of the intimate venues of the supper clubs and piano bars. When Mike read this, it caused him to jump up from the kitchen table and pace around his flat. He then flew out the door and down to the end of the hall, where he spun around on one foot and marched back muttering, "Just wait, just wait, just wait" with each step.

Jesse was wide-eyed at 1:34 in the morning. With less than a week until his wedding, he was more conflicted than ever. Not only was Sarah constantly in his thoughts but the time with Persis was muddying his thinking even more. Why hadn't he met these intriguing women earlier? On top of everything else, Mike had been standoffish lately, and Charlie demanded going for a run more often. He finally "hit the wall" and needed to talk to somebody.

Setting pride aside, he walked down to see if Mike was home from Johnny's. He thought he heard practicing through the door and knocked.

"Come in, come in," Mike hollered impatiently.

Once inside, Jesse went straight to the window and stood a moment. "Mike, I need help."

Mike peered up from the piano, "Of course—you alright?"

Jesse turned around with his heart racing. "I have to make a decision…about Becky so… I can get some sleep."

"Yeah, man, I'm listening."

"I don't understand how I can get married when I keep thinking about Sarah. And the time I spent with your sister was so much fun . . ." He then slumped into the beanbag chair.

"Look...I don't see it with you and Sarah. You don't have any idea how she might feel." Mike seemed agitated, got up and started to pace. "This is it, man—do you love Becky?

Jesse raised his palm to his forehead and squeezed his eyes shut. "Yes . . . I think so."

Mike stopped in front of him and crossed his arms. "Hey, from what I know, it's easy to become infatuated when you meet someone who shows you a fresh perspective, but when you get to know them, you start to see all their faults. Now, as for getting married—isn't it common to became nervous?"

"Yeah, I guess," he said. Then a deep breathe, letting it out slowly through pursed lips.

"Maybe when you get back with your family and friends, it will all come together," said Mike, appearing upbeat.

Jesse shook his head. "I don't think I can convince Becky to move here. She's such a family person. But of course my folks would love us living near them in Minnesota."

"Man, life's a compromise. You give up something to gain something. When you heading back?"

"Charlie and I are driving back tomorrow. Maybe I can get some perspective on the road," Jesse said, a little less frantic.

"And your hound is such a good listener."

"Yeah, he is," Jesse, said reaching for Mike's hand to get out of the beanbag chair. "I can do this," he said, straightening up.

"Sure you can, man, but it has to feel right. Please, talk it over with your dad."

Jesse nodded. "Got it." Then as he reached the door, he added, "I don't understand why you haven't fallen for Sarah. She's so much more than the women who are after you at the club."

"Oh, so now you're a love expert too," Mike said. "Anyway, Sarah's just a kid."

Jesse snorted. "She's hardly a kid, my friend."

Mike narrowed his eyes at him.

"Fact is," Jesse said, looking over his shoulder as he headed out, "I don't think either of us are good enough for her."

𝄞

Jesse closed the door of his apartment, bags in hand, with Charlie at his side prancing with excitement. He hated feeling uncertain. Somehow he had to convince Becky he needed the city to help him get over his writers block and launch his next novel.

With Charlie sitting shotgun in the cheapest rental he could find, they headed out on the twenty-four-hour trip to Minneapolis. As they cruised the Pennsylvania turnpike west, his thoughts bounced around like a billiard ball: from Greenwich Village to the wedding, from the bustling city streets to a quiet lake in Minnesota, from Becky to Sarah to Persis.

It seemed, though, the closer he got to home, the more he looked forward to being with his family, and by the time he reached Illinois he was beginning to imagine what the wedding would be like. And then there was the honeymoon in Europe. He found himself thinking of getting with his college buddies and bragging a little about meeting with his publishers, the new book, and a possible article in the *Atlantic Monthly*. As they reached the Minnesota border on a cloudless but cold

March day, Charlie had had enough of being cooped up, but Jesse was feeling more positive about the upcoming wedding.

Driving into the Olson's gated estate, he considered the possibility of working for Becky's father. He could continue his writing in the evenings and on weekends. Yes, that wouldn't be so bad. Besides, he had made a commitment to Becky, and hundreds of people had made plans.

Parking the rental car behind one of the Olson's Mercedes, he prepared himself for dealing with his future mother-in-law and gave Charlie his marching orders before letting him out.

"Charlie, be good to Becky's poodles. No rough stuff. Understood?" he said, knowing Charlie had to let these poor excuses for dogs run circles round him and nip at his heels. He hoped his dog could take it—again.

Mother Olson met him at the door with a big hug and as usual appeared as if she had just stepped out of the beauty salon, with her big hair, red nails flashing, and gold accessories hanging from every possible location. "Hello, son," she said, "How was your trip?"

"Not too bad. I had time to think—"

"Yes, dear, that's good. Becky is on the back porch. You must help her pick out some colors."

"Colors . . . for what?"

"Oh, there I've done it. It's supposed to be a surprise. Please act surprised when Becky tells you."

He felt his stomach do a half roll as he made his way to the porch. But seeing Becky through the French doors as he approached, reminded him why he had fallen in love with her. Even sitting with her back to him she was beautiful, with her elegant posture, long honey-blonde hair, and slender waist. He snuck up on her and grabbed her from behind.

Becky jumped and swore under her breath. She turned around with a frown. "There you are. Thought you would be here earlier. I had to cancel a meeting with the wedding planner."

"We ran into road construction in Wisconsin." Becky's frosty greeting cooled his loving thoughts. "Hey, aren't you happy to see me?"

"Sure, dear. I'm just trying to get things wrapped up here. Is Charlie with you?"

"Of course. Do you think I would leave him in New York?"

"Hope he's not pestering Toodles and Doodles."

Jesse was beginning to get a headache along with the rolling stomach.

"Charlie has never hurt your dogs. Besides, I put him back in the car after a quick run." Jesse inhaled slowly. "I need to check in with my folks before I get involved with any planning. I'll be back for dinner."

Becky set down a handful of travel brochures and searched his face.

"Is everything okay?"

"Sure," He lied. Then flashed a smile. "I'll be back by five."

As he made his way down the long hall to the front door, the walls seemed to close in on him. *What's going on with me?* When he got in the car, Charlie squirmed back and forth, anxious to leave also. But as Jesse drove the forty-five-minutes to his hometown west of the Twin Cities, he began to relax. Passing the small towns and farms on his way, a flood of memories—mostly good—made him smile. He had loved growing up here with so much for a kid to do. Every season had its joys. Water skiing and sailing in the summer, duck hunting and football in the fall, snowmobiling and ice fishing in the winter, and in the spring, baseball—his favorite sport.

Pulling into the Peterson family farm, he saw lights on in the garage and figured his dad must be working on his truck. Charlie was so excited to be back home, he practically knocked Jesse down getting out of the car. Jesse ran up to the side door of the garage and banged on it before he entered with a big smile, Charlie rushing in ahead of him.

"Pops, the old beater giving you trouble?"

His father pulled out from under the hood. "Good to see you, son, and you too, Charlie," he said, shaking Jesse's hand, Charlie pushing between them to be petted. "Yeah, the alternator needs replacing. Good trip?"

"Yeah, fine. I stopped at Becky's on the way, but I need to get back for dinner. I'll run in to see Mom, but I'll come back out. I want to talk to you about something."

He missed his parents even though it had only been a couple of months. Stopping back at the rental car he grabbed the box of milk chocolates then hustled to the house. He tip-toed in the back door and snuck up on his mom.

"Jesse! You're going to be the death of me." He ducked from a pretend slap from his mom.

"Ma, just giving your heart a little excitement. It's good for you," he said, noticing she seemed older, a little grayer.

"I'm not so sure, you brat," she said with her hands on her hips.

"Sorry. Would a box of your favorite chocolate make you feel better?" Jesse asked presenting the box that was hidden behind him.

"That and a hug." His mom opened her arms wide, beckoning her son. She hung on for a long embrace then held him out for a look. "You have to tell me all about New York and your writing."

"I will," Jesse, said, smiling - thankful someone understood him. "But I have to help dad with the truck and then head back to Becky's for dinner."

"Fine, but don't stay too long at the Olson's. I miss you so," his mom said, with a wave, looking a little sad.

Walking back to the garage he thought about how to put his question. Once inside he saw his dad turning a wrench on the motor and leaned under the hood to get his attention. "You know, Dad, this wedding business is getting to me. I just don't feel a part of it all."

His father looked back with a slight smile. "Son, the fact is, it's all about the bride. You are feeling what every man has felt since time began."

"Yeah I guess. But that's not all. I'm . . . well since moving to New York, I'm seeing Becky and marriage from a whole different angle."

"Well now, that's something else then," his father said, pulling out from under the hood as he wiped his hands on a rag. "Tell me what you mean."

"I've met some people . . . okay a girl—a woman, I mean— that has an amazing outlook on life that is so . . . I don't know . . . freeing."

"Freeing?" his dad said, his eyebrows rising.

"In a good way. And no, we aren't involved. It's just that when I'm with her I feel I can be myself." Jesse paused for a long breath. "With Becky it feels like my life is all planned out, and we aren't even married yet."

His father took a moment to reflect. "Sorry, son. I think what you're feeling can happen when people are from different backgrounds. You have to know exactly what you're getting into."

"You aren't upset with me?"

"Oh, my boy, I don't want you to do anything that doesn't feel right. I'm behind you no matter what you decide. Listen to your heart, and you will make the right decision."

"I hope so," Jesse said. "Can I leave Charlie awhile? I'll be back later."

His dad smiled. "Sure, Son—your mother would like that."

He was hoping his dad would tell him what he should do, but understood he couldn't. After kissing his mom good-bye, he was on his way to steaks and expensive wine at the Olson's. The forty-five-minute trip back to Becky's gave Jesse time to prepare his case for New York. He hated it was still up in the air.

When he came to a stop in the Olson's circular drive, he saw Becky's father coming out of the six-stall garage. Mr. Olson, wearing his dark-blue cashmere topcoat and maroon silk scarf, came up to Jesse's car to greet him.

"Jesse, my good man. How was the trip?" he said, reaching out his hand.

"Some road construction through Wisconsin, but not bad." Jesse liked Becky's dad okay, although he was much the opposite of his own father.

As they headed to the house, amid a light flurry of snowflakes, his future father-in-law put his arm around him.

"Jesse, I would like a minute to go over something with you before dinner."

"Sure," Jesse said, his heart speeding up a notch.

After shaking off the snow and hanging up his coat, he followed Mr. Olson down the hall to the sliding oak door on the left and entered the den. The dark-green carpet, overstuffed brown leather chairs, and wall-to-wall bookcases gave the room an "old-boys' club" feel. Jesse was asked to take a seat in front of the immense mahogany desk, where Mr. Olson held court.

"I know you are thinking of moving to New York when you get back from your honeymoon, but Becky mentioned you haven't decided for sure. I want you to know you have a position at my company if you like. Our management-training program, which takes about six months, would set you up for a great career. Of course there'll be no favoritism, but know if you work your butt off, as I did, it'll all be yours someday."

Jesse pasted on a smile. "Thank you, sir. That's a very nice offer."

"Well, do you have any questions for me?" Mr. Olson said.

"Not really. I have a lot to consider and will make a decision before we get back from our honeymoon," Jesse said, trying to sound professional while his insides churned. With that, Becky's father came around from the back of the desk and gave him a hearty handshake and a slap on the back, then directed him across the hall to the dining room.

Jesse knew something was up when he saw the table set with fine china and crystal glassware. The classically designed solid oak table even with the table leaves out sat eight, so with Mr. and Mrs. Olson at either end and Jesse and Becky across from each other, it gave the whole scene a theatrical impersonal feel. With everyone seated, the maid began serving the first course. Jesse wasn't sure he would be able to eat anything.

He looked across the table at Becky. She seemed to be studying him, so he smiled back appearing as if everything was fine. Talk was all about business, upcoming vacations, and wedding plans. He wanted to feel part of the conversation so shared news about his writing. "I met with my publishers, and they've offered a nice advance on my next book."

Mother Olson smiled and said, "Dear boy, I thought you would have gotten that out of your system by now."

"No, not really," Jesse said. "I've also been asked to write an article for the *Atlantic Monthly*."

"That's nice, honey," Becky said, "but I bet you will change your mind about New York when you see the new townhouse Daddy is giving us for a wedding present."

His mouth dropped. Squinting back at Becky, he blurted, "So that's what this is about." He paused and gulped a breath of air. "Do you care at all what I want?"

Becky pulled back in her chair. "Honey, you can't be serious. What are the chances that you'll write another bestseller? From what I hear, the odds are against it."

Stunned, he sat staring at Becky.

"Jesse," Becky continued, "I can't move to New York. It's smelly, dirty, and noisy. I just can't do it."

Something snapped in his core. "Well, I can't do this," he said, looking around the table. He then set down his napkin, pushed back his chair, and excused himself.

"Jesse, sit down, dear. Where are you going?" Becky said, springing up, leaning toward him.

"I'm going to my new home in New York."

Mrs. Olson dropped her fork, which clattered as it hit her plate and fell to the floor.

"Stop it now, you're scaring me. Daddy—stop him!"

Mr. Olson stood, mouthing something inaudible, seemingly unable to move. Becky's mother gasped and shouted at her husband to do something.

"Sorry, Becky," Jesse said, heading for the door.

Becky ran after him and grabbed his arm. "Get the hell back here!"

"Becky, it's over—let me go." Jesse wrenched his arm away and strode to the hall. He grabbed his coat and burst out the door with Becky stumbling to catch up. When she got to the foyer, she lunged for a vase and chased after him. As he skipped down the stairs toward his car, the vase whizzed past his head, exploding as it hit the front bumper.

Jumping in the rental he slammed the door, cranked the ignition and drove off with Becky's distorted face raging in the rearview mirror.

24
Rehearsal

Mike couldn't believe it. It was seven in the morning on Saturday, and he was wide-awake and moving. Wanting to make a good impression on the group he sprang for new music stands and bought decent folding chairs at Goodwill. And because he encouraged collaboration, he had pencils and pads of paper for notations, along with a full score and description of movements for each player; this he had to admit might have helped the first group. For inspiration he hung posters of some of the greats: Duke Ellington, Dave Brubeck, Mile Davis, and Ella Fitzgerald.

He hustled about to get the room set up before Sarah came over, stocking the fridge with drinks, hauling the mattress into the hall, sweeping the floor, and setting up the chairs and music stands in a semicircle around the piano. He made some coffee and toast and sat at the piano to be ready for Sarah. She was right on time.

"Come in, door's open," he said over his shoulder when he heard her knock.

Sarah peeked around the door like a wide-eyed kid and seeing the room said, "Am I at the right apartment? It's so organized and clean in here."

"I know. Am I dreaming or is this for real?" he said, scanning the room.

She walked up as he sat at the piano and put her hands on his shoulders. "It's for real because you've found your path."

"Yeah, I guess, as long as I don't screw it up."

"How would you do that?"

She sat down in the kitchen chair and faced him. "Are you concerned about your drinking?"

"I don't know. Passing out and starting a fire really scared me."

"Well . . ." Sarah paused with her eyebrows raised.

"Okay," he said, rolling his eyes. "What would Grandma Mae say?"

"Well . . . she would say, 'If it causes problems, it is a problem.' Does it cause a problem, Mike?"

He thought a moment. "Maybe. I don't know. I wish my father were around. Crap, I really screwed up with him. I should have handled that better."

Sarah pleaded, "At some point you've got to let that go."

"Maybe I could talk with my uncle Luther. It's hard to imagine now but he once had a drinking problem." Mike paused to reflect on his uncle. "Hey…enough of that. I want to go over the "Grandma Mae" theme. You have it nailed, but I need to do something better with the backup."

"Hit it, maestro!" Sarah said as she came over and slid in next to him at the piano.

He had just finished the intro, when there was an aggressive knock at the door.

"Come on in—it's open," Mike hollered.

The door swung open and a hairy yellow shape streaked in.

"Charlie!" Sarah yelled, grabbing the dog as he skidded into her. "Did you come back by yourself?"

"He probably would have if he could reach the pedals," Jesse said as he strolled in, looking wrung out. Sarah ran up and gave him a warm hug as Mike looked on.

"Take it you missed the wedding?" Mike said, not crazy about Jesse's sudden return.

"Yes, it was a close call." Jesse brushed his hand across his forehead as if wiping off sweat.

"Let's see if I have this straight," Mike said. "You gave up wealth, status, and a beautiful wife to live like a pauper."

"Yeah," Jesse said as he slumped into a chair, "except I feel lousy about hurting Becky and her family, but in the end I had no choice. No one cared what I thought. I felt invisible."

Mike turned to Sarah. "Man, I have to hand it to him—that took guts."

"I don't know," Jesse said, rubbing his forehead. "It feels like I had to cut off my arm to save my life. I'm still bleeding."

Looking like she was about to cry, Sarah stood up behind Jesse and rubbed his shoulders.

Although Mike wasn't wild about Jesse back on the scene he hated to see him hurting.

"Hey," he said, throttling his jealousy, "we should have a party after rehearsal to cheer up our friend and invite the neighbors to get their buy-in on our practicing here. What'd you think?"

Jesse looked over his shoulder at Sarah, then at Mike. "Sounds okay to me."

Sarah nodded. "And why not call your mom?" she asked Mike. "Wouldn't she like to meet your friends and see where you live?"

"Right. And get a hold of Persis, and call the gang at Johnny's," Mike said, getting wound up. "Just one thing though—who's going to invite the scary-looking artist across the hall?"

"Now that sounds prejudicial," Jesse said. "You have something against artists?"

"You must admit he is a little creepy," Mike said.

"Yeah, you're right…Sarah, you'll have to do it, but we'll be right behind you, girl."

"Hope you two are kidding," Sarah said with her hands on her hips. "Look at you. One with dust bunnies stuck in his Afro and the other looking like he hasn't changed his clothes for days."

"Guess you're right—we are pathetic," Mike said." Okay, I'll go over and invite him. But only if Jesse and Charlie back me up."

Sarah shook her head and moaned as Jesse finally smiled and held out his hand for a little skin from Mike.

𝄞

Roy was the first to arrive with his drum set, rolling it on a cart from the elevator. He muted the bass and snares with pillows and dampened the cymbals with a dishtowel. Then came Morris with his string bass; Willy, a veteran jazz player, with his trumpet; then Garrett with his guitar strapped in a gig-bag on his back. Alice and Diana, who had just finished a morning rehearsal with the New York Philharmonic, arrived together with their violin and cello.

After they all settled in their chairs, Mike introduced everyone and thanked them for coming and being a part of his crazy experiment.

Then he said, "I don't know if any of you have been compelled to do something without knowing where it'll lead, but to be honest, that's how I feel. I have enough in the bank to last a couple of months to see what happens. I know it's a little nuts but—"

"Cool, man, we're with ya," Morris shouted. "Let's jam."

"Alright!" said the others.

"Thanks, Morris," Mike said. "Well then . . . this is how I want to work. I'll read the description of each section that represents the major elements of Sarah's story to give you an idea of the theme. Then I'll play the core melody in hopes you will find your way into the piece the best way you see fit. Sarah and I are almost through writing the lyrics for her parts, which we'll have for next week's session. It's that simple, yet I know it's a lot to ask. Any questions?"

Mike glanced at each musician. "No questions? Great! I'll read the whole description through once, then I'll start with playing the Overture."

$$\&$$

Sarah had to fight back tears as Mike read his notes that portrayed her life. She hadn't realized until now how much he cared for her. What an amazing gift to have her story told in this way—turning her life into living, breathing music. She felt blessed and ached with joy. How had this happened? Only a few months ago she had nothing.

It appeared that Mike's idea of collaborating was going to work. With Mike setting the tempo and playing the core theme for each movement, the others soon felt comfortable experimenting with their parts. At first it seemed chaotic, like the random tuning of an orchestra before a performance, but after a half-dozen runs, it smoothed out with each player making notations on their music. Whenever her part wasn't called for, she took orders for drinks and snacks or just sat back to take in the birthing of Mike's opus.

When six o'clock came and went, there was a knock at the door with Jesse sticking his head in. Mike looked up, seeing it was going on seven, shook his head in disbelief. After finishing the section they were on he stood up at the piano.

"Is anyone here ready for a break and a party?" Mike shouted over the group.

"Gee, do we have to?" Morris asked, sticking out his lip.

Then Garrett got everyone's attention. Letting his guitar hang from his shoulder strap, he held out his hands. "So, what do you guys think—is this going to work?"

A loud roar of affirmation went up as Sarah covered her mouth wide-eyed and rocked back and forth in agreement.

25
Party Time

To get the party rolling, Mike announced for everyone to help themselves to the fridge, which was well stocked with cold beer and cheap red wine. Jesse had earlier set up his hi-fi, and acting as DJ started playing records from his collection that included Miles Davis, Ray Charles, Count Basie, Dave Brubeck, and many other greats. It was the best system money could buy, and the group grooved to the great sound it cranked out. After getting drinks, band members came up to shake Mike's hand and thank him for being part of his project. Mike was so pumped he got on the phone and invited everyone he could think of—even getting Honey to stop by. Next, he went across the hall to check on his neighbor. The artist answered the door wearing coveralls splashed with paint and holding a bottle of beer. Mike had met him when he first moved in, but had only nodded to him a few times in the hall, so reintroduced himself and invited him to the party.

Theo, the artist, thanked Mike graciously and said he would love to stop over and would bring some wine to share. He wasn't at all what Mike expected. *Why do we form opinions without getting to know people?*

With "Take Five" blasting, guests poured into the small flat, overflowing into the hall and down to Jesse's. As Mike surveyed the room, he caught a glimpse of his mother standing at the open door and snaked his way over to her. Wearing her navy-blue floppy Boho hat and three-quarter-length wine-colored cape from the sixties, she looked a little out of place, but she had style. He girded himself as he approached her, not quite sure what to expect.

"Mother, so glad you made it down."

Looking uneasy, she yelled over the music, "Trina and Persis came with me and are here somewhere. You'll have to introduce me to your musician friends. I can't tell who's who."

He took her cape and hat and motioned for Morris, someone she knew, to come over.

"Mrs. Monroe, good to see you again," Morris said gallantly as he reached for her hand.

"Mother, you remember Morris from the Cornell days. He'll get you a drink while I find Sarah for you." Then to Morris, "Please try to convince her this music venture is a good thing."

Morris chuckled, looking at Mike's mother. "Not to worry, Mrs. Monroe. Your son's a genius."

His mother gave them both a look. "Whatever you say, boys."

Mike gave Morris a crooked smile and turned to look for Sarah. He was eager to find her and tell her that Garrett got them a Monday night slot at the Black Diamond. Mike could use the extra cash to put toward promotion *or* maybe a demo tape for approaching record companies *or* for travel expenses, if his agent could line up a tour for the coming fall. His mind whirled from all the possibilities. Moving through the partiers to the door he spotted Mark and Patsy, the newlywed couple that lived across from Jesse. He went over to welcome them and then headed down the hall to look for Sarah.

As happy as he felt, Sarah's health worried him and, having not seen her for a while, thought she might have gone home. *But she would have told me.* With people sprawled all over the floor, he worked his way down the hall and smiled at Runt as she sat happily in the corner with her arms wrapped around Charlie's neck. Peering over and around a mass of people in Jesse's apartment he thought he saw a flash of red hair at the end of the room. Bobbing and sliding sideways, he made it through to the middle of the crowd and with a couple more steps saw Sarah standing at the back with Jesse. She was holding his face with his hands at her waist. Mike's face flashed hot as he watched them embrace. He stood a moment, not able to turn away.

"Sarah . . ." he murmured, then spun around and headed for the door. He snatched another look as his fists clenched then zigzagged out of the room and back down the hall, trying to compose himself. But just as he reached his door, someone went flying into the drum set along with a shout of profanity. People and drinks flew in all directions.

"Keep your hands off my wife, jerk!" Mark bellowed as he stood over the trumpet player.

"What's goin' on?" Mike yelled, seeing Willy sprawled under the drums along with Morris, who was facedown with a gash in his head. Willy struggled to get up and charged in Mark's direction, but Mike caught him halfway and slammed into him with a body block. He pinned Willy down in a flash. Mark grabbed his bride and pushed his way through the crowd to their apartment, slamming the door behind him. Mike's mother seized her cape and hat and stormed out looking for Trina; as Persis bent down to tend to Morris.

Turning Willy over, it was apparent to Mike he was high on something, probably crack.

"Roy, help me get him up!" Mike yelled.

They packed Willy's trumpet, got him downstairs and hailed a cab. When the taxi pulled up, Mike tossed him in with his horn and roared, "You're done, man. Don't bother to come back."

Mike slammed the door and stomped back upstairs with Roy. He had suspected Willy was a druggie, but was so impressed with his playing he'd decided to overlook it. Another lesson learned, but costly, knowing it wouldn't be possible to have the band back for rehearsals.

It wasn't long before the party was back in full swing, the music cranked up and everyone dancing. Honey, seeing Mike alone, went over and sat down next to him as he sipped at a tumbler of bourbon.

"How you doing?"

He peered over at her. "How do you think?"

"Want to take me home?"

He huffed. "Sure . . . great idea," and tossed back the remainder of his drink.

He asked Roy to lock up for him then slipped out with Honey, deciding to hit some of the local jazz clubs on their way to her place. The weather had turned miserable with sleet slicing into them as they made their way from Mike's apartment across the wide-open sweep of Washington Park in search of a cab.

Stopping for a couple more drinks at the Bottom Line nightclub, Mike considered finishing off the night by getting totally smashed – the scene of Sarah and Jesse playing out in his head. But the fire still haunted him. So despite Honey's invitation to spend the night, he walked her home and hoping to sober up headed to his place as the sleet turned into an icy downpour.

Dripping wet and shaking, Mike reached his floor at two thirty in the morning. He found his key on the top of the window frame at the end of the hall, and opened his door to the mess left from the party. He threw his sodden coat and hat across the room, flipped on the single light over the piano, and dragged his mattress to its spot in the corner. Stripping off his wet clothes, he flopped on the mattress in the midst of the clutter. The dark room matched his mood – lying there in his boxers - brooding over what to do next.

About ten minutes into his deliberation there was a light knock at the door. Mike lay splayed out with a pillow over his face.

"Yeah, who is it?" Mike yelled into his pillow.

"You okay?" Jesse said, poking his head around the door.

Mike sat up with a jolt, tossed the pillow across the room—knocking over beer bottles and ashtrays. "You got to be kidding?"

"What is it, Mike?"

He sat a brief moment looking at Jesse in disbelief. Then leaping up from the mattress, he stepped to within a foot of Jesse's face with an angry scowl. "What are your intentions with Sarah?"

Jesse leaned back at the waist. "My intentions? What're you her father now?" He chuckled.

A firestorm began to brew in Mike. He was ready to punch something and it might as well be Jesse. Sticking out his chest, he bellowed, "Someone has to look out for her. She doesn't need some bozo on the rebound from a lousy relationship!"

Jesse snorted. "Get out of my face, Mike. You don't know what you're talking about."

Mike's muscles tightened. "You don't want to mess with me, man."

Jesse held his ground. "You're an idiot. She saw Honey chewing your ear off tonight."

Mike drew back. "She was just playing around—it meant nothing."

"Well, it meant something to Sarah."

"What?" Mike stared at Jesse.

"Yeah, dumbass. She saw you with Honey, and was devastated."

"Don't give me that crap," Mike growled. "I saw you two making out in the corner." Jesse stood a moment with a blank stare; then spoke deliberately slow. "I was having some regrets about Becky. Sarah helped me through the guilt I was feeling." He paused and heaved a breath. "Sarah's the most amazing person I've ever known—but she loves you."

"Loves me?"

"I should say *loved* you. I think she's had enough." Jesse shook his head and turned for the door, slamming it on his way out.

Mike shuddered. The noise echoed in his ears. He got up and went to his piano and sat on the bench with his back to the keyboard. He put his head in his hands, feeling ill.

This was the night he had planned to reveal his love for her.

26

Home

Mike opened an eye and peered out from under his pillow at the chaotic mess. *Crap, it wasn't a nightmare.* Pulling the covers over his head, he thought of all the things he had lost in the past six months: his father, his first love, a place to practice, his trumpet player, the friendship of the person who'd saved his life, and the voice that inspired him to write his opus. The only thing left was to be told he had only a month to live.

All he could think to do, as he shuffled to the bathroom, was to head home to Harlem. He wasn't sure why, he just needed to see his family.

The air was crisp, but the sun warmed his face as he stepped out and headed down to the subway. As he sat on the train watching people come and go, a shabbily dressed man with a dirty bundle got on. Observing the man's aimless stare, Mike sighed, thankful he had family who loved him no matter what.

It was a little past eight when Mike walked into the kitchen, finding his mother at the stove. He gratefully inhaled the aroma of bacon and brewing coffee.

"Morning, Mother," he said flatly.

His mother turned with a jerk. "Goodness—you gave me a fright."

"Sorry. I should have called," he said as he idly scanned the room.

His mother frowned. "Well, good to see you didn't end up in jail."

Mike slumped. "I know—it was a nightmare."

His mother shook her head and turned off the stove. "I don't know, Michael. What is it you are trying to prove with that group?"

He fell into a chair and stared at the floor. "Not sure really. But…it's probably over anyway."

His mother studied him. "Michael, you look terrible. Come here, dear," she said, reaching for him.

He got up and unashamedly walked into his mother's outstretched arms.

"I just couldn't stay at the apartment," he said over her shoulder.

"Might be time to give it up. Why don't you go lie down while I finish up."

His room was pretty much as it was throughout college: a set of bunk beds along the left wall, a desk at the window overlooking the small backyard and alley, and a bookcase to the right with his many wrestling and track trophies along with posters of Miles Davis, Eddie Henderson, Herbie Hancock, and John Coltrane on the walls. The familiar surroundings bathed him in warm memories.

After kicking off his shoes, he lay down on the quilted bedspread his Grandma Monroe had made and looked for solace in the faces of his heroes, wondering if he could survive yet another disaster. And how would he ever reconcile with Sarah? He wouldn't blame her if she never spoke to him again.

Not getting any answers from the posters, he closed his eyes and drifted off for an hour until his sister, seemingly with great pleasure, ran in to wake him up.

"Mikey, it's time for church!" Trina bellowed.

He peered from his bed at his baby sister standing in the doorway with her arms crossed.

"Argh," he moaned. "Runt . . . yeah, alright. Give me fifteen minutes."

After a quick shower Mike descended the stairs, buttoning his shirt. He stopped a moment to take in the three women standing at the door. Although not always happy with him, they were always there for him. He was glad to be home.

The bright April morning had a moist earthy smell as they walked the four blocks to the small Baptist church. After a service of spirited singing and preaching, everyone headed downstairs for coffee and lunch. As Mike strode through the basement fellowship hall, nodding to the many familiar faces, he caught Reverend Robinson's eye and made his way over to see him. The reverend, without his burgundy robe and Bible in hand, could be taken for a New York Giants linebacker if it wasn't for the smile lines at the corner of his eyes and mouth. With a hearty handshake, that bordered on painful, the reverend asked Mike how things were going.

"Some days good and some not so good."

"Sounds like life, son. I've watched you grow up, and I know you can do whatever you set your mind to."

"Thanks, Reverend."

"Sure miss your father." He then inquired, "How's the family doing with him gone?"

"Mother seems a little lost. Trina is busy with school. And Persis appears to be handling the stores okay," Mike said mechanically.

"And how about you?" the reverend said, peering deep into his eyes.

Mike knew this was coming. He sighed. "I don't know. A little lost, I guess."

"When a parent dies," the reverend said, "it can feel like we've lost a piece of ourselves. But really that piece is inseparable and can't be lost. Over time you'll find he is still with you, Mike."

He was about to let out how guilty he felt over quitting NYU and not helping his dad, when his mother called to him.

"Michael, come here." His mother called, waving him over. "Do you believe it? Your uncle Luther, back in church."

Mike glanced over, catching his favorite uncle's beaming face. Mike nodded back, then reached to shake the reverend's hand but got a solid hug instead.

"Keep the faith, son. You'll be okay."

The fatherly embrace of Reverend Robinson was comforting. Mike smiled, thanked the reverend and made his way through the gathering to his uncle.

"Man, it's good to see you again," Mike said.

"Same here," his uncle said in his usual jovial fashion. "Got a good job selling cars in Queens, so hope to see more of you." His six-foot–five frame towered over Mike, but the broad smile with a slight gap in his front teeth revealed a tender heart. Mike felt drawn to him like never before.

After catching up Mike asked his uncle if he would walk back to the house with him. He wanted his opinion on something. As they left the church he tried to think how to pose his concern.

"It's been hard since Father died," Mike said, bowing his head, searching on the sidewalk for what to say. "I'm feeling bad for not helping with the stores and . . . I don't know. Maybe I have a problem with drinking. Father told me you went to AA for a while."

His uncle took Mike's words in stride as they walked. "A couple things," he said. "For me, I had to get over my guilt by making amends when possible to those I hurt and then forgive myself. Basically live the Serenity Prayer. Then I had to find out what I was good at and then do it. For me, I love cars and I love selling, so that's what I do, and ever since life's been good."

"Makes sense I guess," Mike said.

"I knew your father better than anyone. He was a driven man. Opening those stores was his passion. But you need to find *your* passion. You won't be happy until you do."

"I know my passion," Mike said with conviction.

"Then you're halfway there. It might be good to check out AA or find someone you trust that would hold you accountable."

"Oh! I have a couple friends that would love that chance."

"Good, but don't put it off. Carrying around a big bag of guilt will sap your energy and your creativity."

𝄞

After Sunday dinner and an afternoon game of Monopoly with Uncle Luther keeping order and winning in record time, Mike went upstairs and packed his duffle. As he left his room to go downtown, he walked past Persis's room and stuck his head in.

"Hey, Pers, I'm heading out," he said to his sister at her desk going through some papers.

"Michael." She turned around, looking solemn. "You're my brother and I'll always love you, but you have to stop being so self-centered. I understand you weren't cut out for the stores, but now you've crushed Sarah."

"What are you talking about?" Mike said weakly.

"I saw you leave with Honey. How could you? Don't you know how much that girl cares for you?"

Mike stood back with his hands in the air like he was being arrested. "All that's a big misunderstanding. Nothing *happened* with Honey."

Angry, he turned to leave, then stopped and threw down his duffle. "I didn't mean to hurt her, Persis."

His sister shook her head in disgust.

"I know," Mike said. "I'll try to explain it to her when I get back."

Persis dismissed him with a wave. Mike scooped up his duffle and went downstairs. After saying good-bye to his mother, he left, going over what to say to Sarah. As he stepped down from the stoop, Trina ran up to him, hollering like a crazy person with a friend trailing behind.

"Mikey, what a great party," She said, slamming into him with a huge hug.

"Runt," he said, holding on to her for a moment, "it wasn't supposed to be quite that exciting, but I'm glad *you* had a good time."

"Yeah . . . while it lasted—until Mom hustled me out of there."

Mike looked lovingly at his kid sister's face. "I can always count on you to lift me out of the ditch."

"Sure, Mikey—you're the best." Trina smirked.

"I know…I'm your favorite brother," Mike said, reaching for her again.

As Mike rode the A train to the Village, he leaned back with a great sigh, taking in the sprawling graffiti. It struck him in that moment the intense need humans have for affirmation and self-expression; notice me—I exist. He could relate, but what would it cost him?

𝄞

The first thought Sarah had Sunday morning, after the disastrous party, was to check on Mike. Pushing aside her wounded heart, she baked some of his favorite muffins, wrapped them to keep them warm, and walked the six blocks to his place as fast as she could. She tried to think of what to say as she took the freight elevator up to his floor. If he didn't love her, she would just have to accept it.

She knocked at his door but no one answered. She plunged into despair. Frustrated, then angry, she fought back a sob, and stomped down the hall to Jesse's. After a quiet woof from Charlie, Jesse opened the door to Sarah's troubled face drenched with tears. She handed him the muffins and dropped to her knees to give Charlie a hug. Charlie sat steady with his head on her shoulder as Sarah stoked his back.

"What is it, Sarah?" Jesse asked looking pained as he closed the door.

"He's not there. At least, he's not answering," she said with an edge. "Maybe he's completely burned up this time."

"The jerk." Jesse muttered, peering down at her. "Stay here as long as you want."

Sarah got up from the floor and dropped onto Jesse's bed as he returned to sit at his typewriter. Charlie stretched, went to the side of the bed, and propped his head within easy reach of Sarah. As she reached out to pet Charlie, she looked over at Jesse and noticed he was watching her. "What is it, Jesse?"

Looking deep in her eyes, he said, "You know how beautiful you are?"

She suddenly felt anxious. "Why are you saying that?"

"Because," Jesse said, smiling, "I think I'm in love with you."

"Don't say that…please." Sarah sat up, swung her legs out, and gripped the edge of the mattress.

"Why not? It's true."

Sarah closed her eyes, slowly hunched over, and started to weep.

Jesse got up from his typing and walked over and sat next to her.

He put his arm around her. "Sorry. Please don't cry."

After a minute Sarah caught her breath and whimpered. "What do I do now?"

Jesse looked across the room, shaking his head. "I don't know . . . but I'm always here for you." Leaning over, he brushed her silky hair aside and kissed her cheek.

Feeling drained, Sarah laid down and Jesse covered her up. Soon she was asleep with Charlie stretched out on his rug and Jesse back at his typing.

🎼

The sun broke out after a cleansing April shower and splashed through the window onto Sarah's face. The warming rays beckoned, waking her from a brief nap. Suddenly feeling claustrophobic, she got up, got her coat and stopped at the door.

"Thank you," she said, fingering the cross beneath her blouse, "for being a good friend."

Jesse looked over from his typing, slumped a little, and nodded.

Charlie padded up to her with a whine. She stroked his head for a moment then left.

Unconsciously she headed for her favorite spot in Madison Park. As she walked up 23rd Street, soaking in the reviving rays of the sun, the YMCA came in view. She walked up to the front steps of the Y and decided she needed to see Floretta's smiling face and check out the bulletin board. She had been so busy with Mike, she hadn't thought much about teaching or keeping up with her sketching. Finding nothing interesting on the bulletin board, she headed up to the locker room, but as she passed the front desk, the director saw her and called her over.

"Sarah, right?" the director said.

"Yes, you remember,"

"Of course. You were my first choice for the class, but I got overruled. Anyway, we're looking for someone to help with the summer program. Interested?"

"Sure," she said without hesitation. "When would I start?"

"Tuesday, June tenth. Nine a.m. to noon."

"That would be great!" Sarah was so excited that when she leaned over the desk to shake the director's hand, she knocked some books onto the floor.

"Sorry." She bent down and retrieved the books. "Thank you so much. See you on the tenth."

She felt like skipping up the stairs to the locker room, but then thought better of it. Not finding Floretta anywhere, she dug in her bag for her journal and did a quick sketch of "washing" her clothes in the shower and signed it: "See you this summer. Love, Sarah."

Passing Samson's Market on the way to Madison Park she couldn't resist and went in to buy a sandwich, a small milk *and* Twizzlers. After her treat and spending a couple of hours at her favorite bench, sketching and daydreaming of teaching kids at the Y, Sarah felt whole again. She tossed a few crumbs to the birds, closed her eyes and thanked God for giving her hope.

Leaving the park, Sarah hummed happily all the way to her apartment. But as she reached the second floor, she saw someone in the dim hall coming toward her—tall and dark-haired, like her mother. How was this possible? It was her aunt.

"Hello, Sarah."

"Holy cow. Aunt Clara—is that you?" Sarah said, rushing into her aunt's reaching arms.

"Wasn't sure I would ever find you. I was 'bout to head back home."

"What are you doing here?" Sarah asked, gazing up at her aunt, who smiled back with tears in her eyes.

"I need to talk to you."

After Sarah showed her aunt the apartment, they sat down at the table facing each other.

"First, I want to apologize for not com'n' to my sister's funeral. I know you called and left a message with my husband, but we were going through some stuff and I . . ." Aunt Clara couldn't continue and broke down sobbing.

Sarah's heart sank as she recalled her mother's funeral, without any family. Yet, felt sorry for her aunt and her troubles.

After collecting herself, her aunt continued.

"I first went to the apartment where you lived with your parents. They said to check the 31st Street shelter, and when I went there they gave me this address. I had this image of you all alone in this big city. I just had to find you."

Thankful, Sarah reached for her aunt's hand. "I'm all right, really. Thank you for coming."

"You lived out of a shelter?" her aunt asked, sagging forward.

"Yes, but not for long. God's been good to me."

Her aunt stiffened. "How can you say that? You've lost everything."

Sarah didn't know how to answer her aunt, so she just smiled like someone blessed.

"Dear, I want you to come to Kentucky with me. Your uncle Merle finally left—I think for good this time." Her aunt paused and studied her. "It'll be a whole lot safer, honey, and you'll be with family. The twins would love hav'n' ya around."

Sarah pondered the offer. "But I have a job here."

"What kind of job?"

"I sing in nightclubs."

Her aunt shifted forward. "You do what?"

"I sing with Mike, who is an amazing pianist, and we're getting more work all the time. We call ourselves *The Moment* and have gotten some pretty good reviews."

Aunt Clara narrowed her eyes. "Your Grandma Mae would have had a fit about this."

"I don't know. She always encouraged my singing."

Her aunt sat quiet for a moment. "But you don't have family nearby."

"I know," Sarah said, wincing at the thought of Mike with Honey.

"Child, please seriously consider coming home. Your mom told me 'bout your health. Maybe you don't know, but I'm an RN now at St. Mary's, and I can get you the care you need. And, hon, I can tell you aren't doing that well."

"I'm just tired from last night. But that does sound good," Sarah said.

"Dear, I need to get back for the Tuesday night shift, but I can send up one of your cousins to help you move when you're ready."

Sarah's thoughts whirled. "Auntie…you've made me feel so much better by just being here. I never understood why my parents lost contact with our Kentucky relatives."

"Hon, that's all over with now. What's important is you have a home to come to."

Sarah stood up from the table and fell into the open arms of her aunt and clung to her. It had been a long time since she felt so loved.

27

Family

Finding refuge with his family, although prickly at times, Mike sat revived on the subway, going over his apology to Sarah. He really hadn't meant to hurt her. *Maybe I am an idiot.*

Running up a flight of stairs to her floor, Mike saw Sarah and a tall dark-haired woman coming out of her apartment at the end of the hall.

"Mike," Sarah gasped.

"Sorry, I just had to see you," he said, panting as he ran up to them.

Sarah considered him a moment. "Well . . . this is my Aunt Clara. She's from Kentucky."

"So glad to meet you," he said. "I didn't know Sarah had any family."

"Yes, she has, and I hope we can make up for some lost time," Aunt Clara said.

"That's great. Family is important, very important," he said, reaching around Sarah for a one-arm hug. She leaned back peering at him out of the corner of her eye.

"Sarah's become like family. Has she told you about her stunning singing career?"

Clara looked at his arm around Sarah, then back at him.

"She mentioned she was singing in a nightclub—with you, I gather."

"Your niece is incredible," Mike said. "She's an inspiration to me. I only hope I can keep up with her."

There was a moment of silence as Sarah reddened and Aunt Clara studied him. Mike continued. "Will you be in town for a while?"

"Actually, I need to catch a bus by eight, so I need to get going." Then said, "It was nice to meet you, Mike. Sarah, let me know what you decide, dear."

They walked down to the entrance and out to the bustling street. It was dusk. The streetlights were just coming on, and rush-hour traffic was in full press – horns honking and tires screeching. Mike went to the curb and hailed a cab, whistling and waving his arms.

"Will you get back okay?" Sarah asked.

"I must admit, at first I felt like a sparrow in tall weeds. But I think I can get anywhere now, after searching for you. I rather enjoyed the adventure," her aunt said, looking pleased with herself.

Sarah took a deep breath and plunged into her aunt's arms. "Thank you," Sarah choked, her eyes glistening, "for coming to see me."

"Take care. I love you, my dear." Aunt Clara said peering over Sarah's shoulder at Mike.

𝄞

Sarah stood watching the cab disappear as Mike wondered what Aunt Clara's appearance could mean.

They continued on to his place so he could change before going to Johnny's. He wanted to clear up what had happened with Honey, but also wanted to hear about Sarah's aunt. When they stopped on their way at Gino's for a slice of pizza, he pondered what to say as they sat in the cramped restaurant the clatter of dinner hour around them.

After getting their wedges of pizza, Mike opened with, "Your aunt seems like she really cares about you."

Sarah looked straight at him. "She wants me to come live with her."

He caught his breath and fell back in his chair. It never occurred to him she would leave New York.

"Do you want to leave? I thought this was your home now."

"She's family. She's an RN, and she's concerned about me," she said soberly.

"My God, Sarah—what would I do without you?" he said. "I thought we were like family."

"Family?" Sarah said.

Mike pushed back his plate and peered hard at her. "Is this about Honey?"

She straightened and glared at him. "This has nothing to do with that."

He wasn't so sure and reached for her hand. "I'm sorry—"

Sarah pulled her hand back. "Mike, I won't leave until after we perform your opus. I wouldn't do that to you."

Mike fell silent, aimlessly watching the crush of people moving in and out. *Where did Jesse get the idea she loved me?*

Once back at his apartment, Mike made another attempt to explain the misunderstanding about Honey. As he held her hands, pleading forgiveness, a loud insistent pounding thundered from the door.

"Anybody home?" yelled Jesse.

Man, now what? Before he could think of a diplomatic way to turn Jesse away, Sarah went to the door and let him in. Charlie scooted in first to greet them, his tail waving wildly, as Jesse stood in the door frame glaring at Mike.

"Thought I'd stop by and see how ol' grumpy pants was doing."

Mike didn't know how to respond—throw a fit or ignore him. Shaking his head, he finally threw up his hands. "Sorry for being a jerk, man. Why do you put up with me?"

Jesse softened and snickered. "Because you're awesome, and you have mostly great parties."

"Right." Mike snorted. "Come on in. Let me get you a makeup beer."

Just as Jesse walked over to flop in the beanbag chair, Patsy from down the hall stuck her head in. "Hey, can I join the party?"

The small group was struck speechless as they stared back at her. Mike finally got out, "I didn't think you would ever speak to me again."

"Oh, Mike," Patsy said, waving her hand in dismissal, "it wasn't your fault. Mark overreacted. Musicians run in my family. My dad plays guitar, and my uncle played trumpet in the Count Basie orchestra for a while."

Mike and Jesse looked at each other in disbelief.

"You're kidding!" Mike said. "Does your uncle still play?"

"Yeah, but he doesn't like traveling so much. He had his fill in the sixties.

Mike's eyes grew wide. "Well, as you know, we are in need of a trumpeter. Do you think he might possibly consider—"

Patsy titled her head and smiled. "I'll see him this week and pass on your offer. I think it would be a riot. And I would get to see him more."

Mike stammered, "Uh . . . you don't mind if we still practice here?"

"I insist," Patsy said, smiling.

"Grrreat!" Mike shouted. "How about coming for a couple of sets at Johnny's tonight, so you can hear sweet Sarah sing?"

Patsy grinned. "I'll check with Mark, but I'm sure he'd be up for it."

Sarah jumped in. "And I'll invite your dear neighbor Theodore, to make it a total fourth-floor party."

𝄞

Mike felt a growing camaraderie as all six stuffed themselves into a Checker cab and roared off into a wonderful drizzly spring evening. The sparkling refracted light of raindrops on the windows added to the magical feeling of breaking free from orbit as Mike took in the sight and sound of everyone joyfully talking at once. The conversation ranged widely from fine art to fist fights to big band music. He was struck by how sweet the talk seemed. Even though they hadn't known each other long there was a connection, a love for music that strung them together.

Mike kept their first set short so they could rejoin the warm conversation. The second set was made up completely of requests from their new friends. With his arms outstretched at the keyboard and Sarah's smiling eyes upon him as she sang, his spirit soared to new heights. He'd never played better.

Mike was about to end the set, when one last song came to mind. Taking the mic from its stand, he stood at the piano and made an announcement. "I would like to dedicate this last song to someone who saved my life. The most amazing person I've ever known." He motioned for Sarah to sit at the stool next to the piano. "This one's for my beautiful partner, Sarah.

I know she loves Billy Joel, so I learned this one just for her."
Mike sat back down and smiled as he looked over at her and
played "She's Got a Way."

Sarah lit up, holding her hands to her cheeks as she moved
side to side in time to the music. Their friends gave him a
thumbs-up and watched her with delight. When he ended his
song, he stood to a standing ovation as Sarah reached for him.
This was the best night of his life.

The warmth and companionship at the table seemed
impenetrable until an intense well-dressed man came over and
introduced himself.

"Hello, I'm Martin Roake," he began, looking at Mike and
Sarah. "Sorry for interrupting. I represent the Encore Talent
Agency on Park Avenue."

Mike stood, shook his hand, and introduced everyone at
the table, then offered him a chair.

Mr. Roake continued. "I'm on assignment to find talent for
a musical set to open on Broadway this coming Christmas,
and honestly, I've been looking for some time." Then, looking
at Sarah, he said, "I think you would be a perfect fit. Not only
because of your beautiful voice, but your poise and appearance
are ideal for the role."

Sarah looked over at Mike with a blank stare. He looked
back, trying to put a sentence together. The rest of the table
eagerly watched.

"What do you think about Broadway, Sarah?" Mike asked
with mixed feelings.

"I don't know what to think," she said, looking troubled.
"We're in the middle of practicing for Naumburg."

"Sarah, these things don't come along every day," Mike
said, forcing a smile.

The agent broke in. "Sarah, here's my card. Think about it and give me a call." He stood and scanned the club for a moment, then turned back to them. "Bet you two will be getting many opportunities. You're really good."

Mike and Sarah stood. She thanked Martin Roake and said she'd let him know.

With Monday morning closing in fast, after hugs and handshakes, Mark, Patsy, Theo, and Jesse headed back to the Village, leaving *The Moment* to finish out the evening.

After their last set and a wave good night to Rudy, Mike and Sarah stepped out from Johnny's to a waiting cab and rode in silence back to Chelsea. Mike stared out at the deserted streets with his emotions raging, chewing on what would be best for Sarah.

28

Change

By the time they got to Sarah's apartment after Johnny's, she had told Mike about Aunt Clara's visit. He in turn continued his plea for forgiveness, which was met with an unrevealing blank stare. Neither brought up the agent. Standing at her door, he fidgeted with the coins in his pocket, wishing he could just kiss her and have everything return to the way it was before Aunt Clara and the agent.

"You know I want what's best for you," Mike said, practically chewing his lip off.

"What do you think that is?"

"You should get the best care you can, of course."

"And what about the agent?"

"Are you kidding? Go for it!" Mike said with his big-brother voice. "I'm really proud of you. People are finally seeing how wonderful you are."

She studied him, silent, seemingly not hearing what he said. He turned for the stairs as if in a hurry to get home. "See you tomorrow. I need to work on something that came to me tonight."

"Yeah. See ya," she said, watching him head down the hall.

Mike was stricken. When he reached the street he started running the six blocks to his flat, but thought better of it and slowed to a walk. He wasn't in any mood to get stopped and questioned by some early morning patrol.

Back at his floor, he went straight to Jesse's on the chance he might be up. He saw a light under the door and rapped lightly.

"Jesse, it's me."

Jesse opened the door as Charlie lay under the bed wagging his tail.

"Got a minute, man?"

"Sure, what's up?" Jesse said closing the door behind him.

Mike paced around the room as he spewed his concerns about Sarah. "I can see diabetes is weakening her. And her aunt would make sure she got the best care possible. And if she can get her health back, a chance at Broadway is huge—a better opportunity than I could ever offer." He walked to the window with his fists balling. "I know all that is good for her, but I don't know how to deal with it, man."

Jesse blew out a breath and dropped into a chair. "Well, I'm happy for her…but not so for you."

"I can't lose her," Mike said with a gasp.

"I understand."

Mike sat on the edge of the bed, cradling his face. Charlie scooted out from underneath and nestled his head in his lap. Mike sat working all the angles, bouncing his thoughts off Jesse as he petted Charlie. Finally, going on three a.m., exhausted, Mike stood up.

"Thanks, man, for listening. Guess this was better than arm wrestling with Old Granddad." He nodded at Jesse and turned for the door.

"Sorry, friend. I don't know what to say." Jesse leaned back looking pained. "Wish I was more help."

Mike glanced back. "Really…it's out of my hands anyway," he said and let himself out.

𝄞

Mike woke the next morning, anxiety gnawing at his gut, thinking of all the work he had to do. Before Saturday's practice, he needed the next three movements worked out so feeling sorry for himself was not an option.

The Grandma Mae movement was the most challenging but offered the greatest number of emotional transitions, ranging from soaring orchestration to poignant elegy. Getting the counterpoint melodies to weave harmoniously stretched him to the max, but he was thankful for such experienced musicians to help him augment his arrangements, which relieved *some* of the pressure.

Occasionally, when stuck on how to convey a theme, he'd get up and move about the room to physically express what was in his head. Closing his eyes, he tried to visualize what the emotion would feel like as body movements. He thought of it as composing to a dance. As he glided about the room, swaying and moving his arms, he would transpose the dance into music, choosing the instrument or combination of instruments and voice to represent the motif. His greatest fear was that he would lose what was in his head before he could write it down. When he felt he had it, he would rush to the Goodwill table and write down enough musical notations so he could re-create the piece later. The whole process was totally engaging, but often left him drained yet fulfilled.

With building emotional gestures, the "Grandma Mae" theme called for more expansive movement, so he went out into the hall and started sweeping his arms and swaying past

Jesse's door to the fire escape window and back to his place. On his second lap back to his flat, the freight elevator opened with a clunk at the end of the hall by his door with Patsy and someone he assumed was her uncle Jerry - catching him sashaying toward them. Mike stopped midstride and smiled broadly as he bowed to their smirks and applause. Patsy's uncle was a barrel-chested, stocky man in his fifties. His round face was accented with apple-red cheeks and a smile as broad as the Grand Canyon.

"I didn't know you were a dancer too," Patsy called out with eyebrows arched as they walked toward him.

"It's hard to explain. It helps me compose stuff," he said, screwing up his mouth as they met in the hall.

"It seems to work for you. Anyway, I want you to meet my Uncle Jerry," Patsy said.

"Uncle Jerry, so glad to meet you," Mike boomed, grabbing his hand.

"Likewise, Mike. Later I want to hear more about how you create your music."

"I would be honored. Anytime you would like to stop over, I would love to show you some of the things we're working on."

"How about right after dinner?" Uncle Jerry said. "I understand Patsy is doing burgers for us. Oh, and, Mike, just call me Jerry."

Mike got on the phone and called Sarah right away. He wanted Jerry to meet her so he could hear the voice that inspired him. This was big. Someone that actually played with Count Basie might consider playing in his group.

After dinner they all shifted over to Mike's. With Sarah sitting next to him at the piano, they chose to do the opening number, "Morning on a Kentucky Porch," which featured

Sarah's voice welcoming a new day with her beloved family all around her. Mike looked down at his hands as he played for fear of reading something unfavorable in Jerry's expression. It seemed each time they did this piece Sarah tried something a little different, making it even better than the time before. With the final chord, Mike peered hesitantly to catch Jerry's reaction.

"I'm in! I'm in!" Jerry said, standing up and raising his hands in the air. "This could be the most fun I've had in ages. Just use me any way you want, and if I have any thoughts, don't worry—I'll speak up."

Mike and Sarah gazed at each other, grinning wide-eyed.

"Fantastic!" Mike said. "We'll get back to Saturday practices, thanks to your understanding niece. I thought we were done for."

"I'll bring a recorder so I can practice the music at home," Jerry said. "As I understand it, collaboration and improvisation are encouraged?"

Mike laughed. "Encouraged? No, I would say required."

"I love it, man. I have some ideas already," Jerry said.

Mike was back on top with Jerry's affirmation, and after everyone had left, they put more time into the Grandma Mae movement, trying out various renditions.

"Once we've established the theme," said Mike, "you can take the lead, and I'll support it with wispy harmonics. I think Grandma Mae's musical spirit should reappear throughout the composition in counterpoint as well as solo at times. This should hold it all together. I'll ask the others for their input as well."

Sarah stared at Mike. "How do you know to do this?"

He caught her gaze. "I don't really understand it. All I know is, without you none of this was possible." He sighed. "*You* make it happen."

In the middle of their performance, at a packed house in the Lincoln Center, Aunt Clara appeared from nowhere with two other nurses and gingerly helped Sarah onto a gurney and wheeled her out the backstage exit to a waiting ambulance. "Why," Mike moaned, not being able to pull away from the piano. "Come back!" He yelled, reaching out to her, convulsing in agony. Desperate and panting he willed himself awake – his sheets wet with sweat. His heart raced as he sat up wrenching his covers, the nightlights of Bleecker Street streaming in. *That's it…I've got to find out what's happening with her.*

𝄞

Mike knew Sarah was returning to her doctor in a couple days for test results from a physical, so insisted on going along. She tried to talk him out of it, but he demanded - not knowing was driving him crazy.

Mike hated hospitals—the antiseptic smell, the hushed conversations of doctors, the crying of relatives in the halls. Then came the memories of his father's last day.

Finally, after a half hour of fidgeting, Sarah sitting quietly at his side, the door to the cramped exam room opened and the physician came in.

"Hello, Sarah," the doctor said. "And you're Mike?"

"Yes sir."

"Okay, so here it is," he said, sitting down and rolling his chair up to them. "The blood test shows continued degeneration in kidney function since your last test three months ago." He stopped and looked directly at Sarah. "We need to stop this. Next, there is some increase in blood pressure. I expect you're feeling a lack of energy, am I right?"

"A little, but we've been working hard," Sarah said, looking over at Mike.

"And how about your vision?"

"A little blurry sometimes," Sarah said calmly.

"I know, but has it gotten worse?"

"Oh, maybe a little."

"Hmm. You'll need to slow down and get more rest...alright?"

Both Sarah and Mike nodded in agreement.

"Lastly, no more weight loss. You're down five pounds, and that's a lot for you," he said sternly.

Sarah nodded again as Mike just stared.

"Sarah, your kidneys are barely functioning," the doctor said as he reached for her hands, "You're at a critical point here. I want more rest. I'm going to up your insulin to twice a day, and I want to get another blood test to see if there are any changes since the one last week. We have to keep close tabs on this." The doctor paused. "I don't need to remind you what could happen."

"Got it, Doctor. I know," Sarah said.

The doctor made some notes, wrote out a prescription, and handed it to Sarah; then got up to leave.

Before going out the door, he turned and looked at Mike. "See that she takes care of herself."

Mike straightened, "Yes sir, I will."

The reality of Sarah's health smacked him hard. She *was* thinner and tired easier – thinking back to when they had first met. Needing to address his concerns, he asked her to come listen to something he'd been working on.

Back at his flat he idly shuffled papers at the piano and flashed a smile as Sarah sat next to him on the high stool.

"I want you to know how happy you've made me," he said.

Sarah's eyes narrowed, piercing his façade. "It's all coming together and I think everyone is having a good time."

Mike folded his hands and looked down. "But nothing is as important as your health." He peered at her from the corner of his eye. "You need to get the best care possible. You should go live with your Aunt Clara."

Sarah was quiet a moment. She then glared back with a hard-edged sneer. "So. That's what you've decided, huh? Well, I better get moving if I'm going to catch the eight thirty bus to Kentucky." She slid off the stool and headed for the door. When she reached the door, she spun around, marched back and glowered at him.

"Mike!" She scolded, gulping a breath of air. "I know you're concerned about my health, but you can't decide what's best for me. I'm not helpless!" She dropped down at the table with her hands under her chin and glared at him.

"Now, here's what *I've* decided about my health."

Mike sat at the piano in silence as Sarah stood up and strode about his flat, lecturing, like a football coach chewing out his team, down twenty-eight points at halftime. When he attempted to speak, he was shushed. A few more laps around the piano, while he followed her with his eyes, she ended her tirade at the door.

"Now…any questions about how I feel?" she asked.

He remained silent, looking at the piano keys, his hands in his lap.

"Good—see you tomorrow."

Sarah woke to the urgent jangling of her phone. She stumbled from her bed to the couch, picked up the receiver from the end table and answered.

"Sarah, this is Dr. Connelly. I put a rush on your blood test from yesterday." He paused a long moment.

"Yes, Doctor."

"It's not good . . . much worse than I had hoped."

"Okay," Sarah said, leaning back, closing her eyes.

"I need you to check into Bellevue Hospital as soon as possible." He paused again. "This is critical. You can easily go into a diabetic reaction that you'll not survive. Do I make myself clear?"

This was not a great surprise. She didn't need test results to know her time was short.

"Yes, Doctor, I understand."

"Good. Please take it easy until you get checked in."

"Yes, I will, thank you for calling," she said and hung up.

Sarah sat staring into the room. Knowing for sure what she had sensed strangely comforted her. Her thoughts then shifted to Mike and her wild harangue last night. She winced at the thought of Mike's sad face as she stormed out of his apartment. But she had no choice. She had to wrench the responsibility for her life from him—it was out of his hands as well as hers. A peace come over her as she accepted this, but knew Mike could never.

After a hot shower, she got dressed and went to the kitchen. Opening the fridge she got out milk for her cereal…then stopped. She couldn't just go about her morning as if nothing had happened. Mike was hurting. She couldn't stand it; she had to check on him. So along with the milk, she took out eggs and went to the cupboard for the rest of the ingredients needed to make the muffins he loved. After quickly whipping up the batter, she poured it into a muffin pan and put it in the oven. Then she got out her journal and drew a sketch of her holding the muffins on a plate with a caption: "Sorry for yelling at you—Street Urchin." Then she remembered her job at the Y would be starting in a few weeks. She had to call them. Might as well do it now.

When the muffins were cool, she decorated them with blue and yellow smiley faces, wrapped them up with her sketch, and headed out the door. Walking past the trees, bushes, and flowers exploding with color in Washington Square caused her to think of the hope and new life spring brought each year, and this would be the best spring ever with the performance of Mike's opus.

She took the elevator up to his floor and tiptoed to his apartment. She set the tin of muffins at his door with her drawing on top, knocked, and went around the corner in the hall to hide.

"Come in, it's unlocked," Mike yelled. After a moment, he opened the door. Sarah peeked around the corner from her hiding place to watch him. He peered down at the sketch, grimacing at first, and then turned to look to the only place she could be hiding. She grinned at him as his face softened.

"Come here," he said, reaching for her.

Sarah came out and shuffled toward him. He went to her and folded her in his arms. "What are we to do?" he whispered.

Sarah leaned back and looked up at him as she held his waist.

"I know exactly what to do," she said boldly.

"Oh man, now what?" He sucked in a breath.

"Come with me," she said, taking his hand. She led him to his door, picked up the muffins, and ushered him inside.

"I'll get you a glass of milk, and you're gonna to eat the muffins I made as I tell you about my idea."

Mike sat at the table staring straight ahead, his hands clasped in front of him.

"I thought you weren't going to boss me anymore," he said, trying to look brave.

"No. I'm not going to yell at you anymore. I didn't say I wouldn't boss you anymore."

"Alright, alright," he said, starting to get grumpy. "Get on with it—I'm busy here."

"Exactly!" she said. "You're too busy."

"So?" Mike pursed his lips. "Go ahead. Like I'd be able to stop you."

"Thank you," Sarah said, stepping back from the table. Then, pacing like a lawyer in front of a jury box, she pointed out how he was becoming short with the band at practice and actually yelling sometimes. Also, she'd noticed him eating antacid tablets like popcorn—not good. But worst of all, it seemed he wasn't having fun anymore. Wasn't this his dream? Then she stopped in front of him, placed her hands on the table, and leaned forward.

"You need to get away—get out of the city for a while," she said, peering down at him as if looking over a pair of reading glasses.

"Get away? To where? I have to get this thing done!" Mike was at a point of yelling, when she put up her hand and said calmly, "Let's take a little trip. I want to show you something."

Mike sat back, rolled his eyes, and huffed.

She had squirreled away fifty dollars for such an occasion. They would pick up sandwiches, snacks, and drinks at the deli and hire a cab for her little surprise trip. He would just have to trust her on this.

"And if you don't come with me, I'll quit!" she said emphatically, giving him only a hint of a smile.

𝄞

It had been five years since she was last at Breezy Point to watch the shorebirds migrate up from their "winter vacation in the Caribbean," as her father had put it. Her father, being from the hills of Kentucky, hadn't spent much time near an ocean but had a fascination with anything that flew. He told her when he was young he marveled at the soaring flight of the red-tailed hawks, eagles, and harriers. One of his fondest memories was flying homemade kites in the pastures in springtime.

Soon after they moved to New York, he read about the migration of shorebirds through the new Gateway National Park on Long Island. Wanting to share his passion for birds in flight with his daughter, he planned a surprise trip to Breezy Point just for the two of them.

𝄞

Recalling those sweet memories, Sarah reached for Mike's hand and squeezed it with anticipation when they got out of the cab within walking distance of the point.

"See that breakwater ahead?" Sarah said, shaking with excitement as the wind blew her hair back like the tail of a kite. "We have to stand on it to watch the sunset."

Mike groaned. "You're kidding…it's only three o'clock. Sunset's hours away."

Sarah rolled her eyes. "Not now!" she shouted over the roar of wind and surf. "First we'll have our picnic, then we'll fly our kites, then we'll build sand castles and watch the birds fly in and out. Then we'll go stand on the breakwater and watch the sunset."

Mike looked pained. "But what if I have to pee?" he said as he crossed his legs and started hopping around in the sand.

Sarah put her hands on her hips. "Fuhgeddaboudit, buddy," she ordered in her best New York tough guy accent.

Eager to get to the ocean they took off their shoes and socks and tossed them in the tall beach grass, then ran hand-in-hand to the water's edge to let the cool squeaky sand squish between their toes. The endless expanse of the azure Atlantic greeted them with row after row of tumbling white surf on the beach. Leaning into the brisk onshore breeze, Sarah and Mike filled their lungs with the fresh salty sea air as sounds of squawking gulls and rumbling breakers yanked them from their world of traffic, crowds, concrete, and steel.

Once again Sarah had engineered a miracle. All the simple pleasures they shared at the ocean transformed Mike. This huge shift in perspective allowed feelings he'd been stuffing to bubble up, ones entrapped by pressures of the impending performance. While he had at first been simply charmed by this frail yet formidable girl, he now found it impossible to think of living without her.

Thoroughly regenerated in mind, body, and spirit, Mike, with renewed passion, tore into the last days before the performance. He was amazed at the progress. The entire band seemed to catch fire, each contributing so much that he no longer thought of it as his work alone. He considered a number of names for the group, but the idea that came to him first was the best, and it got unanimous approval at Saturday's practice. From now on they would be called *The Gathering*.

Though stretched for time, Mike was determined to add one last section after that joyous day at the beach; watching shorebirds soar, flying yellow kites in a cobalt sky, and splashing barefoot at the waters edge. This movement would be a tribute to the one that inspired his opus, a love theme that took him to a place he didn't know existed. This he kept to himself, calling it simply "Flight."

The music seemed to write itself; letting his feelings flow through his fingers to the keyboard. He got the theme down fairly quickly but felt it needed something more than just him at the piano. This kept nagging at him, until later in the week, while stepping off the train from a solo gig, he was met with the sweetest of melodies, a heavenly hymn that rose high above the stench and grime of the Village subway station. It stopped him cold. The resonance was exactly what he needed to complete his "Flight" theme.

He followed the haunting voice down to the end of the trash-strewn concrete platform.

The reverberation in the subterranean station only added to the rich quality of the instrument, causing his eyes to well up as his heart began to thump. Nearing the end of the platform, he came upon a frail form bent over a saxophone, leaning against the last graffiti scrawled pillar. Mike stopped to take him in. The ebony-skinned old man wore a tattered brown wool sport coat over a gray sweatshirt and bib overalls. His battered sax case lay open, where a single quarter rested, held down with a piece of tape. Next to the case was a white cane.

Listening with quiet reverence, Mike stood with eyes closed and grooved to the beat. He didn't want the moment to end, but when it did, Mike caught the widest toothless grin he had ever seen.

"Man, I wish you could play forever. I'd stand here till I dropped," Mike said in earnest.

The sax player slowly nodded his head. "Thank you, sir."

"No—thank you," Mike said, chuckling. "Say, I'm Mike Monroe. Your name is…?"

"Reggie Green, but friends call me R.G."

Mike smiled to himself. "Playing anywhere besides here?"

"I used ta," R.G. said. "Played most o' the joints in the Village, but it's hart to get around dese days."

"Right." Mike thought a moment. "Don't suppose you'd be interested in a paying gig?"

R.G. shrugged. "I don't know. I kina got burned out with the late nights."

Mike's mind started to churn. "Not a problem. We practice six hours on Saturday afternoons, and the performance is scheduled at six in the evening. You'd get fifteen bucks an hour for practice, and we split any performance money. And I'd pick you up and see you get home."

R.G. titled his head in thought. "Anybody in your group I might know?"

"Most everyone is young, in their twenties, but you might have heard of Jerry Hathaway. Played trumpet for the Count."

"Oh yeah," R.G. said, "I know Jerry. He's good."

Mike sighed with relief. "Well, any other questions?"

R.G. thought a moment, and then smiled in Mike's direction. "No, man—sounds pretty good."

"Great!" Mike shouted, as he did a little dance, pumping his fists, which drew looks from a few late-night commuters down the platform.

While Mike walked with R.G. to his one room flat on 14th Street, he filled in more details about his opus, especially his ideas on the "Flight" theme. Even with just a week left, Mike felt R.G. would work in perfectly—the last bit of seasoning he was looking for.

Standing at his bathroom mirror getting ready for bed, Mike questioned using the last of his money on something as intangible as music – then thought of the old sax player; even though barely subsisting in a cold-water flat, he could still play such sweet music. He stood back, straightened his shoulders, and said to his reflection, "This is good. This is right." Then reaching for the sink with both hands, he lowered his head and said a long overdue prayer.

31

Harlem

Sitting out on the fire escape at the end of the hall, Persis leaned against Jesse, as the moon chased the sun from the sky, and the heat from the last day in May retreated.

"Who'd have guessed I would fall for a friend of my half-baked brother," she said, watching the bustle down on Bleecker Street.

"Half-baked, maybe. Friend, I'm not so sure," Jesse said.

"What? He admires you. He thinks you're trustworthy and stable."

"Oh great." Jesse huffed. "Hope I'm not boring because I'm so stable."

"I like stable. Anyway, how did this happen? I was just minding my own business. I never laughed so hard. I'll always have that image of you in the back of that bus waving frantically with fear in your eyes. That whole day with you was completely amazing," she said with a smile.

"So…I have to make a fool of myself to make you happy?" he asked, looking out over the city. "I guess I can do that."

Persis held up her hand. "Another quality you have is courage to follow your dream." She snickered and kissed his cheek. "Anyone who would turn his back on a flying vase . . . well, you deserve a medal for that one."

He peered at her. "Oh, so my *friend* Mike has been leaking information about me?"

She angled her head and smiled. "He thought it was very brave and honorable to walk away from a life of predictable ease."

Jesse clenched his jaw. "I still feel bad about it. But in the end we each wanted something different." He hesitated and reached for her hand. "I don't think I would have understood that without the help of your brother and Sarah."

Persis looked back doe-eyed. "See—you need them. And me too, I hope?"

"I don't know what you see in a dope like me," he said. "The only thing more uncertain than being a musician is being a writer."

"I can make the money," she said.

His face fell as he thought about Persis supporting him.

"Hey," Persis said, catching his expression, "you're a fantastic writer."

"I'll believe that when I can write another best seller. For now I'm just another one-book wonder."

"Knock, knock," Mike yelled out the fire escape window. "Mind if I join you? It's hot as hell in my room."

Jesse looked at Mike coming through the window. "How you holding up?"

Mike swung his legs through and sat on the windowsill. "Oh, man. I've only got four days left." He paused a moment to catch a breathe and studied the two of them. "Okay, what's goin' on here? Is this getting serious?"

"What? We're just good friends, like you and Sarah." Jesse said.

"Shut up, Jesse," Mike said with a frown.

Jesse, stifling a laugh, decided not to press the issue.

"Persis?" Mike looked into his sister's eyes. "Oh, man. Mother is gonna croak. Isn't this kind of sudden?"

"No, not really," she said. "We've been hanging out on Tuesdays when I come downtown."

Mike gave her a stern look. "Why didn't I know about this?"

"Hey, you guys," Sarah called out as she walked down the hall. "So this is where y'all are hiding." She came up and hugged Mike from behind as she smiled at Jesse and Persis.

"Thought you wanted to get some work done tonight," Sarah said, looking around at Mike's face.

"Yeah, but I could use some help finding a place for our final rehearsal. We gotta have more room to move around like we would at the band shell."

"How about the gym at the Y? If we went early, like five on Sunday morning, we could probably get it," Sarah said.

Mike puffed his cheeks and shook his head. "Realistically, I don't think the group could make it at that hour."

Persis brightened. "Then how about the church fellowship hall? Might be able to get it for Saturday afternoon and evening."

"Yes!" Mike shouted. "Sister, you're brilliant. Do you think Mother would feed us?"

"I'm sure she would do anything for her favorite son."

"I can't help it if I'm her favorite," Mike said, puffing out his chest.

"Oh, you're not her favorite—just her favorite son," she said with a smirk.

"You still have to have the last word, don't you?" Mike said. "Jesse, I pity you if this thing goes any further."

"I hope it does," Jesse replied as he leaned over to kiss Persis.

Mike rolled his eyes and shook his head.

"Don't be dense, Mike," Sarah said. "Can't you tell they want to be alone?"

"Fine. I'm out of here. We've got work to do." He swung his legs around to the hall. "Poor Mother. This could put her over the edge."

♪

After a couple of hours of practice, Sarah sensed Mike was procrastinating. "Aren't you going to call your mother about the rehearsal? It's getting late."

"Yeah, just not sure how to put it. You didn't see her face when the fight broke out. She was pretty disgusted."

"Don't overthink it. You don't know how she feels. Just explain that Willy is gone and you have a new guy who used to play for Count Basie. I'll bet she was a fan of the Count."

Mike's eyes widened. "Yeah, that's it. That'll give us some credibility, like I know what I'm doing. Sarah—only you know I don't really know what I'm doing."

"I don't know what you don't know. But you know what? Just call your mother."

He found the phone under the piano, dialed, and paced the floor with the receiver in his hand, the cord trailing behind.

"Hello, Monroe residence."

"Mother, it's your favorite son."

"I guessed that. What's up?" she said.

"I have a favor to ask," he said with a hopeful smile looking at Sarah.

"Yes?"

"Could you check with Reverend Robinson to see if we could use the church fellowship hall for a rehearsal Saturday afternoon? We need to go through the whole performance a couple of times with more room to move around."

"I don't know, Michael. Do you think it's possible your boys would behave themselves?"

"Mother, they're not all boys, and besides, Willy has been replaced with a guy who played with Count Basie."

"I don't care if he played for Lawrence Welk, I won't have you embarrassing me with some bad behavior."

"Mother, it will be fine."

There was a moment of silence. "Alright, I'll call him, but you are responsible for keeping them in line."

"Great, Mother. And if we stay over Saturday night, we could do a number or two for church on Sunday."

"You'll all go to church?"

"Of course. I'll tell them the house rules. Anyone who stays over Saturday goes to church. It could be a first for a couple of them."

"Well," his mother said joyfully, "in that case I'll cook up some of Georgia's best, but you'll have to check with the reverend about the music."

Mike felt his throat tighten. "I'll call him. Love you, Mother—you've made my day."

"Love you too, my favorite boy."

Mike hung up and plopped down at the piano with a sigh and a grin. Sarah slid in next to him and put her head on his shoulder.

𝄞

With the afternoon sun igniting the stained-glass windows, members of *The Gathering* started showing up Saturday at the small Baptist church in Harlem. A few came by cab, some walked up from the subway, and a couple drove up in a rusted-

out van. Mike stood outside to give them a hearty welcome
and direct them where to set up in the fellowship hall.

After tables and chairs were moved into the storage room,
the space allowed them to spread out much like they would
on the Naumburg stage. The old upright piano along the wall,
pretty much in tune except for a few black keys in the upper
register, was moved to what would be stage right, and the
other musicians set up in an arch to the left of it. When Sarah
and Mike came down the stairs with the last of the band, the
Monroe women were already preparing coffee and sandwiches
in the kitchen at the end of the hall. As Mike crossed the room,
Trina ran up and stood in his path, grinning like a crazy person.
Seemed like every time he saw her lately, she'd grown taller
and looked more like a young woman than the kid sister he
was used to.

"Mikey, I have a surprise for you," she said, bouncing on
her toes.

"Oh, something for me? I know I'm special and all."

"It's not for you. I have a friend I want to bring to the
performance."

Mike stopped a minute to let this information sink in.
"A friend?"

"Yeah, his name is Kevin."

"Kevin?" Mike said, crossing his arms. "That sounds like
a boy's name. Is that a boy's name?"

"What do you think? Michael, I'm almost seventeen." She
gave him the look.

"Why am I never consulted about these things? First Persis,
now you."

"What do you mean 'first Persis'?"

"Oh crap. You can't say anything, Trina, please," Mike
said with frown.

"Five bucks…just kidding. I can keep a secret. Who is it?"

"You'll have to ask her, but don't mention anything to Mother."

"So it's okay if I bring Kevin?"

"It's fine with me if it's okay with Mother."

With that, Trina spun around with a grin and headed back to the kitchen. Mike stood watching her go with a twinge of melancholy. He looked over at Sarah, who had taken in the exchange. She walked over and peered up at him.

"I'm losing my biggest fan," he said.

Sarah smiled. "You'll always be important to her—that's why she came to you."

He pinched his lips and nodded, hoping Sarah was right.

Mike took in a resolute breath and turned to the clatter of setting up and joking with his band. The tuning of instruments began, which always gave him a chill of expectation. But this wasn't some group he came to see perform. It was *his* group, and they were playing *his* music.

He stopped for a minute to look around, to memorize the moment. From across the room among the jumble of instruments and sound equipment, he caught Sarah's eye. She turned to him, smiled sweetly, and threw him a kiss. He reached out to catch it. *I do love that girl.*

Even with the poor half-basement acoustics of the fellowship hall, Mike was astounded how well it went, with everyone groovin', full of energy. His plan was to break for dinner after the first session, then come back at seven for a complete nonstop rehearsal. The only other thing he had to accomplish was a little time with R.G. to tighten up the "Flight" movement. So when the last notes of the postlude diminished, he held up his hands to get everyone's attention.

"What do you think? Are we going to knock them out at Naumburg?"

Cheers of affirmation went up with a drum roll and trumpet blast.

"Now, as a special treat, you're all invited to an awesome Southern style dinner at Mother Monroe's. My kid sister, Trina, will lead you the four blocks to the house, and R.G. and I will be there in a half hour after we go over a few things."

Once outside Trina officiously had the band form a straight line behind her as Mike looked on. But as they started out from the church, they all had fun thwarting her efforts of keeping them in line—a few skipped, some ran circles around the group, while others marched stiff–legged, saluting whenever she walked back to check on them. Mike practically collapsed laughing as he watched the shenanigans before he went back in to practice with R.G.

When Mike and R.G. walked up to the house after their session, they saw the band gathered on the front stoop, laughing and kibitzing as they swapped stories of past performances. Garrett looked up as they approached and gestured at R.G.'s sax.

"Hey, man, I bet you even sleep with that thing."

"Sure 'nough. If I ever lost this *thing,* I would just have to die," R.G. said with a tortured expression and clutching his chest.

"Well, as long as you have it with ya, play us some dinner music, man."

The whole group agreed with cheers and hoots. So R.G. sat down on the steps, got out his horn, and played some sweetness that brought broad smiles. Even people from across the street came over to bask in the tenderness of R.G.'s playing. Sarah soon joined in with her lyrical singing as the others hummed and bobbed to the beat.

"I thought y'all were taking a break," Mike's mother called from the door as she brought out lemonade and root beer.

"This is a break," they shouted.

Then with great flare, Mike hopped to the top step next to his mother and got the crowd's attention. "I believe I failed to properly introduce all of you to my dear mother, Rose. So now that we're all together in one spot, if you would each give your name, tell what you play, and share a little about yourself. R.G., would you start please?"

R.G. stood and politely bowed. "Ma'am, I'm Reggie Green, originally from Brooklyn, and I play the sax just about anytime I can."

Roy popped up next, tossed his dreads over his shoulder, and did a little dance. "Mrs. Monroe, I'm Roy Jefferson, and I play the drums. My claim to fame is . . . well, this may be my claim to fame—if I don't screw up."

This triggered "awws" and hugs of assurance from all the women seated around him as he flashed a cocky grin.

"Ma'am, I'm Garrett, and I play the guitar mainly because it kind of rhymes with my name. I thought about playing the tuba, but it just didn't sound right."

Boos rose up from the group along with waves to sit down. Then Alice shyly stood.

"Hi, Rose, I'm Alice. I play violin with the New York Philharmonic."

"Rose, I'm Diana, and I play the cello also with the New York Phil. Both my parents are musicians, so I don't think I had much of a choice, but I love it."

"Jerry Hathaway, Rose, on trumpet. My latest claim to fame will be playing with this outstanding collection of fine people at the Naumburg band shell; this coming Tuesday!"

Jerry ended by standing up and shouting like the captain of a football team at the start of a game.

With that pronouncement, the whole group stood clapping and chanting, "Naumburg, Naumburg, Naumburg." Gazing around at the joyful faces, Rose lifted her hands to gain order and said, "I know Morris plays bass and doesn't need to introduce himself. But I want y'all to know that if I had another son, I would want him to be just like this fine boy."

"Oh, man. Think I just lost my appetite," Mike said, "but we should probably eat so we can get back to work!"

With that the whole mob headed up the stairs and piled into the kitchen to fill their plates buffet style. Then sitting around the crowded dining room table, they took their cue from the elders, R.G. and Jerry, who waited politely for Mike's mother to come in and sit.

"My, what manners," she said, noticing that everyone waited for her before starting to eat. "Before we say grace and thank God for our *many* blessings, I want you to know you're welcome to spend the night. But there are house rules. Morris, you remember what they are?"

"Sure Mrs. M. No swearing, drunkenness, or smoking in the house, and church is at nine thirty tomorrow."

"Thank you, Morris," she said. "Now for grace and then help yourselves to as much food as you want."

$$\phi$$

With expectations clearly laid out, the chatter of the horde ebbed and flowed as they filled their bellies with fried chicken, sweet-potato casserole, and greens. Gazing about with pride, Mike caught his mother studying Persis and Jesse, who were sitting at the far end of the table. It was obvious to everyone with eyes that something was going on between them. His mother caught Mike's attention, and before he could look away she nodded in the direction of the kitchen. Mike got up and followed her, knowing he was about to be interrogated.

"Michael, is there something I need to know about Persis and Jesse?"

"What?" Mike said, trying to look clueless.

"I have eyes, Michael. I see how Persis is treating him."

"You also have amazing ears, as I remember." He smirked. "Mother, what are you worried about?"

"What if this leads to marriage and they move away... to Minnesota?"

"Whoa, now, Mother—"

"I know Persis, and she's *never* looked at anyone the way she moons over that guy."

"If it's any consolation, he's about as solid as they come," he said confidently.

"I don't know. It worries me."

"Okay, as long as you're already worried, what if I marry a redheaded homeless girl?"

"Michael, don't mess with me."

"Mother, I think I love that girl—"

"Oh, Lord Jesus, give me strength," Rose said with her hands to her face. "Lewis, why did you have to leave me?"

"Mother, calm down before you have a stroke," Mike said, reaching for her shoulders.

"What're you doing to upset her now?" Trina said, drawn into the kitchen by her mother's raised voice. Not far behind were Persis and Sarah. Always quick on her feet, his mother said, "Now that I have your attention, how about some of my Georgia peach pie?"

"That sure sounds good, Mother," Mike said. "I'll get the plates."

"Head to the dining room now, while Mike and I serve up the pie," she said, shooing them away.

$$\text{\clef}$$

For a final rehearsal, the timing was still a little ragged, but Mike intuited he had to let it go and not overwork the group. After having some fun with "Amazing Grace" and "When the Saints Go Marching In," the two numbers they would do in church tomorrow, the group packed it in for the night.

Walking back to the house, without the law and order imposed by Trina, the members strolled casually in pairs. Mike could tell something was buggin' Roy, so he checked in with him on the way home.

"'Sup, man? Look like you're chewing on some gristle," Mike said as he came up alongside him.

"Man, do I have this right? Is that cracker goin' after Persis?" Roy said.

Mike stopped to let the others pass so they would be alone. "Dumbass, that cracker is solid and a good friend. What's your problem?"

"I don't know 'bout a fine-lookin' sister datin' a white boy."

Mike glanced away for a moment, then back. "Roy, have you ever dated a white girl or thought about it?"

Roy peered up at Mike through his eyebrows. "Yeah, I've thought about it. I know what you're gettin' at but—"

"Man, I don't want this to be a problem," Mike said, cocking his head to look Roy hard in the eyes.

"Yeah, okay. I guess if he is one of the *good* ones."

Mike groaned. "Yeah, man, he is one of the good ones."

♪

Sunday morning service started with a bang at Harlem Baptist with the congregation clapping wildly and singing "When the Saints Go Marching In" with *The Gathering* swaying as they played spread out behind the pulpit. Reverend Robinson led the children in, parading down the aisles as they gleefully sang and danced.

The band sat mesmerized throughout the reverend's powerful message as preacher and flock communed with the Holy Spirit - amid spontaneous shouts of "Amen." Sarah closed the service with a heartrending version of *Amazing Grace* – the congregation growing quiet, many eyes glistening with tears.

After the church had emptied, with Mike's mother sitting in the front pew watching the band pack up, Reverend Robinson came up the aisle to thank them. He shook the hand of each member, then stopped at Sarah and gazed upon her.

"Dear child, you blessed us so with your singing. Please come back soon."

Sarah stood a moment, and then reached to hug the stocky preacher as she put her head on his chest. "Thank you, I will."

Glancing over from the piano, Mike exchanged looks with his mother. Her face softened as she smiled back with a slight nod. Joy filled his soul. All the loose pieces of his life were finally coming together.

Back at the house, with hearts and souls healed, Rose put out another spread mostly made up of leftovers. Then gradually, with hugs and farewells, the group split up as they had come, leaving in cabs, subway trains, and a rusted-out van.

When everyone had left, Mike stayed out on the stoop to be with his mother; the others went inside to clean up and do dishes. He wondered what it would be like to wake up Wednesday not feeling the stress of getting ready for a performance that could make or break his career. As he gazed off down the street, his mother's instincts seemed to kick in.

"Mike, this is so wonderful. Everyone in the band is having such a great time. I think it's because of your music."

He scooted over and leaned against her. "I don't know what I'll do when I wake up Wednesday without this madness."

"Oh, I think you'll find something to torture yourself with," she said, rubbing his back.

"Why do I do this? Why can't I just be happy playing at Johnny's?"

"Why couldn't I be happy having just one child?" she said.

"You trying to confuse me?"

"No. We just do what we need to do. I have to try to raise good kids, and you have to make good music and maybe some kids too—at the proper time, of course." She smiled as Mike groaned.

"Actually, Mother, I don't know 'bout bringing kids into this screwed-up world."

"Michael," she said, "this world's been messed up since the beginning. It will always need more good people, and that's the kind of children you will have."

Mike was warmed by his mother's words and tried to imagine being a father some day.

𝄞

Needing to get back to his piano, Mike sprang for a cab to get the three of them downtown. As they piled into the taxi, Persis ran up to Jesse, pulled him back toward her, and planted a long passionate kiss on him. Watching the scene, his mother just rolled her eyes as Trina whopped and jumped up and down like a cheerleader at a football game.

"I don't want there to be any doubt in *anyone's* mind how I feel about you, my pumpkin."

"My pumpkin?" Mike said, pulling Jesse into the cab by his shirttail. "Driver, get us out of here quick before I lose my lunch."

32

Requests

The three sat quietly in the cab ride back to the Village. Mike gazed out the window behind the driver, Jesse stared out the other side, and Sarah sat between them leaning against Mike, holding his arm.

Pulling up to the "Palace," Jesse looked over at Mike and pointed at Sarah, mouthing that she was asleep. Mike nodded and mouthed that he would take her home. Jesse seemed concerned as he looked at Sarah and then got out.

The drizzle that had started in Harlem was now a full-blown storm, with flashes of lightning and raindrops hammering the roof and hood, as they pulled up to Sarah's apartment building. A clap of thunder jolted Sarah awake, and she noticed Mike smiling down on her.

"What is it?" she said, responding to his tender look.

He wished he could stop time and simply gaze on her forever. The driver peered at them in his rearview mirror with a faint smile.

"I know I've been distracted lately with everything going on, but you have to know…I'm hopelessly in love with you," Mike said in a whisper.

Sarah closed her eyes and looked as if she was about to cry.

"Sarah, what's wrong?"

"I know. I love you too . . ." she said. She reached up to hold his face and kissed him. His chest swelled as he enfolded her and savored her warmth. Then, pulling back with a smile, he slipped off his jacket and covered her. After leaning forward and paying the cabby, he slid over and opened her door and swept her up in his arms into the streaming rain. He bumped the cab door closed and dashed to the awning entrance as she nestled her face in his neck. For a brief moment Mike fantasized he was Superman and could glide off into the air saving his Lois Lane from an unspeakable disaster. Sarah had saved him—he now needed to save her. But his dream was fleeting.

Although he had never picked her up before, she seemed too light. *Has she lost even more weight?* His moment of ecstasy suddenly vanished, replaced with a sense of foreboding. His pulse raced. He chided himself. He's been in denial.

Walking up to her apartment with her still in his arms, he fought to keep his dread under wraps. He set her down at her door, and Sarah turned and faced him with an angelic look. Her love light soothed the rip in his heart as she stood on her tiptoes and kissed him passionately. She then settled her head on his chest.

"I loved you the first night I looked into your caring eyes at the soup kitchen," she said, tightly reaching around his waist.

Mike drew in a long slow breath. "That night was magical for me too. It just took a while for my heart to make sense of it."

Once inside her apartment Sarah settled down at the small wooden kitchen table appearing at first tired but then contemplative. "I need to rest a minute. Then I'll fix you something to eat."

Mike sensed her weariness. "Are you kidding? I'm cooking," he said, going to the refrigerator and looking in. "I see you have everything I need, so I'm gonna fix ya ma famous cheese and bacon omelet my mama taught me when I was just a tot." Mike got out the ingredients, trying his best to be bright and cheerful. Then going to the little gas stove, he stood thinking about what to do next.

Sarah groaned and grabbed a dishtowel from the table, wadded it up and threw it at him. "Why do you care for me?" she moaned. "All I can do is sing a few songs." She paused, dropped her head into her hands and started to weep. "You shouldn't love me . . ."

Mike's eyes widened as blood rushed to his temples – throbbing. A bolt of rage shot through him like an electric current. He grabbed the sides of the stove, wanting to rip it from the wall and throw it across the room, then let out a heartrending cry of hopeless despair.

"I can't lose you!" he yelled at the wall over the stove.

"But *why* do you love me?" she yelled back as she sobbed.

Going from maniacal wrath to distraught spent exhaustion, Mike slowly closed his eyes and eked out, "You've given me my life. A life I didn't know existed." He threw his head back and gasped, "I can't do *anything* without you."

Lacing his fingers behind his head he looked around without seeing and started pacing about the room. His mind clouded. He was near panic. He went to the window, stopped and took a long breath. Standing silent for a minute, he dropped his arms and gazed at the adjacent buildings trying to gain control. "Why do I love you?" he said, peering down at his hands. "Because you are you. You're like no one I've ever known.

You are joyful, sad, funny, stubborn, and hopeful, and have a voice that inspires me." He paused and scanned the horizon. "Why does anybody love anyone? I think it comes down to trust—having someone to share your life. You've captured my heart and opened it to your love."

Sarah watched him at the window with one hand covering her mouth and the other sweeping away tears.

He was suddenly struck by how powerless he was. She had saved him, but he couldn't do anything to help her. He spun from the window and started stomping around the room. "I have to go for a walk," he said, and practically ran to the door.

"Mike, stop!" she shouted. "Please don't go." Sarah paused to catch her breath. "Do you trust me?"

He hesitated, then turned in disbelief "Do I trust you? Of course I trust you!"

"Then listen…please," she said, trying to gain composure. "You have a God-given gift. You tell wonderful stories through your music. The world needs good stories so people can better understand their lives and feel hopeful. Your music does that." She got him to look her in the eye. "I'm always amazed how it seems you create art out of thin air. But it's not really thin air, is it? It's listening and having the courage to act on what you hear." Mike nodded in agreement. "I see how you explain your ideas—you're a natural teacher."

"Okay . . . so?" Mike said, scrunching his face as he stepped back to the table and dropped down in a chair facing her.

"You could share your gift and knowledge by teaching others who need encouragement and someone to believe in them. You know exactly how it feels to discover and develop your passion, so you could help others gain confidence and explore their talents."

Mike leaned back with a frown. "What are you getting at?"

"You had teachers in school that encouraged you. Without them you probably wouldn't have discovered your gift."

"Are you suggesting I teach? I can't teach! Teach what? I don't understand what I'm doing myself, so how would I teach someone else? I don't have a degree, I don't even know if I like teaching, I don't—"

"Stop!" Sarah shouted. "You love people, especially the underserved. You love music, especially music that comes from the heart. And you love sharing your gift by playing to all kinds of people." Sarah smirked. "Even people that aren't paying much attention."

Mike pulled back in his seat, paused a moment and stuck out his lip. "Wait a minute. I think a couple regulars at Johnny's actually listened."

Sarah smiled and reached across the table for his hands. "Please, at least give it a try. If it doesn't suit you, then by all means move on. If it works out, your gift of music will be passed on."

Squinting his eyes closed, he searched for reasons he wouldn't make a good teacher. But after a long pause, he nodded, resigned.

But now it was his turn to make an appeal. He thought it only fair. "I'll consider it," he said, searching deep into her eyes, "if you will go to your Aunt Clara's after the performance and stay as long as it takes to get healthy."

Sarah's face softened, radiating love and nodded in return.

After they ate the dinner Mike prepared, they sat at the table and talked nonstop for hours as if making up for lost time. When Sarah started to fade, Mike insisted she get ready for bed and lay holding her in his arms until she fell asleep.

When he stopped at the door to let himself out, he turned and gazed back on his sweet Sarah. His heart went numb.

33

Regrets

Monday should be a day to kick back and relax, but no, Mike woke with a hangover of dread. He got up and couldn't think of one thing to do. There wasn't any work to be done on his opus, and his worry over Sarah was making him sick. "Okay, this isn't good," he said out loud to the vacant room. After a blazing hot shower and a cup of coffee, he called Sarah, and then went down the hall to Jesse's to ask if he could borrow his dog.

"Jesse, I need to do something. Can I take Charlie for a walk?" Mike asked.

"I don't know. Charlie, would you like to take Mikey here for a walk?" Jesse said, looking down at Charlie.

Charlie stood up from his rug, stretched, found his leash under the bed, and dragged it over to Mike.

"Well, there's your answer."

"Thanks. We'll go pick up Sarah and head to the park for a while."

The massive arched entrance to Washington Square Park was like a gateway to an oasis. It was a sparkling warm day with crab apple trees blooming pink and green grass beckoning.

Couples dangled their feet in the fountain pool, chess players huddled over their games, and a street musician strummed from a park bench. Mike chose a spot on the grass to be near the music and the sound of water gurgling in the fountain.

"Isn't New York great? Look one way and you see magnificent steel-and-glass skyscrapers, the other way, a lush Garden of Eden," Mike said, determined to remain upbeat as he watched Sarah set up their spot.

"You've never been to Kentucky, have you?" she said with a sophisticated air.

Mike chuckled, bending down to stretch out. "No, but I hear the skyscrapers there are really something."

Sarah frowned, and instead of lying next to him quickly turned and sat on his chest.

"Umff," Mike grunted.

"I was referring to the natural beauty, not steel and concrete," she said, bouncing a little to emphasize each word.

"Okay . . . you win . . . I'm sure . . . it's heavenly," Mike said, gasping for air. He then grabbed Sarah and rolled her onto the blanket.

Charlie seemed annoyed with their roughhousing, so got up from his spot and headed off to check out the nearest tree. As Mike and Sarah watched him trot away, a trio of punks walked over and stood within a few feet of the blanket, peering down at them. Mike didn't care for the vibe he was getting.

"What's up with you people?" a towering Neanderthal said to Mike. "Can't you find women of your own kind?"

Mike looked up, trying to make sense of what was happening. He closed his eyes in disgust and pondered how to take this jerk down. Fortunately for everyone, Charlie appeared out of nowhere and sat between Mike and Sarah. He picked up on the evil intent of the grunts and bared his fangs, a deep rumble coming from his powerful chest.

Charlie inched toward the not-so-confident thugs.

Mike sprang up and clipped Charlie's collar to the leash. "Gentlemen, I'm sorry you don't like me because of my dark skin. But we are all God's children and need to get along. I don't have a beef with you. And Charlie here . . . he's just doing his job."

"Yeah, right," Neanderthal man said with a scowl. After a moment of consideration, he turned and led his small band of misfits away, across the lawn.

Sarah, looking relieved, hugged her hero around the neck. "Charlie, you were wonderful!"

Mike dropped back down on the blanket with a frown. "Say, what about me?"

Sarah reached for his face. "You did good too," she said, and kissed him tenderly.

He felt better. "Wow, that was nice. What do I need to do to get another one?"

"I'll let you know," Sarah said nonchalantly.

"Well, in the meantime, shouldn't we have that *fine* lunch you prepared?"

"Oh, I don't know. Shouldn't we go?" she asked.

"Hell no, I'm not going to let some jerk spoil our day. You said you made something special, so I'm not moving till you show me what it is."

Sarah had used Grandma Mae's secret meatloaf recipe to make a pre-performance dinner, but when Mike called to go to the park, she quickly turned it into her all-time favorite lunch: meatloaf and mashed potato sandwiches, using thickly sliced homemade bread, with fresh chopped green onion and bacon whipped into the potatoes, and packed with butter pickles and plenty of ketchup. By the time Mike picked her up, she had two sandwiches, a bag of chips, molasses cookies, and two bottles of Mike's favorite root beer all packed in a small tote cooler.

As Mike lay back with a groan of satisfaction after devouring her special layered concoction, some chips, and a molasses cookie, Sarah gazed upon him thoughtfully.

"Okay," Mike said warily, "I know that look. What's on your mind?"

Sarah looked at him out of the corner of her eye. "Tell me more about your father—you rarely talk about him."

He squirmed for a moment but couldn't think of a way to change the subject. "Fine. What do you want to know?"

"To start with, how did your parents meet?"

Mike frowned as he tried to dig back in his memory. He was saddened he didn't really know a lot about their past—his uncle Luther providing most of the interesting details.

"Let's see, they met at a dance hall in Columbus Georgia just after Dad got back from Korea in 53. According to Uncle Luther, he was plenty smooth with the ladies, the life of every party – playing his guitar and singing all the latest songs." Mike paused, reflecting on his own words, trying to envision his father as the center of attention at parties. He looked up, noticing Sarah studying him, and went on.

"My mother was from a well-to-do family in Atlanta and got a degree in teaching from Spelman. She became involved in the Civil Rights Movement in the fifties, and was teaching third grade when she met my dad. I guess my father pretty much swept her off her feet with his guitar slung over his shoulder, can-do attitude, and looking like a hero in his dress uniform. He wasn't quite what her parents had in mind, but after they eloped, begrudgingly accepted him into their tightly knit family."

Sarah flashed an impish grin when Mike paused to sip his root beer.

"What?" he asked, his brow furrowing.

Sarah chuckled. "Oh nothing. Would you say your dad was stubborn?"

"You could say that. *Determined* might be a better word," Mike said with a snort.

"I see . . . tell me more," Sarah said, lying down on the blanket - propping her head up with her hand.

"Well, not too many months after they got married, Persis was born." At that point Mike sucked in his lips and gave his eyebrows a little wiggle at Sarah.

"They lived on base at Fort Bragg, North Carolina, where my father entered Special Forces training. I arrived two years after Persis. Trina, the whoops baby, came eight years after me. After Vietnam, Dad retired as a colonel in the Green Berets. That's when we moved to Harlem to be near his family. After two years in a cramped apartment he used his savings from twenty years in the Army to buy a run-down townhouse on Strivers Row and open a grocery store."

Mike was silent a moment, then said, "That's pretty much it."

Sarah sat up and asked, "Sorry, but you never told me what happened between you and your father."

Mike stiffened. Why was she doing this? He looked around as if checking on Charlie then moaned, "I let him down when I quit NYU. He was counting on me to get an MBA and take over the stores."

His words hung in the air for a moment. "But that wasn't you, was it?" Sarah said.

"No, but I didn't know that until I got to NYU and started at Johnny's," Mike said. "But what kind of a person walks out on a father who has done everything for him—even died for him? I should have . . . dammit, it's too late now," he said, squinting and rubbing his forehead.

Sarah reached over and stroked his back. He sat hunched, picking at lint on the blanket. "If your father walked up and sat down with you now, what would you say to him?"

Mike slumped. "I'd ask him to forgive me . . . say I'm sorry."

"And would he forgive you?" she whispered.

After a period of silence, while he stared at the ground between his legs, he murmured, "Yes," then wept bitterly.

Sarah reached for his arm and leaned against him as his chest heaved with sobs. When his breathing slowed and he lifted his head, she said, "Do you think he ever made mistakes?"

Mike looked at her over his shoulder. "I suppose he did." Then he shook his head slowly from side to side. "There you go again. Where do you get this stuff?" He paused as a faint smile crept up his face. "You know, if this singing thing goes south, I'm sure you could make a fortune as a shrink, especially here in New York."

"I can only think of this *stuff* because of you," Sarah said as she reached to stroke his cheek. Just when she was leaning in to kiss him, someone walked up to them.

"Hello there."

With Charlie stretched out with his head on his paws, Mike and Sarah looked up to see a smaller version of Neanderthal man standing in a posture of contrition.

"I . . . I want to apologize for what my big brother said earlier."

Mike was astonished. Sarah nodded at him with an encouraging smile.

"Well, thank you for that," Mike said, straightening as he tried to collect his words. "Man, that is the kindest thing that's happened to me today, besides Sarah's meatloaf-and-mashed-potato sandwiches. Sorry, my name is Mike, and this is Sarah. You met Charlie earlier. I see he likes *you*. What's your name?"

"Jeff," he said. "I like dogs. He's a beauty."

"Yes, he is. Say, if you like *good* music, you should come to the band shell in Central Park tomorrow to hear the premiere performance of *The Girl in the Yellow Scarf* featuring this up-and-coming star sitting before you."

Jeff said he would try to make the concert and after shaking Mike's hand smiled and strolled off.

"Wow." Mike shook his head. "That was a cool thing to do. I hope he comes tomorrow."

34

Glorious Day

Mike woke Tuesday with a jerk and sat up bolt straight fearing he was late for something. Then, realizing he was dreaming, fell back in bed and thought about the glorious day ahead. The group had survived lost tempers and disagreements of vision, but that was unavoidable with any collaborative effort. Then, considering all that could go wrong today, he jumped up, squashing his anxiety with a vision of sweet Sarah, and went about making coffee. With cup in hand, he paced the hardwood floor, considering what might help set the mood and spark the group to play with inspired improvisation and empathy.

As he went about his morning routine of showering and shaving, he thought back on the time they got the most heartfelt reaction from an audience—that first night playing together at Johnny's. As he stood looking in the mirror, it came to him. Halfway through the overture Sarah could come up out of the audience wearing her yellow scarf and that old raincoat of her mother's, and upon reaching the stage take the mic and start singing in her mesmerizing style. Throughout the performance she could change into different outfits from her eclectic collection.

That's it. With shaving cream still clinging to his chin, he rushed to call Sarah. She was thrilled with the idea and wanted to hang up right away so she could get started packing her suitcase with outfits.

Mike had another surprise: "Flight," his celebratory love theme inspired by the soul-reviving trip to Breezy Point. This one he had kept from Sarah, practicing it with the group in secret, featuring R.G. It would portray soaring seabirds, flying kites, sandcastles, and the eternal throbbing of the sea on a sandy beach. He could hardly wait to see her face when, on cue, the ensemble would surround and play just for her.

It was weird to think all he had to take to the performance was his dad's old briefcase full of his music and a small package for Sarah in his pocket. Mike hailed a cab and picked up Sarah and R.G. Together they rode in excited silence to East 72nd Street, where they walked the short distance to the Naumburg band shell.

Mike could hardly believe it. He was about to play on the same stage as Duke Ellington and the Grateful Dead. The massive Romanesque columns and huge sculpted arch of the band shell were intimidating. When he stepped onto the stage and looked out at the plaza that could hold an audience of thousands, he really got nervous. To make things more stressful, station WBLS decided at the last minute to broadcast the performance and had just arrived. Sound people were running all over the stage setting up equipment and laying out cable.

As Mike stood fretting in the middle of the chaos, Trina ran up and demanded to be involved in some way. Trying to compose himself, he put her in charge of caring for Sarah's outfits and helping her change between numbers. Thankfully, Jesse had stepped up to take the role of stage manager and roadie, and was now helping to set up chairs and equipment, while Charlie seemed content to lie out of the way beneath the concert grand piano. Mike's mother and Persis arrived wide eyed, with a huge bouquet of wildflowers in shades of Sarah's favorite color—yellow—as nervous as if they were the ones about to perform. Mike had a couple of chairs placed stage left for them, which made them happy beyond measure.

With all the band members now on stage and setting up, Mike was feeling a little more confident and composed. He went over to the piano, where Sarah was sitting watching the whole operation.

Mike smiled as he looked down at the young woman who was responsible for all this wonderful madness. As he took a minute to catch his breath, he suddenly turned his head to the sky. "No…that's not thunder, is it?" he said. "Sarah, you've been more faithful. Please pray to God it doesn't rain."

She just shook her head. "Oh, so I'll stay dry and the rest of you get soaked?"

"Sorry, just ignore me. I'm a bit nervous."

Mike had put the last of his inheritance money and all his soul into this performance and was determined the show would go on, so he had the musicians move to the back of the band shell, where they could stay dry as a late-afternoon squall moved in fast from the northeast.

"Oh man! Is this an omen, Sarah?" Mike asked as the rain started to splatter on the front of the stage.

"I don't know about you, but it's not going to stop me!" she said, standing up and reaching out as if welcoming the shower.

Facing each other, just under the huge arching lip of the band shell, Mike heaved a great sigh and choked out, "No matter what happens, I want you to know you have given me a priceless gift. You have given me my dream." He then fished around in his pocket, pulled out a small-hinged felt box, and got down on one knee. With raindrops showering his face, Mike looked up into Sarah's widening lavender eyes, opened the lid, and said, "My sweet Sarah, I love you so. Will you marry me?"

Sarah seemed to stop breathing. "You still want to marry me?"

Mike held out his arms in dramatic fashion. "Yes I do—without a doubt."

With his gaze locked on her, the world around him momentarily vanished. Sarah's infinite faith and love had rescued him and would live in his heart forever.

The blissful moment was abruptly interrupted with a screech from Trina, who charged up the stage steps, yelling, "The program director needs everyone to take their places—you're live in thirty seconds!"

"Well . . .?" Mike said, turning back to Sarah with a hopeful, pleading look. Ever since that stormy night in the Yellow Cab, he knew for certain she was the only person he would ever love—really love.

35
Opus in the Park

At the last minute as the members of the band spread out, poised to begin, Mike held up his hands. Taking the microphone, he strolled forward from under the arching shell to center stage. He stood for a moment to form his thoughts. In the drizzle he looked up to the heavens and then out to the small huddled audience. "Thank you so much for coming today despite the rain. This is the first performance for our group called *The Gathering*. We've worked on this composition for almost three months, and I feel blessed and honored to be in the presence of such outstanding musicians. I'd like to tell you how this opus came about. Nine months ago I met the most amazing person with an equally amazing voice. When I first met Sarah, I was puzzled how someone so young could possess such a rich mature understanding of life. Then, after hearing how her circumstances, family, and faith shaped her life, I was inspired to tell her story in an eight movement composition, which is the piece you are going to hear today—*The Girl in the Yellow Scarf.*"

Mike paused and looked out to find Sarah in the clustered knot of people facing the stage. He smiled when locating her. "I love this girl so much, I asked her to marry me just a few minutes ago," Mike said, grinning helplessly. "And she said yes!"

The small audience erupted into applause as the band broke into an impromptu "Here Comes the Bride." Mike, hardly able to contain his joy, rocked back and forth - laughing. After a moment connecting with the audience he raised his hands and continued. "Sarah's story has changed my life. Maybe it will be meaningful to you as well."

$$\oint$$

Gray clouds wept, as Sarah stood among the dripping umbrellas in her rumpled raincoat and yellow scarf. Pulling her eyes away from Mike she gazed down at the amethyst and gold ring on her finger - her heart ripped in two - half drenched in joy, half doused with melancholy. Quivering from fatigue she steadied herself and prayed she could survive the day. This was all she asked.

$$\oint$$

The overture began with a single sustained note from Diana on the cello. Faintly, Alice joined in on the violin with sweet wispy harmony. Then piano, bass, and other instruments contributed rich chords and countermelodies, depicting the morning mist slowly rising like a lifting shade. There were fewer than a hundred people in an area that could hold thousands, as Sarah approached the stage. When she reached the steps, Trina handed her the microphone for her opening song: "Morning on a Kentucky Porch."

The quizzical looks from the gathering changed to fascination as her indescribable voice began to radiate over them like waves of warm sunlight. Sarah's red hair hung down in wet ringlets from under her yellow scarf - her face beaming with joy and wonderment, causing the small audience to break out grinning. As she sang, she reached out her hand to the persistent drizzle, using it like a prop to enrich the performance.

The "Beloved" movement emerged next, with descriptions of each family member on the sundrenched Kentucky porch, represented by different instruments lightly taking the lead, then weaving a pattern with rifts and counter-melodies, giving each musician an opportunity to improvise as the spirit moved them. The opening scene of security and warmth in the Appalachian Mountains led into ominous tones that introduced "A Life Lost, a Life Saved." Challenging, heavy chords reflected the unfolding scene of a small wooden boat sinking on the Ohio River of what started as a birthday celebration for Sarah but ended in the drowning of her brother after he had saved her life.

The small orchestra's depiction of despair from a life lost mingled with the introduction of the "Grandma Mae" theme as only Sarah could portray it. With the orchestra gradually stepping back, Sarah took over, a cappella, painting a vocal picture of Grandma Mae—provider, protector, and savior—teaching Sarah life skills that nurtured her mind, body, and spirit, but then dying of a stroke in Sarah's arms while working in the garden.

The funeral for the beloved matriarch followed, expressed as a cathartic celebration of a life well lived. With eyes closed, perceiving the unseen, Sarah gently swayed as she summoned from somewhere over the heads of the audience her wordless song, taking them on a heart-wrenching journey. Beginning with hopeless, painful isolation, the portrayal slowly evolved to a place of total embracing love. Couples turned to each other with expressions of utter disbelief at this completely unique experience. The movement closed with a duet of voice and sax, part wailing and part celebration, at the passing of Grandma Mae. With empathetic expressions, the audience seemed held captive by the kaleidoscope of emotions and lyrical images, as each movement dovetailed into the next.

"NYC Hope" opened with Roy thumping a funk rhythm on drums to create the heartbeat of the city. Garrett and Morris then mix in a hip-hop beat on the guitar and bass, creating a clamor of discord, mystery, and anticipation. The percussive sound of drums and guitar bumped along like a swarm of yellow taxis on Madison Avenue; sax, trumpet, and piano joined in to scurry like ferrets, each in their own world yet somehow blending. Gradually violin and cello calmed the city throb with a hopeful melody, characterizing Sarah and her parents moving to New York looking for a better life after the death of Grandma Mae. For a while all is good as Sarah discovers and develops her artistic gift.

Mike was so engrossed in the melding of their musical spirits; he hadn't noticed the gradual increase of the audience. People began arriving with transistor radios pressed to their ears, while others huddled under trees for the small shelter they provided. But most—now more than three hundred—just stood in the open, being bathed in sublime sound and a cleansing light shower. Mike imagined this was not what the listeners of WBLS were expecting on their evening commute. The music from the Naumburg seemed to act as a pied piper, leading them away from their daily routine to the historic band shell.

The "Survival on the Streets" movement emerged with cello once again taking the lead, the bow creating a haunting drone with Mike joining in, playing a searching melody that laced in and out with warm then chilly tonality. Sarah's voice reintroduced the "Grandma Mae" motif as a backdrop, braiding a cord that not only joined them musically but also in spirit.

The drifting theme slowly expanded into bright overtones of strings and sax, featuring Jerry on trumpet moving to center stage. With an unexpected blast of celebration, depicting Sarah's extraordinary talent, "The Gift" was introduced as *The Gathering* began to play and groove to a gospel rhythm.

Mike was barely able to contain himself as the entire audience, now well over five hundred, he guessed, started to sway to the music. He could have shot up into the sky and burst like Fourth of July fireworks! In all his joy, Mike looked over to where Sarah was standing at the microphone. Again for this number she wore the old raincoat and scarf, but seeing the way it hung from her shoulders suddenly made him heartsick. It seemed even from behind she was withering before his eyes.

He became so caught up in anguish; he couldn't begin the next movement, "Flight," his surprise love theme. Sarah looked over at him as if a hand had tapped her on the shoulder - his tears trickled down his face and dripped onto the keys. Catching his shameless weeping, she shuffled over to his side and gazed upon him with lavender pools that spoke of love and grace. Feeling he was about to collapse, Mike put his head down to hide his sobbing. Sarah slid in next to him, leaned in, and kissed him on the cheek.

She then tenderly wiped Mike's tear-streaked face while the band and audience watched in suspended silence. Lifting his face to hers, she sang an intermezzo that portrayed her abiding love, raising him from despair to a place of redemption.

Many in the audience were now sobbing while embracing one another. As Mike slowly straightened, nurtured by Sarah's song, *The Gathering* moved in for the closing number, "Deliverance," which reintroduced the various themes in miniature. Mike, braced by Sarah's beaming face, was able to join in the finale with exuberant riffs and flowing arpeggios.

As if on cue, the shower stopped, the clouds receded, and slanting golden rays of sun sparkled on the wet pavement, leaves, and tree branches of Central Park as *The Girl in the Yellow Scarf* came to a close.

$\oint$

The WBLS station engineers, realizing they had just witnessed a groundbreaking musical event, grabbed an auxiliary microphone and went to capture the joyous reaction of the audience rushing the stage in hopes of an autograph and a touch of history. Mike's mother, Trina, Persis, and Jesse ran up shouting with joy and encircling Sarah and Mike, embraced them.

The band flowed to Mike and Sarah to join in the love feast. They hugged one another while the audience, now at well over a thousand, cheered as they swarmed the band shell stage.

Jesse, seeing R.G. corralled in the corner, went over and led him through the mob to Mike and Sarah at the piano. When Mike saw R.G., with his hand on Jesse's shoulder coming toward him, he thought, *Why not?* Mike reached out to R.G. and spoke in his ear. R.G.'s face lit up and motioned for Jesse to bring him his sax.

With a huge smile, Mike jumped up on the piano bench and whistled to get everyone's attention. As the roar of the crowd ebbed, Mike scanned the audience, soaking up their adoration.

Gazing down at Sarah, Mike grinned. "I have one last number I need to play, if you folks wouldn't mind. It's called 'Flight,' and was inspired by a magical day at the seashore when I realized I was hopelessly falling for the girl in the yellow scarf." Mike paused to look over at his sax player. "However, nothing would have come of it without the influence and mastery of Mr. Reggie Green, who gives my spirit *flight* with his playing. Thank you, R.G."

The audience hushed to a murmur as Mike stepped off the bench, sat down, and began the intro with Sarah at his side on the bench. R.G. soon swooped in with the sweetness of honey dripping from a honeycomb and together wove a tapestry of love with themes of reviving onshore breezes, cirrus-streaked blue skies, and sparkling waves splashing against a seawall.

Then for the next ten minutes, with the band joining in, "Flight" held Sarah and the audience captive with lyrical visions of that day at Breezy Point, rendering seabirds flying, castles in the sand, and the steady heartbeat of the ocean pounding the beach. As the last notes of Mike's declaration of love floated off into the cityscape, Sarah reached around Mike and pulled him to her with a clutch that took his breath away - his family looking on with beaming faces.

The crowd once again erupted into wild applause as Mike and R.G. took bow after bow – Mike deflecting the adoration with outstretched arms toward Sarah, the inspiration for his opus.

Mike had arranged for a horse and carriage to pick Sarah up in front of the Central Park stage, and when it arrived he stood up from the piano and offered his hand to Sarah, who was still sitting on the bench. She reached for his hand but did not stand. Instead, she just continued to sit gazing up at him, with a far-off expression. He paused to peer deep into her eyes as if trying to read her thoughts.

Something like a jolt of current flowed through him, making him shudder at first, but then *that* smile appeared and swept away the mysterious tension he had felt. Reaching with both hands, Mike helped her up for a tender embrace. Then holding her out to look at her, time seemed to stand still. With senses heightened, he became aware of every nuance around him: the blood-red sun setting through lush green leaves, the chitter of birds in the linden trees, even the earthy smell of rain-soaked soil and stone.

Helping Sarah through the crowd, down the stage stairs, and into the carriage, it seemed they were held in a bubble of time that would last forever. Climbing in after her, all he could do was look upon her as she leaned back in the seat. When the carriage started with a jerk, he saw the musicians following the clip-clop of the horse and carriage, singing and playing "Everything is Beautiful" with an entourage of audience. Shortly after starting out, he saw a flower vender cart and had the carriage driver pull up and stop.

Mike bent down and kissed Sarah as he held her face. "You've made me the happiest man on earth this day. The rest of the evening is going to be all about you. Stay put—I'll be right back."

Sarah smiled softly as she sighed and leaned back into the corner of her seat. Mike reached for the carriage door and stopped to look back and take her in. His heart filled to bursting. He then hustled to the vender and scanned the many varieties of bouquets. Should he get all white or red or just stick with yellow? He paced in front trying to decide. Not able to make up his mind, he got two of everything. He dug into his coat pocket for his wallet and counted out seventy-four dollars for six huge bouquets.

With his arms so full, Mike could barely see his way back to the carriage. The driver saw his predicament and jumped down to help. Holding on to three of the bouquets, Mike climbed back into the carriage and peered down at Sarah. She was leaning back against the corner with her eyes closed as if asleep. But then as he looked closer, his heart began to race.

The flowers dropped from his hands, hit the carriage step and tumbled to the ground. He tried to speak but nothing came out. He fell into the seat next to her. Was she breathing? He couldn't tell. He touched her pale face.

"Sarah," he pleaded.

Nothing. He jumped up, banged his head on the metal bar of the roof, and yelled, "Driver! Get to the nearest emergency room fast. Sarah's in trouble."

As if watching a silent motion picture from above, Sarah saw herself resting in the corner of the carriage as Mike, frantic, soundlessly waved his arms at the driver, then sat down and drew her to his chest.

People scattered as horse and carriage galloped along the Central Park path with the coachman standing and rattling the reins. Coming to the entrance of the park, a mounted policeman stopped the driver briefly and both looked back at Mike holding Sarah in his arms. The policeman pulled his horse around and led them out the entrance, stopping rush-hour traffic so they could cross to another section of the park.

Sarah could taste Mike's warm tears as he sobbed and held her face to his cheek.

"Sarah . . . Sarah," he gasped. "Oh, Lord . . . please . . ."

Looking down from above, Sarah watched as the mounted policeman and carriage turned off the park path and floated across a grassy meadow, picnickers springing to their feet, scurrying to get out of the way. Weaving through hedges and park benches, the officer led the carriage to an opening in a stand of trees that bordered

5th Avenue. He again held up traffic so they could clomp across the busy thoroughfare to the Urgent Care entrance.

Emphatic shouts brought Sarah back to herself as nurses carefully lifted her out of the carriage. Charging through the Emergency entrance, she felt the warmth of Mike's hand in hers as he ran alongside the gurney being pushed by emergency staff. She slowly turned her head toward Mike, and pondered what all this meant, as he gradually faded from sight . . .

36
Deliverance

Mike sat through the night at Sarah's bedside, holding on to some part of her. He was so exhausted, he didn't know if he was awake or if this was all a horrible dream. He would sit there forever if need be, willing her to breathe, matching her breath for breath.

As he held Sarah's hand just below the IV in her wrist, a golden light entered the room. It gradually made its way down from the ceiling, along the wall, and onto Sarah's bed. When it struck Mike's face he realized he had been sleeping sitting up. The yellow glow of sunrise touched him in a profound way, causing him to feel hopeful amid all the tangle of tubes, wires, and monitors. The steady blip-blip-blip on the display was somehow comforting as Mike said a prayer, asking for strength and reconciliation.

"Good morning," the nurse said as she breezed in to check on Sarah's vitals.

Mike looked up from his prayer to catch the soft smile of the shift nurse. "Morning."

"Why don't you take a break while I attend to Sarah? The cafeteria will open in a few minutes, and I'm sure they'll have something delicious to eat," she said, winking.

Mike snorted and cracked a smile. "Delicious hospital food—that's a good one. Maybe some coffee."

He stood up from his post, not wanting to leave.

"Go ahead—she'll be okay."

"Alright. I'll be back in ten minutes," he said and headed down to the café.

Exiting the elevator into the front lobby, he saw a bundle of the *New York Times* being dropped off at the front entrance newsstand. It dawned on him he should at least check if there was a review on the Central Park concert. Digging out a quarter, he bought the paper with the latest bad news plastered on the front page: riots in Miami, President Carter deals with hostage crisis, gas lines running for blocks.

He walked to a nearby bench that overlooked a garden with bulging blooms of purple irises rising above a tangle of weeds. Sitting down, not really expecting to find a review of his opus, he turned to the Variety section and scanned down the page till he came to the music section.

"Naumburg Tuesday Evening Concert: a stunning début by The Gathering*; out-of-this-world performance by all connected with* The Girl in the Yellow Scarf*. The composition broke new ground, and the voice of Sarah— magnificent! Who are these people? We want more!"*

Mike read the words, but they were just words without meaning. Then gradually, the significance hit him. The opus was a success. This was good, right?

He leaned back with a great sigh and gazed at the flowers fighting to survive the encroaching weeds in the unattended garden. Why was everything a struggle? How would he survive the reality of what was happening in the room above him? He couldn't make sense of it, yet whenever he envisioned his sweet Sarah, all he felt was her peace—a peace that surpassed all understanding. Buoyed by that peace, Mike stood, tucked the paper under his arm, and headed back inside and up to Sarah's floor.

Approaching her room, numb from lack of sleep, he heard her voice floating toward him. He stopped walking and held his breath to take in the sweet sound. Needing to appear cheerful, with tears threatening, he straightened his shoulders and pushed on a smile as he entered.

The nurse left the room when Mike walked in and Sarah slowly turned her head to follow him with her eyes. He caught a sob just before it leapt from his throat. Her soft lavender eyes locked on him, and he fell into their purple pool - he was suddenly afraid, alone. She was leaving him.

Unable to move, he stood gazing at her. He wished he was strong, but all he wanted to do was to run out the door and keep running until he dropped.

"Mike . . ."

Sarah's voice was like oxygen that gave him life. He would live as long as he could hear that voice. He tried to speak but couldn't. He just stood, savoring the sound of his name.

"Come sit with me."

Mike moved as in a trance to sit in his chair next to the bed.

"I never had…a chance to tell you…how much the ring meant…to me." Her voice was shallow but sweet. "You made me so happy…beyond words." She took a long breath and rested a moment. "All I can say is…I love you more than anything…in this world." She gave Mike a Mona Lisa smile. "I have…something to give you…too." She lifted her arm and rested her hand on her chest. "I want you to have…Grandma Mae's cross."

Mike looked down at the handcrafted cross. He involuntarily shook his head from side to side, knowing what she was implying. Mike brought his fisted hand to his mouth, trying not to break down. But when he looked back into Sarah's eyes, he was strengthened, feeding on the peace that radiated from her.

"The box my Grandpa made for the cross…is in the top drawer…of my dresser. It has…the history of the cross written…by Grandma Mae."

Her halting speech caused him to choke up. He looked back at the cross.

"Take it, Mike…please," Sarah said, reaching for him and lifting his chin so he would look her in the eye.

Her touch was a life force that enabled him to carry out her wish. Like an angel touching his soul, empowering him to stand and reach for the braided silver chain. He unhooked the clasp and with both hands lifted the cross from her flawless ivory neck.

Sarah watched him as he examined the cross. A raw sense of connection struck Mike as he ran his finger along the hand-trimmed polished edge. He could picture the love that had gone into the shaping of the silver. When he looked back at Sarah, she reached over and softly held his hand – smiled tenderly and closed her eyes to rest.

When Mike sat back down, sleep threatening to overtake him, he heard a whisper from the doorway. He turned to the smiles of his mother, sisters, and Jesse. Each day they brought flowers and a little something for him to eat, knowing he wouldn't leave the room for long.

The four tiptoed in and stood around the bed, transfixed as they looked at Sarah. She lay so still, Mike would have thought she was gone if it weren't for the weak but steady sound of the monitor. With the white bed covers tucked under her arms and her satiny red hair spilling over the pillow, she appeared as an angel, delivering peace to all in the room.

After a half-hour of silent vigil, with everything that needed to be said expressed by the warmth of their presence, Mike stepped into the hall for hugs and good-byes from his family and friend.

He had insisted on staying through the evening despite *Sarah's* insistence that he go home and get some proper rest. So as she slept, he quietly paced about the room, reliving the days they had spent together.

He had known from the first moment she was someone special in the world. But why had he been chosen to be blessed by her? And not just him, really—his whole family. And anyone who heard the music she gave him. Whatever the reason, instead of feeling bitter, a spirit of thankfulness flowed through him. Before her, his life had had little meaning. He'd been on the edge of an abyss, and she saved not just his life but his spirit as well.

Throughout the long night of watching her sleep, he began to feel he would never really lose her, that she would remain a part of his life. Then at one thirty in the morning, as he dozed in his chair, Sarah's gentle stirring woke him. He leaned over to hold her small soft hand, and at that moment she turned and looked up, smiling as if someone above him was greeting her. She then closed her eyes, and the room emptied.

37
Spoon Cross

After consulting Aunt Clara, Sarah's funeral was held at the Harlem Baptist Church. She was buried in the small cemetery next to the church with a simple headstone etched with her name, the years she'd lived, and the inscription: "May God Receive the Girl in the Yellow Scarf."

After burying his sweet Sarah, Mike languished in his flat for days. What would he do without the exasperating sweet spirit that had become the focus of his music and also his life? Mike had received a flood of calls after the Central Park concert, but he put a hold on everything until he could sort out his life without Sarah.

Persis and Jesse stopped by to check on him after the funeral and gave him their full attention as his expression of loss flowed like a river. The three connected as never before through their shared grieving. With their support, he wanted to go to Holy Apostles soup kitchen to show them where he had first met Sarah.

Al immediately dropped his paring knife and went over to embrace Mike when he came through the kitchen door.

"So sorry, my friend," Al said.

As his knees went weak, Mike hung on to Al. A couple of regulars came over, putting their arms around them both. Persis and Jesse turned away with tears in their eyes.

As if trying to retrieve some part of Sarah, Mike went out to sit in the dining room at the same spot where he first heard that incredible voice. "Can you believe it? It was only nine months ago when we met," Mike said, smiling up at Persis and Jesse as they gazed back with compassion.

Mike turned his attention back to the table, trying to envision her next to him. "When I sat next to her, even though she didn't say much, I felt I was in the presence of someone special." Mike chuckled to himself. "And, man, was she ever special."

Sitting still for a moment with his eyes closed, Mike got up and indicated he was ready to leave. Heading out from Holy Apostles, arm and arm with Persis, he needed to make one more difficult stop—Sarah's apartment.

After getting the apartment key from the landlady, Mike opened the door to Sarah's little home flooded with bright yellow light streaming in through the window. Stopping just inside, they stood a moment in reverence as each took in the belongings of their precious friend. Mike caught his breath upon seeing Sarah's clothes washed and placed in boxes for Goodwill. Biting his lip, he walked over and slumped down at her small wooden table and put his hand to his mouth. *She gave me all she had to give.*

Catching Mike's look of despair, Jesse came over, stood behind him, and placed his hand on his shoulder.

Then, with a nod and a smile from Persis, Mike got up and went to the dresser. Opening the top drawer, he saw the little battered wooden box, maybe three by five inches, with a simple leather hinge and hasp holding the lid. The sight of it sitting alone in the empty drawer caused him to grin in spite of himself. It looked so small yet exuded such great significance, much like Sarah.

He reached in and picked it up. It was heavier than he'd expected. Carrying it with both hands, he sat back down, with Persis and Jesse watching over his shoulder. He pulled up on the leather hasp and opened the lid. All six eyes peered in with fascination.

The lid was made from a solid half-inch piece of rough-hewn hardwood, as were the sides and bottom, giving the box its weight. The inside was lined with a dark-green felt that added a treasure-box quality to the contents. Their wonderment turned to puzzlement over the tiny photo of a smiling couple looking out at them.

Mike took it out and held it up to look at it closer. After handing it to Persis, he pulled out a folded scrap of paper yellowing at the edges. He opened it and saw that it was a note addressed to Sarah's mother.

My dear Jean Marie,

I want you to understand the significance of the "spoon" cross. Your father made it for me from the handle of a teaspoon his great grandmother "stole" from the larder of her master just before escaping north sometime in the 1850s. She didn't take it as treasure but as a memento for the unborn child she was carrying. I can't imagine all the trials Isaiah's family went through, but the significance of the teaspoon and the cross that was cut out from it, using only a coping saw and a file, makes it a treasure beyond any amount of gold.

When you think the time is right, please give it to Sarah, your blessed child, who I love more than life itself. She will know what to do with it.

Love you forever,
Mother, Proverbs 3:5–6

Mike sat back in his seat as Persis and Jesse went around the table to sit facing him.

"Wow," Mike said, looking at them both.

"So that's her Grandpa Isaiah with Grandma Mae," Persis said, holding up the picture. "Appears he was high yellow."

Mike chuckled as he shook his head. "Sarah never mentioned anything about her grandpa being mixed blood. Could be what caused the friction in her family."

Speechless for a while, the three studied the box, admiring the simplicity of its pegged construction, rough-hewn surface and oiled finish. Then without speaking they got up, and with one last look around, closed the door and went to tell the landlady they would return the next day for Sarah's belongings.

Back at his flat, as Mike aimlessly paced about the room, Persis asked him to play something for them. "You know, Sarah was a gift to all of us, but she especially lives in your music, and she will always be with you."

After a long moment of considering his sister's words, Mike went to his dresser drawer and pulled out Sarah's yellow scarf that was buried beneath some clothes. Draping it over the piano lid, he slid in behind the scarred but resonant grand and started to play an impromptu memorial to his beloved.

As his hands moved about the keyboard with visions of his arms enfolding her in the back of a yellow cab, it seemed that Sarah had entered the room, smiled and embraced them.

Manhattan, February 1982

Heading out from Harlem, his family surrounding Mike with smiles, the stretch limousine made its way to Broadway and the premiere performance of *The Girl in the Yellow Scarf.* Anticipation filled the car – everyone looking out the windows as if seeing the city for the first time. But before going to the Plymouth Theater on 45ᵗʰ Street, Mike had the driver continue to 23ʳᵈ and the YMCA.

After almost two years, Mike had found Sarah was right about how well teaching suited him. When the limo pulled up in front of the Y, Mike got out and sprinted up the stairs to drop off tickets for his students to opening night of his Broadway musical.

With Franklin's prodding, and encouragement from Jesse and Persis, Mike had begun to implement his promise to Sarah. Drawing on his own experience and success, he initiated a program at the YMCA that encouraged kids on the fringe to explore and develop their love of music. At first he just volunteered a couple of afternoons a week, but soon the mentoring program caught on, and he needed more resources. He applied for, and received, a grant from the city under the leadership of newly elected Mayor Koch. As the program grew, he brought in other musicians from around the city to contribute their time, which enabled them to reach even more children.

The endorsement by the city and the challenge and joy of seeing kids gain self-confidence in expressing their gifts filled his cup to overflowing. As if that wasn't enough, a WBLS executive proposed and financed a collaboration between Mike and one of New York's foremost playwrights in writing a Broadway musical based on his opus. With his newfound celebrity, he was able to leave the piano bar circuit and compose music full-time along with managing his after-school program.

After wading through the crowd in front of the theater, Mike sat staring open-mouthed at the murmuring audience about him. With his family seated arm and arm next to him, he smiled to himself recalling the many times he and Sarah played and sang together. Mother and Trina sat next to him, looking about with anticipation and sharing thoughts of how Sarah might be portrayed by the lead actress. Persis and Jesse came next, sitting silently, leaning into each other for support.

As the lights lowered and the curtain rose, Mike had a sense of deliverance and leaned forward to take in his family. With the silver cross, cool, against his chest, he sat back and watched an *almost* perfect performance. For him, however, there could only be one perfect performance—the one that featured Sarah, the frail sweet girl in the yellow scarf.

The End

Sample chapters:
The Piano Man - Book 2 - Opus Series

When the cab pulled out of sight, she peered down at the small handcrafted cross in her hand.
Caressing the smooth uneven surface, she was struck by an equal amount of hope and fear.

1

Dream – Los Angeles, April 1982

"**H**ello, Mike."

Exhausted from a late night of performing, Mike had collapsed onto his bed and dreamed he was beckoned to his hotel room door by a light tapping. In a fog, he shuffled across the room and opened the door as far as the security chain would allow. He peered through the four-inch crack. What he saw caused him to stare back with a gasp.

"I said, Hello, Mike."

It was still dark when the hotel phone jangled on the bedside table, snapping Mike out of his sweet dream. He sat up trying to make sense of where he was, scanning the room in a haze. He located the source of aggravation and did a half roll to pick up the receiver.

"This is your wakeup call, Its 5:30...have a good day."

Squinting, Mike clunked the receiver onto the cradle and rolled over on his back, forcing his eyes to stay open. *Thank God this is the last of it.* Playing live to a massive audience was the best; everything else was nothing but a grind.

As he tried to muster energy to move, he heard pounding on his door.

"Mike...only got forty five minutes."

Jesse, short term travel manager and boyfriend of Mike's sister Persis, was making his rounds to roust the musicians and get them to LAX airport on time.

Following the premier performance in February of his smash Broadway hit, *The Girl in the Yellow Scarf,* Mike and his band, *The Gathering,* were launched on a five-city tour to promote the musical the producers were hoping to take nation-wide. After playing to a packed Orpheum Theater in downtown LA, the last stop on the schedule, the band was headed home to New York.

Mike dragged himself to the hotel patio café. After a bite of coffee-dunked bagel, he glanced sideways to catch Liz sauntering toward his table.

"Morning lover," she said, coming up and ruffling his unruly Afro.

He smiled wearily up at her.

"Where's everybody?"

"Ask Jesse," he replied. Then, studying her a little closer added, "How do you do it? Always beautiful, even at six A.M.?"

She beamed as Mike gazed at her – the emerald-eyed redhead who inspired his thoughts of a future together.

The rest of the band sauntered in, dragged chairs up to Mike's table and, after multiple cups of coffee, became somewhat alive.

"Oh man, here he comes," Mike said, rolling his eyes.

"Ok everyone, out to the van. We're in the air in a couple hours," Jesse said, seeming to relish his role as straw boss. With moans and grunts the group slugged down the last of their coffee and ambled in the direction of the waiting van.

Stopping to take a last look at the tropical grounds with its bougainvillea, red-orange hibiscus and gurgling pond, Mike reached around Liz and pulled her in for a morning kiss before they trailed behind the motley bunch. She gazed up at him with a glow and a questioning smile he was coming closer to answering.

As Mike stared out the van window at the passing world of palm trees, car top surfboards and shorts, a sweet ache settled in with the thought of Sarah's dream visit early this morning. Not since saying goodbye two years ago as she passed from this world had he seen her so clearly. He desperately wanted her to stay, but the material world wouldn't allow it.

2

Mike – Manhattan, May 1982

"**N**ow what?" Al asked. "I hear you're *the toast* of New York and LA as well."

Even with his sudden success, upon returning from California Mike was back to mentoring young musicians at the 23rd Street YMCA and Wednesday evening serving at Holy Apostles soup kitchen.

"Today, I'm just burnt toast man," Mike said. "Really, you can't leave a guy alone, can you?"

Al gave Mike a piteous look and shook his head. After eight years managing the soup kitchen in lower Manhattan, his understanding of human nature was pretty spot-on.

Mike frowned. "Al, just say it."

"Alright. What are you doing here? I know you love me to pieces, but what's going on with you these days?"

Mike looked around the kitchen he had cooked in once a week for almost four years – the counter and sink where he peeled mounds of potatoes, the huge commercial gas stove where he cooked hundreds of pounds of hamburger and onions – and had to admit he felt lost. After Sarah died – his career-saving muse, anchor, and soul mate – the only thing that kept him going was keeping in touch with friends at the kitchen.

"Okay, dammit," Mike said, stretching his five-foot-ten body out full. "I miss her. I don't know if I have anything left. Maybe it was all her."

Al was silent, waiting for him to continue.

"Man, what do you want?"

"I just asked," Al said, holding up his hands in surrender.

Mike spun on his heel and pushed through the kitchen door into the large basement dining hall and stopped behind the very chair Sarah sat in the first night they met.

What the hell. He had success. A Broadway hit, record contracts, and his agent, Jimmy, could probably line up engagements into the next century. Mike pulled out a chair, dropped down with his elbows on the table and held his head, falling into a deep reverie. He had gained much, but had lost much. Before sinking further into sickening self-pity, he pushed himself up and headed back into the kitchen.

"Hey man," Mike said, rubbing his forehead. "I appreciate you checking on me."

Al strolled up to him. His six-foot-five frame towered over Mike as he held him by the shoulders. "Everyone handles grief differently," Al said, his ruddy face conveying compassion. "It still hurts plenty when I think of losing my brother in Nam, and that was over ten years ago."

Mike's eyes misted as he leaned in for a monster hug from Al.

"Thank you, my brother," Mike said, his voice waning.

Leaving Holy Apostles after cooking and cleaning up from serving several hundred homeless folks, Mike meandered through Washington Square on the way to his apartment in Greenwich Village. He smiled at visions of picnic lunches with Sarah on an old bedspread, with the smell of turned soil, fresh cut grass and blossoming crabapple trees. He thought these memories would have faded by now.

After walking up the four flights to his studio apartment on Bleecker Street, Mike stood in the doorway looking at the mess in his room. It was time. Most of this needed to go, except of course his pride and joy - the ebony grand piano with the scarred lid that took up the middle of the room. He had to get the mattress in the corner up off the floor and get a proper bed frame. The tattered beanbag chair that leaked little white puffs of foam needed a home in the dumpster. And what about the Formica-and-chrome table and chairs from Goodwill? No, that was where he wrote the music for *The Girl in the Yellow Scarf*. That would stay. Maybe a new couch and a couple of easy chairs? He'd call Liz and get her help, but first he had to get on with the auditions for young musicians from around the city at the YMCA.

A couple of students from his after-school program were interested in the youth competition at Radio City Music Hall, but he had posted notices in all the boroughs to cast a broader net. After meeting with a dozen kids last week, he would listen to them today and pick eight for an ensemble to take to the music competition the end of July.

With his newfound celebrity Mike was able to convince the director at the Y to convert a large storage closet into a music practice room. The second floor space had one small window at the far end overlooking an alley and floor-to-ceiling shelves on either side filled with boxes of supplies and reference books from the library. Under the window, a large sink and countertop piled with pails, mops, and jugs of cleanser always gave the room a whiff of disinfectant. All in all, with hundreds of cardboard boxes and books, the room didn't need any soundproofing. It was perfect. With an old but in-tune upright piano, donated by a neighbor of Mike's mother in Harlem, the room could pack in their combo of eight young musicians.

The next morning on his way down 23rd to the auditions, Mike stopped at Samson's Market in memory of Sarah and went in to buy her favorite treat: strawberry Twizzlers. He couldn't walk past the cramped little store, where she used to shop, without going in. Why were his thoughts of her always bittersweet? He missed her so much he could cry, but when he thought of her amazing voice and that sweet smile, he had to grin. He kept telling himself she was a gift but the thought never kept him from missing her.

Sitting on the steps outside the Y, Mike finished the last of his Twizzlers and looked up at a small patch of blue sky to say good morning to Sarah.

"Morning, sir," Cobi said, walking up the stairs flailing his arms at a virtual drum set, snapping Mike back to the present. Travis followed close behind lugging a trumpet, French horn and trombone.

Mike nodded. "See ya upstairs in a few." *Since when did I become a sir?* Crap, he was still in his twenties. It must be a sign of respect – that's it. Then looking into the faces of the remaining kids as they arrived, a paternal sense stirred in him; knowing what they couldn't – their potential.

Acknowledgements

First thanks to my early readers and encouragers who were exceedingly kind to read a very rough draft without snickering in my presence: Tom Minor, Shar and Ed Boerema, Karissa Godel, Sherry Rybak and members of my family. Special thanks to Tiger Hayden-Bracy who, having lived 1980's New York, contributed particulars of the Black experience. Then to editors and agents who were indispensable along the way: Laurie Harper, C. S. Lakin, Pamela Illies and Cherry Weiner, but most importantly my wife Janet who read the many drafts and remained encouraging.

Book Club Discussion – Story Elements and Themes

1 - Story hook: Appears in the first few pages and introduces the reader to the story with a question that begs an answer. What is that question in this book?

2 - Color: Used to symbolize an emotional state, event or character. What color often comes up and what might it represent?

3 - Character arc: The transformation or inner journey of a character over the course of the story. What are the character arcs of Mike, Sarah and Jesse?

4 - Setting: Is the location and time in which the story takes place. But can also include historical period, weather, immediate surroundings and social statuses. How are these elements shown and what effect do they have?

5 - Motif: A story element (object) that has symbolic significance. What motifs appear and what could they represent?

6 - Protagonist: Hero, main character. Mike owes much to other characters in the story who at times are allies and/or irritants. What are some ways he was helped by the supporting cast?

7 - Antagonist: Often is a person who opposes the main character but can also be a negative force. What are some antagonistic forces that affect the characters?

8 - Backstory: Is what happens before the story opens. What are some backstory elements of the three main characters and how does it affect them.

9 - Theme: The theme of a story is its underlying message(s) that comes out in the central conflict of the characters. What might be a common theme for each of the main characters?

10- Dialogue: Dialogue reveals character. How does the interaction between the main characters show their personalities and beliefs?

11 - Race: Is race an integral part of the story? Why or why not?

12 - Plot: The sequence of events that draws the reader into the character's lives and helps to understand the choices the characters make. What elements (interests/passions) are woven into the plot and run throughout the story?

13 - Subplot: What are the secondary plots that run parallel and support the main plot?

14 - Faith: How does faith affect the worldview of the main characters?

15 - Conflict and Inner Demons: What issues do the main characters face that hold them back from reaching their goals?

16 - Stakes: What is at stake for the main characters?

17 - Redemption: How do the main characters find redemption?

18 - Resolution: Does the story reach a convincing conclusion? What might be an alternate ending?

About the Author:

C. R. Frigard has written two books on creative problem solving along with the Opus Series, is a creativity educator, artist and inventor. He has four grown children and lives with his wife in Mound Minnesota.

Website:

www.crfrigard.com

Inspiration for the book:

While following a disheveled couple into an upscale mall in Minnesota, I witnessed a smartly dressed shopkeeper sincerely greet them. In that moment, having not seen their faces, it struck me I was judging the couple without knowing anything about them. Upon getting home, I told my wife how moved I was by that exchange at the mall and thought I wanted to write a story about who the couple might be. She encouraged me then and continues to do so. After five years, that story has led to the three books of the Opus Series. TGTG

Made in the USA
Columbia, SC
23 January 2018